Lessons with the Mothman

MONSTER SMASH AGENCY
BOOK THREE

KATHRYN MOON

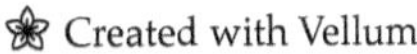 Created with Vellum

To Whoop and her Elias

Contents

Content Information

This story was originally shared with chapter by chapter updates in rough draft form on my Patreon in starting in July of 2024.

The Monster Smash Agency series is sex positive and features sex workers as main characters. Content includes consensual smut with light kink! You can find more information at kathrynmoon.com

Lessons with the Mothman

MONSTER SMASH AGENCY 3
BY KATHRYN MOON

CHAPTER 1
Elias

"TRY THIS."

"Needs more yuzu," Rafe replied with no more than a glance at the cup I held in front of his nose.

"I said '*try*' it," I parsed out.

Astraeya cut in, perched on the high stool, looking like a delicate pink and purple doll someone had placed incongruously in the chaos of Rafe's rental kitchen, "What about a weekend away with Gabriella? She's attending her ex's wedding in Cabo and wants to convince them she's moved on."

My antennae twitched, and I turned in the succubus's direction.

"I don't have to try it. I saw you balancing out the sour with sweet, and I'm telling you I don't want it even. It needs to find balance with the food, not without it," Rafe answered me, as stubbornly hard-headed as his gargoyle stone form.

"It needs balance with both," I said, but Astraeya's question was busy rolling through my head.

A fake date? Feigning emotions and acting on the premise of being already coupled had potential for creating a romantic entanglement between myself and a client, certainly. My brow furrowed as I considered this. Gabriella was a lovely woman with a bit of sylph mixed into her human family line. At our appointment through the Agency months ago, she had levitated at her climax, floating right off my lap in her throes of pleasure. She'd been pleasant company, but I hadn't experienced any hints of real attachment. According to my research, an attachment was something that grew exponentially with time and proximity, but there was usually an inkling to start from one or both parties. I wasn't sure what that inkling ought to feel like, but I imagined I would know when it occurred.

"I'm looking for something more…long term," I told Astraeya.

Specifically, I was looking for love—first love, as it turned out, in spite of my many decades of life. Centuries, perhaps, but who was counting? Love was rare for any fae, and a moth fae like myself was rare amongst the general populace. When I was very young and inclined to fanciful thinking, I'd imagined love would find me when the time was right. With time, I'd grown more skeptical of the concept, eventually losing interest in it entirely. There were more compelling pursuits, and sex was thrilling regardless of any emotional entanglement.

Lately, however, the evidence in favor of a loving relationship had begun piling up around me. I'd found myself distracted and surprisingly…wistful. If love wouldn't find me, I would go in search of it directly.

Rafe choked softly at my claim, and I rustled my wings out to hide any expression he might be wearing from Astraeya's too keen stare. Not that my answer didn't make her skeptical in her own way, her precise eyebrows rising over her milky lavender face. But I had always been particular when it came to the clients I partnered with at the Monster Smash Agency. I was one of their few sex worker staff who was freelance, and the only one who had final word on who I partnered.

It paid—generously—to be exceptional at what you did.

"Oh, really? Because you managed to worm your way out of the last three long-term clients I booked for you," Astraeya parried.

I bristled. "I did not *worm*. If anything, I helped you pair them with even more fulfilling partners."

Astraeya puffed out an annoyed breath and snapped her file shut, shuffling it to the bottom of the stack. "Why don't you go through these yourself while I make us some tea?"

"Tea?" Rafe murmured distractedly, glancing around his kitchen. "Tea notes…Hannah likes pu-erh and caramel…" He trailed off, thinking of his werewolf mate, a softness smoothing over his previously anxious frown.

Love seemed to have that effect on people, I noted.

"With miso," I suggested to the gargoyle, who made a bright, excited sound in the back of his throat as he shot over to the refrigerator.

The pair of them left my side, setting to their own tasks, and I drifted over to the pile of bland manilla folders Astraeya had left behind on the steel counter.

"Isn't it a violation of company policy to let him rifle through those?" Rafe asked Astraeya, head clearing from some new recipe idea.

"Not strictly," Astraeya said, but her voice was a little tight. "Not if I'd have to go through the entire stack with him anyway."

"I signed a very thorough NDA," I said, shrugging a velvety, light wing at my back.

I flipped through a profile about a recently divorced human seeking to fulfill long buried fantasies and explore their personal identity. It would've been a client I'd taken a few years ago; the human fascination with discovery was always a source of entertainment for me. Out of the corner of my eye, Astraeya's foot tapped impatiently against the linoleum tile as the kettled purred with growing heat.

"How are the new recruits?" I asked her, opening another file.

"Fine."

Rafe's eyebrows rose as our gazes met over the littered kitchen counter.

"Well, we lost one, but the other two are doing all right...so far," Astraeya said, fiddling with mugs and tea bags.

"Lost one?" Rafe repeated.

I'd already heard about the event, but I waited for Astraeya to answer, watching the brief parade of emotions that flashed over her features—frustration furrowing her brow, a stubborn moue of her lips, the proud hike of her chin, and finally a wince and slump of her shoulders.

"Marguerite mated," she muttered.

Rafe tilted his head in question and looked to me.

"I didn't know vampires could mate," I said, feigning innocence as I closed another file, adding it to the discarded stack.

Astraeya rolled her eyes. "Vampires don't, but the selkie I paired Marguerite with did."

Rafe snorted. "Monster Smash? More like Monster Match, am I right?"

I pointedly opened another file and left Rafe to suffer under Astraeya's piercing glare. He was lucky he was a gargoyle. A succubus's wrath could snatch years off the average lifespan.

A role-playing request, with somnophilia—standard fare.

"How many matings is that now?" I asked, trying to sound disinterested.

Astraeya sighed. "Five."

Rafe straightened. "Oh."

"My supervisor's starting to think I'm doing it on purpose."

"It's not strictly bad, what you're doing," Rafe said. "I mean, people are happy."

"The mated couples are happy. The abandoned clients, not

so much. The cases we can't take because we're understaffed aren't happy. The company losing clients and staff isn't happy," Astraeya said, her voice rising with the tone of the boiling kettle. She huffed a breath as it clicked off and stared balefully at the steam rising out of the slender spout. "But I can't exactly regret accidentally pairing mates together, no."

Do it for me, I thought. Which was ridiculous. Fae didn't mate. But in spite of the absence of the experience thus far in my long life, I had hopes of finding the strange phenomenon of pointed affection that seemed to exist between my friends and their partners. Love, as they put it. A contrary emotion that seemed to change its definition with every individual recounting. A puzzle, one I was eager to solve.

"I understand the complications it causes, but it just sounds to me like you're more than usually good at your job," Rafe said, passing Astraeya a spoonful of caramel.

She hummed as she sucked on the spoon, and Rafe poured the hot water into mugs.

"I have *tried* to cool it a bit," Astraeya admitted. "But then Breugger's dad died and they had to go to the funeral, and then Gretchen ended up taking Hank as her client anyway, and you know how fast selkie mating instincts are. They didn't even bother with the appointment—just went directly back to Hank's apartment and didn't let any of us know what happened for weeks."

"Gretchen's having the wedding reception at Nightlight," I murmured.

"I didn't get invited?" Astraeya squawked.

"Strictly speaking, you *didn't* set them up, did you? Why does it seem as though we only get the same requests over and over again?"

"Because that's what Monster Smash Agency is, Elias. Fulfilling a biological need, or a psychological one, or both. We don't cater to *puzzles.* We cater to sex. Which, generally speaking, isn't all that curious when you really get down to it." Astraeya's fists were clenched at her sides and she shook her ire out like a wet dog, refusing to meet my gaze.

"Not exactly what you expect to hear from a succubus, especially one with a penchant for matchmaking," Rafe mused.

"Sex is sustenance for a succubus. That tends to shake off some of the mystique," Astraeya said with a wave of her hand.

"Food is sustenance to me, but that doesn't mean it isn't also art," Rafe parried.

I tossed another file onto the increasing stack, ready to open the next and be equally unimpressed by its contents, until a flash of neon yellow caught my eye. A small sticky note was dislodged from the back of the folder I'd just discarded, flipped aside by my careless handling and landing face down on the steel countertop. I lifted it, ready to paste it back on the folder it had fallen loose from, eyes skimming the words once without intention, and then again.

Victoria Dempsey. Independent Masters study for NWU. Monster sexuality, looking for interview subjects. Possible demonstrations?

"What's this?" I asked, holding the note up.

Astraeya and Rafe both turned, and Astraeya frowned, her stare blank.

"It's in your writing," I pressed.

She stepped forward, and I fought the impulse to pull the note out of her reach, keep it for myself.

"Oh shit," Astraeya murmured. "I forgot about that. Where did you find it?"

"It was stuck to a file. What is it?"

"My office has been a mess with all the reorganization lately," Astraeya said.

What is it? I wanted to shout, wings rustling impatiently at my back, antennae twitching.

"It was an email to the agency that I found in the unassigned stack. A woman looking for collaboration from companies like ours to help her research monster sexuality and interspecies relationships. I just thought it was..." Astraeya trailed off, staring at me. "Oh!"

"You thought it was *interesting*," I said, looming over the petite succubus slightly. "And you didn't mention it to me?"

Across the room and from under his breath, Rafe sang an ominous, "Dun, dun, duuuun." Rafe could stir soup and shit at the same time, apparently.

Astraeya rose—slightly, she was still very short—to Rafe's bait, and I resisted the urge to sigh. A succubus was no slouch, and I hadn't been trying to pick a fight. The fine and sensitive hairs on my body all rose to attention as an oppressive throb of energy pulsed in front of me.

"Contrary to what you seem to believe, Elias, I don't actually report to you. I occasionally *enjoy* working with you, and you have always served the agency's clients to extreme satisfaction, which is why we are so willing to cooperate with your whims, but I don't have to share every one of my notes or files or thoughts with you," Astraeya said, prim and powerful all at once.

"Of course not," I said, surrendering the note to her slim fingers, in spite of the urge to tuck it away in my pocket. There wasn't any useful information on it anyway, aside from the woman's name—Victoria Dempsey, old-fashioned and teasingly sweet. "Is the Agency interested in assisting her?"

Astraeya relaxed and shrugged. "She's not really asking to be a client, although she could certainly book an appointment to watch, but pairing the right workers together to create something authentic would be—"

"Is there anything stopping you from *referring* her to a connection through the agency?" I asked.

Astraeya blinked and then stilled, studying me. I wasn't entirely sure of the entire breadth and limitation of Astraeya's ability as a succubus. I wasn't *aroused* exactly at the moment, but I was excited, intrigued, and perhaps she was able to sense those emotions as well.

"Honestly? Probably," she said, frowning. I opened my mouth to object, and she raised a hand to pause me. "In *most* cases, referring an employee of the agency for outside work would be a breach of contract, even if Miss Dempsey has no intention of utilizing them in the same manner. However, you're a freelancer."

"I am."

"And a highly connected one. With a studious nature," Rafe chimed in from the background.

I dipped my head in acknowledgement, but kept my gaze on Astraeya. She wasn't convinced yet.

"I don't want to get you in trouble with the Agency," I said, which was true. It didn't mean I wouldn't act even without her assistance, or that I would feel especially bad if Astraeya did suffer consequences, but it wasn't my *goal* to create a problem for her.

"It's not that," she said softly, eyes narrowing. "You've been…flighty lately."

"Is that a pun?" I asked, my wings flaring briefly at my back.

She rolled her eyes. "You reject most clients, take a few and then change your mind about them. I just want to make sure you'll take this woman and what she needs for her work seriously."

Taking someone seriously, offering them what they needed, was exactly what I was looking for.

"I will," I said. "This interests me."

"Even if all she wants is an interview?"

I can offer so much more than an interview, I thought, recalling the note perfectly. Testimonials. Demonstrations. She needed someone with a connection to the world of monsters, one who could cast a wide web for information and willing participants.

"I certainly have plenty to offer in an interview, more than what might be conveyed in a single session," I said.

Apparently this didn't reassure Astraeya, because her eyes narrowed further. "I don't understand why this is the one."

The one. A commonly used phrase in regards to loving partnerships. Were the words a coincidental slip of the tongue? Probably. And yet…

"It's different," I said. Which was also what Rafe and our other friend Khell said about their own accidentally arranged matings with clients Astraeya had paired them with. That Hannah and Sunny were just…different. "You know I like the cerebral cases. But we should involve the Agency. I may be a freelancer, but if she wants demonstrations, hiring through the company would be an easy resource."

"We'll risk pricing her out, but it would curb any complaint the Agency might have about me referring you," Astraeya said, relaxing at last and nodding.

"I'll waive my fee," I said, shrugging, trying not to make my eagerness too obvious. I was likely failing, or Rafe remembered too well the conversation I'd had with him almost a year ago, because he was staring at me fiercely.

I'd like to try it…falling in love.

I'd expected it to be easy—pick a client, get to know them, enjoy a frenzy of sex, discover…emotions of some sort. If Rafe and Khell could manage it, surely I could. But there was a missing ingredient, and no matter how I quizzed my friends, they offered no explanation. Or at least not ones that offered tangible solutions.

"You haven't even met her yet," Rafe said, a thread of caution in the words.

Which was true. My expectations were premature. Perhaps that was my problem? Khell and Rafe hadn't been *seeking* love when they met their mates. It had struck them unexpectedly. I frowned over this potential muddle. Perhaps there was a cupid somewhere in Chicago I could discuss the intricacies of the process with.

"I'll pitch your offer to the Agency, and we'll arrange a meeting," Astraeya said. She pointed a perfectly manicured acid yellow nail in my face and narrowed her eyes. "*Don't* do anything until I tell you."

I raised my hands in innocence. "Wouldn't dream of it."

"SO, how many hours did you spend last night scouring your potential new client's social media?" Rafe asked the next day, settling down on a bar stool across from where I was counting inventory.

I scowled at him. I hated doing inventory. Generally, I had my vampire night manager do the task after closing. Today, I was in the mood to be annoyed and disagreeable.

"None," I said, which was technically the truth.

"Restrained of you. I would've peeked. What was her name again?" Rafe asked.

"Shouldn't you be cooking?" I volleyed back.

"Chefs have to eat too," Rafe answered. His kitchen wasn't far away from Nightlight, my bar, and it wasn't the first time he'd come to visit when he needed a break or someone to brainstorm flavors with.

"Isn't the point of being a chef to cook food? You can make your own lunch," I muttered.

"No one likes to cook *their own* food. And Hannah's on her way to meet me here," Rafe said.

I straightened at that. Rafe's mate was fascinating. A couple years into her life as a werewolf, the daughter of rock royalty, Hannah was decidedly...*cool*. She was quiet, watchful, and stylish. She and Rafe seemed startlingly different from one another, until suddenly, they stood shoulder to shoulder, magnetically attracted to one another and existing in a kind of harmony that made sense for two people whose work revolved around flavors and music. Compared to our other mated pair of friends, Sunny and Khell, Rafe and Hannah's romance was subtle, their touches casual and secretive, but the looks they gave one another were no less potently loaded with private meaning.

Also, Hannah happened to be one of the only people I couldn't get a read on when it came to drinks. Every time I made her something unique, her thanks was polite and her response mild. What was her *flavor*, damnit? If Rafe knew, he had too much fun keeping it from me.

"Victoria…Dennis? Davis?" Rafe continued to puzzle. "I bet I could ask Astraeya."

Astraeya would tell him to mind his own business, but— "Dempsey. But don't bother. There's no sign of her anywhere online."

"Picsapp account is private?"

"As far as I can tell, it doesn't even exist."

Rafe's eyebrows rose, and his smile crooked at the corner. "Ahh, I see. That's gotta be…" *Frustrating, annoying, surprising,* I thought. "…Exciting for you," Rafe finished.

"Exciting?" I repeated, antennae twitching at the suggestion.

Rafe nodded, grinning now. "You love a mystery. And you think social media is asinine. Now, when you want it to work for you, it can't."

"It doesn't matter. Astraeya got approval from the Agency. She's setting up a meeting." I would meet Victoria Dempsey soon enough. I turned away from Rafe, studying the array of bottles on my shelves. "Will Hannah want a mocktail or cocktail?"

"Hannah will want to *order* a drink," Rafe said. "She's funny like that, wanting to make choices for herself."

I huffed. A mocktail to start. Something smoky this time, subtle. I would solve the mystery sooner or later.

CHAPTER 2
Victoria

I SUCKED in a breath as the back door of my parents' home clicked shut behind me. A beautifully air-conditioned breeze enveloped me, cooling the sweat under my breasts and down my back in an instant. I pinched the loose fabric of my blouse and flapped it for a moment, letting my body adjust after the sweltering heat of high summer. My car's AC had barely made a dent in the temperature, but even the movement of hot air was better than roasting alive.

A head ducked around the corner of the kitchen, with thick gray curls and soft wrinkles around blue eyes. "Victoria."

I sighed, managing a smile for the stalwart housekeeper I'd grown up with. "Rebecca. I would hug you, but I'm disgusting. Is there—"

"A change of clothes for you in the laundry room. They're a bit old, but they'll do," she said, waving a hand toward the door on the left side of the mudroom. "I'll get you some water. Or would you prefer—"

"Water is perfect. And all the ice the party can spare," I said.

Rebecca laughed and slipped away. My father was notoriously paranoid about the ice supply of a party. Or he liked to have an excuse to duck out a few times, to leave the oppressively chummy energy of the gatherings my mother organized and grab a moment to himself at the convenience store just a mile away.

Mom always said I took after him too much.

I grimaced at the dress I found, folksy and sweet and covered in flowers, but the round collar came up to my neck and I supposed it was the best Rebecca could do. I hadn't left behind clothes I actually *liked* when I'd moved out. At least I was mostly the same size. The zipper fought with me but finished the journey up without threatening to split any seams. I shimmied out of my jeans and left them folded on the top of the washer for when I left.

My body felt too exposed as I walked out of the laundry room and through the hall to the kitchen, my arms bare and the skirt ending higher on my thighs than anything I'd worn in a year or more. When was the last time I had shaved my thighs? At least my hair there was light, a blonder version of my red.

"Vicky, there you are."

My throat tightened and I stopped in the doorway, the high, sunny windows streaking light through my favorite room in the whole house. Were kitchens always the heartbeat of a home, or was it simply because this was Rebecca's domain and she had more warmth than the rest of us combined? But even the glimmering streaks of sunshine and my proxy maternal figure couldn't stand up against the icy slash of energy that ran from me to the older woman standing in the doorway to my left. Had Rebecca summoned my mother, or had she come into the kitchen to add another splash of vodka to her lemonade without the rest of the party watching?

"I can't stay long," I said reflexively, adding for effect, "I have a meeting, actually. That's why I drove out."

My mother arched a brow, lips cutting up at the corners in

a sardonic smile. "How lucky for us. Come and say hello to the Grahams, at least."

She turned, her own dress loose and simple, a short silk sheath—it had to be short; she was as petite as I was, and longer styles swallowed us and dragged on the ground—in a shade of blue so refreshing it cooled the heat on my cheeks. Her blonde hair—it should've been gray by now, but my mother was religiously devoted to her colorist appointments—was twisted into a low bun, a few strands brushing against her smooth cheeks.

She let out a soft laugh halfway down the hall, a heady sound that heralded her arrival back to the party. "Look who I found creeping in through the back door."

I straightened my shoulders, and my lips formed a smile that I'd learned from the hostess herself—warm and welcoming, delighted to be here, to see you, to enjoy such a beautiful summer day with such wonderful friends. "As long as there is air-conditioning of course," delivered with a chuckle and a wink.

In the corner of the parlor, curled together on a chair not meant for two, a young couple turned their gazes away from mine.

———

"I SUPPOSE someone has to be the academic," Wendy, one of my mother's clique from the country club, said with a laugh. "Save the rest of us from our ignorance."

"I'm not personally so confused about my gender that I need a study on it," Wendy's husband, whose name I could never remember, chimed in, before reaching around my back and squeezing me twice to his side, his fingers groping the side of my breast.

"Oh, Bobby," Wendy huffed.

Bob. Of course. There were at least three Bob's here this afternoon in some variation of Robert.

"It's a wide umbrella of study," I said, my smile growing tired as I ignored the warning glance from my mother. She wouldn't want me getting specific.

"Only really leads back down one road, though, doesn't it? Academia is just feeding itself a work force of the over-educated…"

My mother took my elbow, peeling me away from the group with a gentle excuse that didn't interrupt Bob's great thesis on academia and gender. Neither of which really had much to do with my actual field of study.

"There's some mail for you on our bed. You're leaving soon?" Mom murmured under her breath, her arm looping through mine, head bowed close. We looked cozy like this—a charming mother-daughter relationship. At least she was giving me the opportunity to leave the room. My mask must've started to slip, and she wouldn't want them to see me without it. I glanced at a clock. I had time to spare, but I could always find somewhere to get a coffee on my way.

"Sure, I'll go grab that now," I said, glancing back at the room.

I'd lost track of my sister, Emma, during the conversation with Wendy and her husband, but I searched the room now, hoping to grab a moment before I left. Hopefully, without an audience. Just enough to say hi, to offer the same chance to get coffee or dinner together in the city. She would say yes and then make her excuses with every gently probing text message I sent, but it was worth a shot.

My mother and I parted ways as she caught hold of one of my father's law office friends, and I slipped down the hall and over to the curling set of stairs near the front door. Sunlight was at an angle now, painting the floorboards and well-worn carpet with the stained glass panels of the door. Most of my parents' friends had moved out of the historic district and farther out from the city, giving up the upkeep of a classic home in favor of more space and modern amenities with larger yards. I could see the itch to do the same in my mother's eyes sometimes, but Dad loved Oak Park. He'd grown up here and spoke of the history of his family and the city with pride.

If my parents ever did decide to move, Emma would probably get the house. It was a house for a family, after all, and she was on the right path for that sort of thing. The path I'd almost taken. I paused at the top of the stairs, arrested by a low, familiar rumble.

The same path. The same man.

I was jolted back into movement by the tight giggle that answered, darting into my bedroom directly on the right. I paused inside, closing the door as quietly as I could behind me, my gaze drifting absently around the space. Sky blue wallpaper with delicate daisies, whose yellow centers matched the bright lace curtains hanging over the two windows that looked down on quiet Elm Street, on the old oak at the corner of the lawn, and the tire swing Emma and I had painted pink, now chipped and scarred with time. My twin bed faced me, wood frame painted white with modest posts topped with round bulbs. I'd begged for a canopy—*too tacky*, my mother refused—and settled instead for draping chiffon from the ceiling, but that had long since been removed in my absence.

There were all the signs of the teenage girl who'd once lived in this room—torn out magazine pages pasted to poster boards, and the brief resurgence of polaroids pinned around the window, the faces of friends I'd lost touch with staring back at me with huge grins and bold makeup, smeared after long nights in the city.

A moan and a hitch of breath slipped through the old vent at the corner of the room where my wall connected to my sister's room. The hair rose on the back of my neck.

A small stack of envelopes rested against the pillow, all advertisements and credit card offers. It'd been years since I'd lived at home, and nothing important came here anymore. All I had to do was cross the small space, grab the mail, and leave again.

"Uhn, baby, yes, that's it."

This room belonged to a long-lost acquaintance now, but I still knew every creaking floorboard on my way to the bed, and I moved slowly and carefully, face flushed as I listened.

"God, yes, you're so close now, aren't you, baby?"

"Y-yes, Brett. Please!"

I cringed at my sister's voice. This was sick. *I* was sick. And fascinated. Was she lying, the way I had? Had she learned to fake pleasure for him? I doubted it. He'd been able to tell with me, and it had been a strange start to a crumbling finish between us, every false moan chipping away another piece of any connection we might have had.

"Yes, yes, you're gonna come so hard for me. I can feel it starting. Such a good girl. You're so greedy for my cock, aren't you?"

I blushed as I made it to the bed, my fingers closing numbly around my mail.

"Fuck. Fuck, you get so tight. Holy shit, baby." My former fiancé's voice took on a broken whine as he spoke to *his* current fiancé, my younger sister.

Messy, I thought, a dry voice in the back of my head. It was the same voice that had privately mocked Brett's attempts at dirty talk, words stolen right out of the cheapest porn. *You're so tight. You like that, don't you? Come for me*, as if it was as easy as ordering me to do so.

I ducked my head as their voices grew ragged and breathy, words of praise and gratitude tumbling together. I needed to leave. If Emma caught me sneaking away after having heard them, it was only going to make her more uncomfortable around me.

Everyone thought I was the injured party, even though I was the one who'd broken off the engagement with Brett. I think they had a hard time believing the truth. Why would I give up my devoted, handsome high school sweetheart with a lakeside condo and a seven-figure income? Why would I choose to live in a cramped apartment in an unstylish city neighborhood, toiling at a useless degree? Why wouldn't it sting to see Brett move on to my younger sister in a matter of months, to see a bigger, shinier diamond on her hand than the one he'd given me?

I wasn't exactly *happier* without Brett, I supposed. My parents and all of our family and acquaintances were right about that. But at least I wasn't promising to spend a lifetime with someone who made me unhappy.

Brett was happier without me. Emma, who'd had a crush on my boyfriend from the moment he'd picked me up for junior year homecoming, was happier with him. And in spite of what *everyone* wanted to believe, I was glad for that.

I snuck out of my old bedroom, out of the house, without another word to anyone.

———

THE MONSTER SMASH Agency headquarters were only a twenty-minute drive from my parents' place, and I arrived too early for my meeting, once again sweating in the blouse and jeans I'd changed back into. The building had a discreet sign on the front lawn, declaring it simply as MSA, and looked like one of the beautiful old Victorians of the neighborhood that had been converted into an office building when the upkeep for such a home became too much.

I pulled the key from the ignition and watched as a massive green orc lumbered out of the building and down the stairs. She was wearing a pretty wrap dress and shrugged a gym bag over her shoulder, long dark braid swinging with her steps, tusks gleaming white as she raised her face to the sunlight.

Uptown was one of the more mixed-species neighborhoods in the city, but between school and my commute, I didn't spend much time there outside of my apartment. The only other species I'd really interacted with much was my incubus friend, Lyle. He was the one who'd given me a number of places to reach out to for help.

Monster Smash Agency was the only one who'd agreed to arrange a meeting.

The chance of air conditioning in the waiting room of the building—and the potential for people watching—was more tempting than sitting in my car, so I grabbed my tablet and purse and headed for the front door. It was quiet inside. An older human man was leaving as I entered, eyes bright and hair mussed—a satisfied customer. He winked as he passed me, and I turned my face away, heading toward the counter.

"Can I help you?" The receptionist stared up at me as I gave my name, slitted black pupils in vibrant blue eyes flicking across my face. Golden ram's horns curled back from her temples. "I'll let them know you're here. Can I get you anything to drink while you wait?"

"We're ready, actually, Gwen," a silky voice called, before a petite woman stepped through the doorway. She was exquisitely beautiful, with high cheekbones and a full pout, pink hair rolling over her shoulders in smooth waves, and two opalescent horns high on her forehead. A succubus. "Elias got here early for once. It's nice to meet you, Victoria. I'm Astraeya."

I caught my breath, a rare bubble of excitement building up in my chest. Standing in front of this perfect confection of a woman made me too aware of the sweat sticking my blouse to my skin; of the thinned patches where my thighs rubbed together and wore away my jeans, threatening to split the fabric at any moment; of the ragged edge of my nails, no longer maintained with regular manicure appointments. I shook her hand and tried not to shiver at her cool touch.

She smiled warmly, and I swallowed hard. "Thank you for answering my email," I said, wrapping my arms around myself, my tablet cradled to my chest.

She waved a hand. "You have Elias to thank, actually. I'd lost track of it, but he found it in the mess of my files."

Elias. She'd mentioned the name in my email. A fae who was interested in assisting me. I followed her down a cool hall, a gust of cold air rising up from a grate.

"This meeting is to introduce the two of you, and also to discuss terms for where the Agency might be able to help, if you decide you need us." She paused outside of a closed door for a moment and then turned to me, lowering her voice. "The Agency will make those terms sound like a requirement, but they aren't."

I opened my mouth to question her, but she swung the door open before I had a chance to speak. Huge dark eyes were the first thing I saw, staring out of a sea of gold and amber, a monstrous face taking up an entire wall. And then the figure turned, and the eyes stretched and shifted, and I shook my head. Not eyes, but the pattern of beautiful, glimmering, and enormous moth-like wings.

My mouth dried at the sight of him, ethereal and eerie, tall and entirely inhuman, with large onyx eyes and shimmering antennae. A thin layer of skin closed from side to side as he blinked, and his head tipped, cheek brushing into the thick and so wonderfully soft looking mane of deep, brassy fur that circled his neck and shoulders.

"Victoria, this is Elias, who I mentioned in my reply to you," Astraeya offered. "And Juno will be discussing various options to you about how the Agency might be able to assist your research."

I spared a glance at Juno, who appeared to be middle management, dressed in a full pantsuit with a curiously writhing and hissing turban atop their head and intensely black glasses that blocked their stare. They sat at the head of the table, with an intimidating stack of paperwork and an open laptop. But I couldn't keep my gaze off the mothman figure across from me, the late afternoon sunlight illuminating his partially open wings and making him almost holy in appearance.

"A pleasure to meet you," he said, bending at the hips, *bowing* slightly to me, a smooth and refined edge in his voice that my body responded to with uncharacteristic eagerness.

Intrigue and caution flared in equal measure, and I stepped into the meeting room as he straightened. Black eyes crinkled at the corners, and a hint of canine fang flashed in his smile.

CHAPTER 3
Elias

A FIERY LOCK freed itself from the tuck behind a small ear, grazing down a pale cheek marked with a streak of freckles. Sunset was blazing into Victoria Dempsey's brilliant hair, and my gaze was riveted to the sight, a hint of amusement striking me at the cliché. She was a perfect flame to lure me in. Short, with generous hips and what I suspected were small breasts beneath the loose flare of her blouse, and her petite frame was entirely overwhelmed by a mass of scorching red and orange hair, barely restrained in a thick braid. She was modestly dressed, especially for one of the hottest days of the year, and had played the role of observer through most of the meeting, asking occasional questions and offering her own pieces of information in well organized thoughts.

Aside from her initial stunned response upon seeing me, she'd been calm and nonplussed, even reserved.

"You'll pay the Agency this referral fee for any personal demonstrations you receive from our employees, and then a separate fee to the individual, based on your demands. We'll leave that to personal negotiation between you and the party," Juno explained.

"I've already started collecting a list of those who'd volunteer their time for an interview or demonstration," I interjected.

Victoria's face lifted, her soft blue eyes searching my face, a daze of discovery passing over her features before clearing with a slight furrow between her brows. How old was she? She looked young, but she carried herself with authority, and she'd mentioned earlier that this would be her second master's degree.

"You have?" she asked.

It'd been two long weeks waiting for this meeting to manifest, but I hadn't waited idly. I might not have been able to learn anything about this woman, but I'd started the work of preparing as much as I could for her.

"I have. I've made my own study of this subject, just out of personal curiosity. I'm eager to help you in any way I can," I said, watching a blush rise, her lips parting to reveal they were fuller than I'd initially measured. "I know quite a few willing parties outside of the Agency's circle as well."

"Competitors? Former employees?" Juno asked. They were a canny gorgon, and already deciding if they had a financial angle they might work on this news as well.

"Personal acquaintances," I said.

"Thank you," Victoria murmured, before turning back to look at the paperwork.

Astraeya hadn't told me how much the Agency would charge for their involvement, but it seemed to give Victoria some pause. I wondered if it would be disconcerting if I offered to assist with the fee, but before I settled on a decision, she was signing the document. The scratch of the pen over paper created a racing thrill that ran up my spine and down into my wings, shivering at my back and drawing Victoria's absent glance.

Juno's snake strands hissed in restless agitation under their covering. They no doubt felt as though they'd accepted the bare minimum on behalf of the Agency. "Please keep us abreast of your work and any further involvement you might require from us."

We want to know if we can wheedle any more money out of you.

"I should be more than up to the task of offering Miss Dempsey what she needs," I said smoothly, pleased with the color that bloomed briefly on her cheeks. She didn't give much away with her expression, but the blush at least offered me some indication of response.

Was I experiencing attraction, or had I manufactured too much anticipation for this meeting? Were the pink stains rinsing over Victoria's features arousal or embarrassment? *Would she enjoy the two in combination? Shame could be potent.*

"I believe that settles the Agency's end of this," Astraeya said, pushing her seat back and giving a meaningful look to Juno.

"I appreciate your assistance, and I'll be sure to reach out to you as well as share the final paper and cite the company in my findings," Victoria said.

Astraeya's lips twitched at the offer. Academia wasn't *generally* MSA's first audience as a company, but Juno's shoulders relaxed and they seemed satisfied by the gesture, nodding and shutting their laptop. "Then we look forward to hearing from you. It was nice to meet you, Miss Dempsey."

"Victoria."

Noted, I thought, not bothering to disguise that my stare hadn't left her in longer than was considered polite. She hadn't looked at me in minutes, and I was growing impatient. I rose from the chair, and her eyes skittered briefly toward me and then away again.

"Can I walk you out to your car?" I offered. I'd seen the thing roll up and park from where I'd been standing by the window earlier—a plain and old but serviceable model that seemed to be well cared for.

Aside from her hair, she isn't very flashy, is she? My wings rustled self-consciously.

Victoria hesitated for a moment and then nodded, stepping back from the table and waiting for me to round it and meet her. She was uncomfortable, and I wasn't sure if it was nerves, or if it was something I had done. *You flirted with her when she asked for academic help.*

"I have you to thank for this working out," she said, hands sliding into her jean pockets as we exited the room. I held the door for her, and she walked through without pause, used to the courtesy.

"Astraeya has you to thank for giving me a task that actually interests me," I said.

She kept her stare forward, but subtle shifts and twitches around her eyes and mouth revealed the racing thoughts she kept hidden. "You aren't interested in your…usual work with the Agency?" she asked.

I glanced over my shoulder and flashed the ever watchful Juno a fanged smile. "On the contrary, sex always interests me. And yet, at the same time it can become…monotonous," I said, lowering my voice as we entered the lobby. We were walking too fast. We'd be at her car before I learned anything at all about this woman.

"I'll want you to explain what you mean by that," Victoria said, lifting her chin and meeting my gaze at last.

An opportunity. I nodded and bent slightly, trying to hold onto this brief moment of connection. "Gladly. Are you free tonight?"

Little lines of flame rose above her eyes in surprise. "Tonight?"

"I own a bar, Nightlight, in Wicker Park. We can speak more there. You can tell me what research you've started, and where you'd like to explore next."

I hadn't clearly read the tension in her before, I realized, because it released now, shutters opening in her eyes to reveal anticipation and pleasure—relief too. It would be a challenge to wage a seduction while remaining professional…perhaps impossible. I tried to adjust my expectations in my mind. Victoria Dempsey's project interested me, with or without the potential of romance. Better not to alienate her with unwanted advances.

"That would be perfect, thank you," she said, straightening with a hint of a smile.

I would simply keep my eye out for any hint of *wanting* advances.

VICTORIA DREW BACK, frowning slightly at the drink I'd slid across the counter to her.

"I didn't order anything yet," she said.

I'd taken a train back into the city and then flown to Nightlight, and I'd still managed to beat her time in traffic. I'd spent an excruciating half hour laboring over what drink to make her, realizing upon arrival that I'd gotten little to no sense of her as a person, less even than what Hannah generally offered. I'd settled on a sidecar, the rich color reminding me of her hair. Her response would at least give me a sense of what direction to go in if I'd guessed wrong.

"I hazarded a guess," I said.

She reached back, freckled arms hefting a mass of wild russet hair off her shoulders, orange lashes tipped with gold fluttering shut for a moment as the bar's air conditioning rushed over sweat dewed skin. She smelled like salt and cloves, and it was a struggle to keep my wings from ruffling impatiently. She sighed, dropping her hair once more and reaching for the drink I'd made her, twirling the glass by its stem.

"Why did you agree to help with my study?" she asked, staring into the amber liquid.

"I did more than agree. I *demanded* the privilege," I said, lips curved to their perfect angle.

Her stare flicked up, guarded and slightly narrowed, and my smile faltered. "Same question."

An unfamiliar prickling teased its way down my back—caution, yes, but excitement too.

"Not very many people would consider what I do with the Agency as problem-solving, but I do," I said, watching some of the wary shutters of Victoria's gaze crack open with interest. "I don't take cases where the problem is simply sexual relief. That's too…easy."

Her lips twitched with a hint of a smirk. "Too skilled, are you?"

I shrugged. "It isn't really about skill. It's about observation—paying attention, noting and repeating what works, actually being able to read a person's body language accurately, and understanding that while there are patterns, language isn't necessarily universal. Your species is curiously contrary. You lie more than others."

"I've heard fae don't lie," she said.

"Not outright," I agreed. "We work our way around a lie."

Her head tipped as she raised the glass to her lips, and I pretended to scan my attention around the bar, turning my head but keeping my inscrutable gaze on her as she sipped. Her lips pressed flat, jaw ticking slightly, and her tongue flicked out to lick away the remnants. There was no flinch, but she didn't like the drink. Too sweet, I suspected.

"So what cases do you take?"

"The ones where the client doesn't necessarily know what they want, or they're ashamed of what they want, or they're wrong about what they want," I said.

Her brow furrowed. "How do you know they're wrong?"

"The succubi and incubi run arousal diagnostics on incoming clients. Being aroused by something doesn't necessarily indicate it's what you *want* to experience, but it will catch a lie."

"Why would someone lie in that case?"

"Why do people usually lie?"

The bar was bustling tonight, and Lulu was busy running to and fro around me, serving the rest of my customers. Conversation was humming thickly in the air, the music low, enough to be heard but not force everyone to shout. The sun was still out, although tucked behind the city, and it gave the street outside a golden cast to match the low watt bulbs filling the long bar. The light made Victoria's hair into long licks of flame, loosely tamed at the nape of her neck, and her bow lips were still damp from her lick.

"To keep a secret, or...because they want something else to be true," she said, taking another slow sip of her drink.

I nodded and shrugged. "I assume the same."

Her gaze refocused on me, shades of blue and gray ringed with dusk. "Does that mean you see my study as a problem to solve?"

No, but I might see you as one, I thought. "I assume your research is approaching a problem, seeking a solution. That's what interests me. For instance, why are *you*, a human, researching monster sexuality?"

She stiffened, stare drifting away once more, shields up. It ought to have deterred my interest in her. "There are studies regarding what people consider sexual satisfaction and how often they achieve it. Kind of a basic information study for my program, but I found...I found variations of the study where the results were vastly different. The rates of satisfaction spiked well outside what might be considered any margin of error."

"What was the difference?"

She wet her lips and looked around the bar. "Whether or not the population studied was confined to human or all species."

I released a laugh. "Ahh, I see."

"I was able to grab the data of two of the studies. As soon

as I added a filter between humans and all other species, the human data matched all other studies."

"You want to know why monsters are so much more sexually satisfied," I said.

"There's really so little research done, and I know there are so many species that it might not be universal. I'm just looking for possible patterns, or at least places where experiences differ outside of the human standard," she said, her speech growing quick and determined, as if she were trying to speak the full thought before someone could interrupt her. "I've already put together a question based data model, and it's being shared across the country. It provides a wider pool of subjects, but it's a very limited mode of retrieving information."

I kept quiet, watching this still and vivid woman grow animated and determined, as if she were in the middle of an argument. She'd been talked over, dissuaded in the past. By professors, perhaps, or those close to her?

"I prefer an interview model, but there are questions I'm still learning to ask, and I don't have the thesis of *why* there's such a difference yet. With humans, it's often the difference between considering sexual satisfaction an orgasm versus an intimate and pleasurable connection. The less emphasis put on an orgasm, the better time we seem to be having. But so far, with monsters, the two seem a closer match. I can't tell if that means monsters are achieving orgasm more easily, or finding emotional intimacy more achievable," she finished, brow furrowing and holding my stare.

"The former," I said.

She blinked, sitting back, and it was as if she'd thought she was carrying the conversation with herself, like she hadn't expected me to be listening. "Really?"

I nodded. "This is based on environmental observation rather than data, so take it with a grain of salt, but I haven't seen any special inclination to other species falling in love more easily than humans."

"That's not...quite the same thing, but I'll take your point," she murmured, an elbow landing on the bar to prop her chin in her hand, gaze distant and thoughtful. She looked disappointed. "Is it a biological difference then?"

"While the biological differences are plentiful, I suspect not," I said. I had a few guesses as to the source of the difference, but it wasn't *my* research project, and I wanted to watch this woman work through the problem on her own.

Her lips pursed. "Well...then I still have questions that need answers. Where do you suggest we begin?"

CHAPTER 4
Victoria

"I'M NOT SAYING demisexuality doesn't exist, Margo. I'm asking you to make the *supported* argument with evidence that's more than anecdotal. This is what we're here for."

I stared down at my notes as Phillip clapped his hands together. At my side, Lyle muttered the word "prick" under his breath, the harsh word still silky in his voice.

"Sam, Kate, you're up next week. Have your points emailed to the class by Friday. Everyone, come ready with your questions. I can *tell* when you come up with them on the fly," Professor Stanton called over the sounds of us shuffling our laptops and notebooks and phones into bags. I kept my head down as I turned for the door.

"Victoria? A word."

Shit, Phillip. It's the first day.

Lyle stalled at my side, catching my eye, and I nodded him toward the door. "Wait for me?" I asked, loud enough for it to drift to the desk at the front of the classroom.

Lyle shrugged, but he checked on me once more before sliding out of the open doors with the rest of our seminar. I moved slowly through the scattered desks, down the shallow tiers of the amphitheater style classroom. It was too big a space for a class of seventeen, but I'd taken a spot as far from the front as I could reasonably excuse.

I stopped my approach at the last step, well out of reach from Professor Phillip Stanton, not that I thought I was really in any danger of him reaching out.

Lyle had left the classroom doors open. He was the only person who knew about the affair I'd had with our seminar professor in our first year. He hadn't even mentioned knowing about it until last spring, after we'd tried hooking up. Hiding sexual tension from an incubus was useless, apparently. Trying to pretend that you're about to have an orgasm was also useless.

"I can't really come unless you can, Vic. Want to order food and watch Secretary?*"*

Lyle was a good friend.

Phillip leaned back against his broad cherry wood desk and crossed his ankles, and contrasting, illogical tendrils of arousal and disgust flitted through me. "It's good to have you back in class again, Vic."

"Thank you, Professor Stanton."

"Even Eddie calls me Phillip."

Not because he respects you, I thought, but I tipped my head, waiting for him to get to his real point.

"I saw the update on your study. A volunteer assistant in… What exactly is this *Elias* offering you?"

Phillip was less than a decade older than me and his sandy hair had a little more gray in it now than it did three years ago, but it didn't lessen his appeal physically. Truth be told, I was still *attracted* to this man, visually speaking. He was tall, slim, and conventionally handsome. He also dressed the part of a professor, which I now suspected was an intentional effort. His tweed patch elbows were every bit the costume as the pleated skirts I'd worn to his class had been at the time.

I'd been looking for a fantasy, searching for something to

feel explosive—or maybe just something to cause my life to implode. As much as he'd told me he wasn't attracted to students, that it was *my* intelligence that ensnared him and my maturity that made his desire for me "helpless," I figured it was safe to say he was enjoying the stereotype as much, if not more, than I had.

"He's arranged four interviews already," I said. *One of which has the potential to offer a demonstration*, I reminded myself, a warm thrill growing in my belly that was entirely inappropriate to the spirit of the study, I suspected.

"He finds you subjects," Phillip said. "You weren't able to do that on your own?"

"Some. Not as many. He has the non-human perspective too. I've edited my questions with his help."

"It's risky of you to bring an outside force to influence your study. Its reputation is already fragile enough with the department."

Isn't it your job to protect that? I wanted to ask.

"Elias is very conscious of the boundary. He offers information based on my prompting. The work I present will be my own, Professor."

"I'd like to sit in on some of the interviews."

It hit me harder than such a demand should've, and I fought to hide my flinch. My relationship with this man had dissolved as undramatically as an affair between student and professor might manage. I'd never told Brett about cheating on him, and I'd miraculously managed to avoid another class setting with Phillip Stanton for two and a half years. But the program was too small for that to go on forever. He was the only figure in the department qualified to advise my work as it was now.

"Of course. I'll send you the schedules. Accommodating the subjects will be my first priority, of course," I said. "But I can always record the interviews."

"I'm only trying to prepare you for the department's push-back," he said, not quite succeeding to disguise his smug pleasure at my discomfort. "Friction is good for a study, yeah?"

Bastard, I wanted to scream.

"I appreciate that," I said, nodding. "See you next week, Professor."

"Enjoy your lunch," he said, calling toward the door where Lyle had shifted into sight.

The incubus didn't bother smiling back at our professor, his preternatural beauty managing to emphasize cool dismissal.

"Off campus?" I suggested, almost breathless. Was I running away from the room? I forced my steps to slow, and Lyle matched me easily, looking back over his shoulder with a narrowed gaze.

Lyle was quiet, and I glanced at him. His pale, almost translucent skin shimmered under the old fluorescent lights that glowed intermittently along the ceiling of the hallway, deep blue lips twisted in a grimace.

"I have my next psych in forty minutes, but—"

I waved my hand. "No, that's fine. I have something to eat in my bag. Let's just get outside." *Preferably before my skin crawls right off my body,* I added privately.

"You should report him," Lyle murmured, not his first time suggesting. "At the very least, you could get a new advisor."

I shook my head. "It was years ago. I'd just look like I was trying to work my way out of a conflict over my study. And no one else would—"

"*Someone—*"

"Lyle, I'm fine," I said, my voice smooth and controlled, a little too close to my mother's own tone.

His expression softened to a smile, eerie aquamarine eyes crinkling at the corners in amusement. I found myself smiling back, some of the tangled tension in my spine easing. I'd always been good at lying. The value of appearance, both in terms of physical and also social, had been persistently enforced in my growing years.

My mother wasn't cruel, but her will was stronger than my own as a child. Her words were the stubborn rose bush that had stretched their strong roots and thorny branches inside of my mind for two decades. And she had taught me that at the bare minimum, I should always be *fine*. For a long time, *fine* had been my baseline, a status so innocuous I'd fooled not just my family, but Brett, and even myself. It was a reflex deeper than my own nature to say that I was fine.

And it was a relief beyond measure to now have a friend incapable of being tricked by a lie, no matter how good.

"When do you meet with the moth again?" Lyle asked, offering me an easy change of subject.

I glanced over my shoulder as another class let out, this one full of undergrads. They looked shockingly young to me now, although I could remember how mature I'd considered myself at the time. I'd been in a relationship for four years already, and I was too tightly wound at parties to enjoy myself, especially with Brett checking in by text every hour. Maybe he'd always known I would stray eventually.

"Tonight," I answered Lyle.

"At his bar again?"

I'd been to Nightlight three times so far, and each one had started with a new cocktail waiting for me, and a quiet exchange of notes between myself and Elias. He was an interesting bar owner by my estimation, somehow both entirely in command of the space and people around him, and yet also fairly uninvolved. No one greeted him as they took their seats, and he seemed to take very little interest in the general management.

I wasn't sure if he *needed* to meet there so he could keep working, since I hadn't really seen him doing anything that seemed to qualify, or if it just felt like easy neutral territory. I'd considered suggesting meeting elsewhere, like a library or coffee shop, except that the patrons of Nightlight fascinated me. The variety of monster races was wider in a small Wicker Park bar than anywhere else in the city I'd encountered, all mingling together over drinks and food. Humans were frequent too, but never so many that they outnumbered any other race.

I nodded to Lyle. "But late tonight. We have our first interview after the bar closes."

"Are they a vampire?" Lyle guessed. "How old?"

I found myself smiling. His own work was focused on fear as a sexual stimulant, and a vampire would be an excellent subject to interview.

"Decades, not centuries," I said.

Lyle drooped slightly. "We shouldn't really be swapping, anyway."

"True, but I can ask if they might know anyone qualified for you."

Lyle's long arm swung over my shoulders, squeezing briefly. "I'd owe you."

I wasn't sure that was true. My friendship with Lyle often felt lopsided, but at least a small favor might help even the scales a little.

———

A HORN BLARED from the street, barely muffled even from the back porch of my apartment. The kitten in front of me stiffened and yowled in warning.

"Yes, I know," I murmured, silky and low. "How rude of them, hmm?"

The kitten hissed. Behind him, the black tomcat I'd named Hubert yawned and stretched, finishing with a lick of his jaw and a patient glance at the wet treat I held out in front of me. He knew he would get his turn.

The kitten warned me once more, arching its tiny, bony

spine, but it pounced closer another few inches, and its eyes flashed between my face and the treat.

Seraphina, a svelte tortie, brushed up against my side and butted her head into my elbow. My knees and ankles ached from squatting for so long, but any attempt at settling myself would no doubt end in the kitten fleeing.

It was a dusty, dirt stained white, with spots of brown on one ear and the tip of its tail, and it had been following Hubert here for three nights, gobbling the bowls of food I left out and growling at anyone and everything. None of my other regulars paid any heed. The kitten was a scrap of fur and bone, and we'd all been through this routine before.

A soiled paw with preciously small black beans slapped ruthlessly at the end of the plastic tube, and a glob of wet treat flew out and landed on the floor of my porch. Seraphina helped herself, ignoring the kitten's outraged howl at her nearness.

I sighed, and it leapt away, scurrying into a dark corner. Growls and crunches of dry food commenced, and Hubert strolled closer to me with a lazy pace, stretching his back legs one at a time.

"Good baby," I whispered, scratching his head as he licked at the end of the treat tube.

Hubert looked like a miniature panther, with muscular broad shoulders and a long sleek frame. Unlike many of the other tomcats who visited, Hubert seemed to have considered his options and decided to settle down, accepting the hospitality of my food and the top cubby of my overly elaborate cat tree within a day of arrival. Lately, he spent more time inside the apartment than out.

"You want in while I'm gone?" I asked.

Both Hubert and Seraphina, the loyalest pair of strays I'd tamed and fixed and vaccinated, wandered to my back door obediently. They didn't always come in, but they had beds and litter boxes and food bowls when they were in the mood. I took their presence as the compliment it was.

Checking the water and food outside once more, I turned off the porch light and picked up my bag from where I'd left it at the door.

With a parting rumble and a hiss, the new stray kitten watched as I took the backstairs down to the alley, calling a car for my trip to Nightlight. It was after midnight, but the bar wouldn't close until two. I'd have time to kill there, but I found myself strangely eager.

I'd never liked bars much before. They'd been places I went with Brett and his friends and their girlfriends—noisy and crowded and inevitably the scene of someone else's personal argument, drunken tears, or vibrant shouting. After Brett, I'd found myself without a social circle that really belonged to me, without anyone to call me out for a drink. It hadn't occurred to me that I could do so on my own, that there might be a place like Nightlight, lively but not oppressively loud, where the drinks were little works of art and the crowd that frequented was anywhere from mid-twenties to centuries old.

A dark car pulled up to the curb where I waited, and I slid into the backseat, wondering what Elias might have waiting for me on the bar top when I arrived.

On my way. I texted.

Good, there are people here I'd like to introduce you to.

CHAPTER 5
Elias

A FLICKER of fire out of the corner of my eye, and I set the bottle I'd been pouring from down on the bar, turning toward the front door.

Victoria walked past the windows, her gaze already searching through the glass, studying the bar. She wore a loose blouse and long pants, and she had her tortoiseshell glasses on. I'd seen them before—she seemed to wear them at night, her eyes tired from contacts perhaps. Her hair was twisted up, barely contained by a claw clip, curls frizzing into a bright halo around her face.

She didn't look toward the bar, toward *me*, as she entered, instead taking in the rest of the long room. Her steps faltered briefly over the threshold, and I wondered if the wave of sound, loudest now in these final hours, overwhelmed her like it sometimes did me.

A stone hand reached for the drink I'd been preparing, and I pulled the glass out of Rafe's reach.

"I assumed you were finished," he said.

I looked down and frowned. "There's only vodka."

"It's a good vodka," Hannah said, seated next to Rafe.

I turned, trying to recall what I'd been preparing for my

friend but unable to resist glancing back once more. Victoria's progress was slow, partly because we were packed and partly because she didn't appear to be in any rush, weaving through the crowd, looking into the faces of those who paid her no attention. I didn't understand how every head in the room managed to avoid looking in her direction.

Moth, flame, a soft voice mocked in my head.

"Move your bag now," I said to Hannah when Victoria had almost reached us.

Hannah's eyebrows raised slightly, but she reached to the bar stool next to her and lifted the bag I'd instructed her to place. I waved to Victoria, pointing to the seat, keeping an eye on the crowd to ensure no one else grabbed it. From the counter below the bar top, I lifted a cut crystal highball glass and slid it across to Victoria before she even sat down.

"Old-fashioned variation," I said, comparing the amber of the liquid to the shade of her hair in the low watt lighting. "Victoria, these are my friends, Rafe and Hannah."

I turned back to the mirrored wall, watching the three exchange hellos and handshakes as I finished Rafe and Hannah's drinks.

"He doesn't allow us to order our own drinks either," Hannah said.

"It's his way of showing he cares," Rafe said, and I considered shoving him off the bar stool.

"I always assumed it was his way of trying to prove he could read you at a glance," Hannah muttered. Which was ironic, considering I could hardly read Hannah at all.

I frowned as I returned with their drinks, regretting asking them to stay to speak with Victoria.

"I assumed it was your way of getting to know me."

I set the drinks heavily in front of Rafe and Hannah, staring back at Victoria, her eyes a little larger behind the lenses of her glasses.

"Perhaps all three," I said, and it was too transparent an answer for my liking, but Victoria smiled. It was a barely there smile, hardly a curve and a faint softening around her eyes, but from someone so remarkably unreadable, a little went a long way. "Hannah and Rafe met through MSA. He's a gargoyle, clearly, and she transitioned into a werewolf several years ago. I think you may find a great deal of information about their relationship useful."

I hadn't planned on asking my friends to participate in Victoria's study. I hadn't planned on introducing them at all, not so soon, not when Rafe was all too aware of my own ulterior motives. But in explaining myself to them, how I was helping, what Victoria needed, Hannah had suggested the meeting herself. Which was unexpected.

"Do you allow for anonymity?" Hannah asked.

"I won't be using any real names, but personal details may be relevant," Victoria said, that momentary softness subsiding under academic professionalism. "If at any time you're not comfortable sharing information, or you feel what I need might be too revealing, I can exclude you from my material. If nothing else, an interview could help guide me with another subject."

"You can use my office," I suggested.

Victoria blinked and glanced between us. "I'm not sure an interview after social drinking—"

"She doesn't drink alcohol, and he metabolizes it too fast to get tipsy," I said.

A shield went up in those dusk blue eyes, and I bit down on my tongue.

"Either way is fine," Rafe said lightly. "We're in town for a few months at least."

Victoria was silent, and I resisted the urge to beat my wings. It'd been a very long time since the vice of impatience had possessed me.

"Three interviews in one night is incredibly efficient," she said, taking a sip of her drink. She paused, and my stare sharpened as she rubbed the rim of the glass against her bottom lip, tongue flicking out. She liked that drink. "As long as you don't mind the late hour."

"We're used to it," Hannah said, smiling.

"Do we tell you about our sex lives together, or separately?" Rafe asked, grinning. "Did you bring a recorder? I'd hate for you to wear out your hands trying to write it all down."

Hannah rolled her eyes, and Victoria shifted her bag on her shoulder. "Separately to start. The office?"

I started to move, but Hannah waved her hand at me, sliding off the bar stool. "I know the way. Entertain my mate."

Victoria's eyes lit up with interest at that declaration, and the crowd parted slightly for the pair to slip away. I had no need to follow them. Victoria likely wouldn't welcome my interference in the interview, and Hannah certainly wouldn't.

"She doesn't like me," I said, partly to myself and partly to Rafe.

His expression was too innocent as he sipped his drink. "Which one?"

I scowled, knowing and hating the answer to his question.

"Too much of a puzzle for you?" he asked, raising his eyebrows.

I found a glass to wipe down, whether it needed it or not, and Rafe hummed.

"Ah, no, exactly the kind of puzzle you wanted. This is you *excited*."

I made sure that Hannah and Victoria were long gone before leaning onto the bar, my arms crossing.

"It only took Khell and Sunny five days."

Rafe snorted. "That was how long their appointment was. I don't think it took them much more than five minutes to start falling in love."

"Was it that fast for you and Hannah?"

Rafe laughed. "I don't know. I mean, no, but in retrospect, it does feel like the conclusion was inevitable. Elias, are you sure you're not..." He trailed off, gaze sliding away.

"What?" I snapped.

Rafe sighed. "Projecting. You decided you want to try falling in love. You find a reasonably attractive woman—"

"Reasonably," I scoffed.

"—who is reserved enough to present a bit of a challenge, which you like, in getting to know her. I mean, would you *want* it to take five days?"

I frowned. I didn't know—that was the point of experiencing love in the first place. Victoria did fascinate me, and in spite of Rafe's concern, I did understand that didn't equate to romance.

"So you're saying it *should* take longer for me?" I asked.

Rafe's mouth hung open for a moment, and then he let out a heaving breath, falling forward and placing his face in his hands. "Oh dear."

———

"CONSUMING a lover's blood is very sensual, just as most demonstrations of physical trust with a lover are sensual. But the act itself can be as mundane as eating a sandwich in mundane spaces," Andre offered with a shrug. "Sex itself is a slightly heightened version of the human experience, from what I can recall. And that's if I'm well-fed. If I haven't had blood in a while, it can be muted, or even sluggish or impossible."

"You rely on blood for arousal," Victoria said, looking up from her notes.

"In the same manner a human requires basic nutritional maintenance."

Victoria blinked, head tilted, and then hummed in acknowledgement. It was almost dawn, the sky the color of a thick layer of dust, and the conversation with Andre had been circling toward its conclusion for at least an hour. Every time Victoria seemed prepared to call it a night—or a nearly morning—another small detail was introduced and she followed the thread with inexhaustible curiosity.

"Another necessity for vampires is, of course, avoiding daylight," Andre said smoothly with a glance at the windows.

Victoria stared blankly back at him for a moment, her head no doubt filling with new questions, and then she followed the line of his stare, startling. "Oh! Of course. I'm so sorry—"

"Not at all. I live very close by, and I was enjoying your attention too much to interrupt you."

I was surprised to see a spreading blush on Victoria's cheeks at the compliment.

I stood, and Andre did the same with a smile, dipping his head to me. "Good day, Elias."

"Good day. I owe you a favor," I said.

The young vampire paused, as still as a statue for a moment. "I should accept, but...no, you really don't."

"A very small one then," I offered, shrugging, impressed that he would even consider refusing.

"If you insist," he said. Victoria had risen to join us, and she shook hands in parting with Andre, offering him a faint smile, perfectly formed and serene in spite of the tired red that had crept in around her eyes.

"I'll be in touch," she said as Andre moved to the back door of the bar.

I'd turned off all the lights in the bar after closing, and the three of us had tucked ourselves into a sheltered booth, well out of sight. Andre lived in an industrial styled garden unit just down the alley and would be home within minutes. Victoria, on the other hand...

Her eyes focused into the far distance, past the walls of the bar, and she swayed slightly in place, her body exhausted even if her mind refused to settle.

"Would you like to get breakfast?" I asked. It was too early for anywhere but a twenty-four-hour diner to be open, but Rafe swore by the hashbrowns of those sorts of places.

"Coffee," Victoria murmured, and then blinked, looking surprised to see me at her side. I tried not to be too offended that she'd apparently forgotten my existence while interviewing Andre. "You offered him a favor. And if I understood the context, that wasn't lightly done?"

"Not amongst fae, no," I admitted.

Victoria wet her lips and then started gathering up her things, checking the recorder she'd been using, skimming through her notes. "You can't indebt yourself to every interview subject you find me. It isn't practical. And I suppose it muddles their motives for speaking with me."

"Fair enough. But this was useful?"

"Three interviews in one night? Yes, Elias, this was very useful," she said. There was that unshuttering again, humor and familiarity and softness in her expression. I wanted to catch her face before it turned away, and I had to tuck my fingers into my pockets to resist.

"I hadn't considered what a difference it might make to those who were born human," she said.

"I believe the increased exposure to human values and society makes a difference to those—"

Victoria raised a finger and pressed her lips flat, shaking her head, but she didn't look angry—that hint of a smile was still in her eyes. "No, don't tell me. I have to reach my own conclusions. Where are we going?"

———

VICTORIA STUDIED the other patrons of the diner we'd walked to with the same intensity she had Andre, sipping on the single mug of coffee she'd ordered. I'd ordered enough food to feed us both and felt a surge of triumph when blatant hunger widened her eyes as the plates hit our table.

"Help yourself," I said, arranging sides of bacon and sausage, hashbrowns, biscuits, gravy, and pancakes evenly between us.

Our weary waitress in an outdated uniform and apron paused at the periphery. "Anything else for you two?"

"Fruit?" Victoria asked, sitting and glancing back at the spread I'd offered her. "And a western omelet...and the bagel and lox platter."

The woman's eyebrows raised as she turned away from us.

"I had to have something to contribute," Victoria said, grinning and creating what could only be considered a rare miracle.

I sat back, stunned by the force of that smile, the brightness, the laughter in the corner of her eyes. She ate a slice of bacon, licking the grease off her fingertips and lips.

"Why are you doing this?" I hadn't meant to ask the question. In a way, I'd asked it once already.

Victoria's guards went up once more, but it was easier to look at her when she was hiding herself halfway—the full reveal had been blinding. Dazzling. Disarming enough to have me blurting out questions I'd meant to decipher the answer to in secret.

Then she sighed and lifted up a pancake with her bare fingers, folding it like a taco and filling it with a sausage link and a pile of hashbrowns. Rafe would've approved. I wondered what the two of them had discussed, jealous of their time alone.

"I suppose, with all I'm asking others to share, it's a good lesson in empathy to do the same," she said. When her eyes blinked, they did so slowly, as if threatening to remain closed and let her fall asleep. She was tired, and perhaps vulnerable to sharing more than she might usually. I should've apologized and changed the subject. Instead, I leaned forward, waiting for her answer.

"I have trouble achieving orgasm," she said plainly.

"Many do," I answered.

Her lips turned down, and I made myself a small plate of food, glancing at her as she ate.

"That's true. I *don't* achieve orgasm with a partner. Or I haven't in many years. I find the expectation to be...oppressive during intimacy," she continued.

"Is sex uncomfortable for you? Physically?"

She shook her head. "No. And I don't think I have issues with arousal."

"You don't think?"

She stared somewhere in the distance, past my head. "I was in a long-term relationship. From high school until a few years ago. I thought I was losing interest in sex altogether, and then..."

It was a struggle not to drop my fork, to fix myself to every word, to leave room between us for her to answer. Such honesty was shocking, most especially from this woman, who sometimes appeared to be all facade and reflection.

"I had an affair," she said.

I wanted to offer her my opinion—that a relationship formed as a child, one where she was losing interest and feeling obligated, was not unlikely to make her seek satisfaction elsewhere. But she didn't need an opinion.

"And did you orgasm during the affair?"

She sighed and shook her head. "I enjoyed sex again though. Craved it. And the person I was involved with was less concerned about getting me off. Perhaps that's what I liked."

A selfish lover? I frowned at that. That would prove challenging. What I enjoyed sexually was learning about the other person, discovering what aroused them and then what satisfied them. Selfishly chasing my own release was too easy—boring, really.

"If you were satisfied with your inability to reach orgasm, an equally disinterested partner wouldn't be so difficult to find," I said, tipping my head.

Victoria snorted, resting her chin in her hand and her elbow on the table. "That's true. I want too much."

Tell me what you want, I thought. "I don't think that's true," I said instead, hazarding a guess. "You want a partner who cares about your pleasure, without making you reach some arbitrary marker of that as a means to prove their own skill in sex."

Victoria's back hit the squeaky booth leather with a slap, and she glanced around the nearly deserted diner and then back at me, blinking rapidly. I swallowed hard and tried to look nonchalant as I ate. The waitress returned with another tray, negotiating new plates onto our buffet, all as Victoria stared at me in startled silence, as if she'd just woken in the conversation and realized all she'd shared.

I waited for the server to return out of earshot, and then continued, "Any luck with masturbation?"

Victoria grabbed her coffee, taking a gulp, and then settled in her seat. "Sometimes. Rarely." She shrugged. "It still feels good either way."

I nodded. Then it was the dynamic of the other person. Was she too guarded to relax around a lover? I helped myself to an underripe piece of melon and let her relax back into the silence.

"The study interests me on its own merits," she murmured, quickly foraging the pineapple out of the bowl, staking her claim. "But I suppose I was hoping there might be something for me to learn."

I nodded. "Naturally. I imagine there will be a great deal."

She blushed and shifted in her seat. "I take it that other

species are much more comfortable speaking about sex than humans."

"It varies. On average, I imagine so." What else had the long-term partner instilled in her? Was it really just a matter of his frustration about getting her off, or was there more? Cautious this time, as one would be when approaching an injured wild animal, I continued, "Less to consider taboo, certainly. What humans refer to as a kink is less scandalous and more a matter of personal preference."

She paused, cheeks spotting with red, and then nodded and took a bite. "Personal preference still allows for incompatibility."

"Of course, but not shame as an accompaniment. I may not find a particular act exciting, but that doesn't mean I couldn't be accommodating for my partner."

She tilted her head. "You don't think that trait has more to do with your professionalism?"

I huffed and waved a hand. "I didn't learn that working for MSA. I simply offered my talents to them."

"As a favor?" she asked, her lips twitching.

"To their clients," I said, answering her hint of a smile with a suggestive one of my own. Finally, we were flirting. "And to the company's reputation."

She laughed at that. "You're that good?"

"I'm the best," I said, leaning back to lounge into the patched and tacky pleather seating. The fine hairs of my wings caught against old adhesive, but I kept my wince buried, refusing to break this tenuous tether of attraction between us.

Her eyes glittered. "I take it you don't just mean at MSA."

I preened as if she'd made the claim herself. "Well, now, that would take an entirely different kind of study on your part."

She laughed softly, shaking her head and returning to her food, but the blush on her cheeks spread down her throat into her collar. It was all teasing, a casual and predictable line of flirtation, but it would plant the seed.

Imagine me in your bed, Victoria, I thought, watching as she arranged herself a bagel half with cream cheese and lox with a degree of precision that showed a force of focus, a determination not to think of us together.

It was a start.

CHAPTER 6
Victoria

"VERY GOOD, *Victoria. A little wider now.*"

I shuddered, my breasts flattened and aching against cool, smooth wood. A tickle of heat raced down my spine. In front of me, on a wall that surged forward and back with the pace of my uneven breaths, an orange kitten clung to a tree branch with too huge eyes, liquid and cartoon.

My hands were sliding over the surface of the desk I was bent over, even as my cheeks spread behind me, revealing too much. For a flash, I viewed the room from above, my bare body spread over a desk, paperclips the size of bananas, and rulers scattered like mulch around my waist. A gleaming, vibrant figure hunched over my back, massive monstrous eyes flashing on metal wings.

"Are you learning the lesson?" the rich and liquid voice purred, snapping me back into my body with a hot pulse and a scratch over my tender ass.

"Th-the lesson?" I moaned and twisted, hard wood softening beneath me, a familiar scent beneath my cheek as thick pressure built in my core. I rocked in place.

"How to come all over my cock, Victoria."

I woke with a whine, my body slick with sweat and the throb of arousal immediately easing. A golden smile and the fantasy of soft, silken fur between my fingers lingered.

I groaned, my hips grinding down into the mattress that dipped away without offering friction.

Inappropriate, a prim voice warned.

"He started it," I whispered to no one, then stretched my arm out to my bedside table, fumbling in the shallow top drawer for my vibrator.

Instead I found soft, thick fur.

I sat up abruptly, startled at the piece of my inappropriate fantasies appearing in the waking world, and then huffed at the sight of Hubert rolled onto his back, belly exposed for my attention.

I sighed, digging my fingers in as he stretched his front legs up over his head and smiling at the resulting heavy motor of a purr.

It was probably better *not* to try and get off to the thought of the mothman who was acting as my research assistant. Surely it would blur the roles between us too much…or something to that effect. I wasn't exactly clear on what the roles between us were, and Elias had remained silent and observant during last night's interviews.

It would be an inconvenient distraction, I told myself. And likely a bitter disappointment in the end. I grimaced, thinking of all I had overshared, and rolled to the edge of the bed, giving Hubert a last pat on the belly. My stomach rumbled, and a pinch of a neglected caffeine habit panged between my eyes. A drip of sweat shivered down my back, and I squinted out of my window at the sunlight clawing through the leaves of the trees.

I needed coffee, a shower, and food that wouldn't upset the strange balancing act I'd created at the diner, probably best arranged in that order.

In the quiet of my not quite studio—the very first place I'd ever lived alone—flickers of the night before organized in thoughts. Three interviews with three different species, two who had crossed over from human to monster. The hazy walk from bar to diner.

My coffee rested on the windowsill of my shower, every sip easing the stabbing in my head and making it easier to recall the details. The incongruous elegance of the moth fae across the table from me, illuminated by dusty, stained glass lampshades, glittering in those black orb eyes of his.

The water of the shower was cool, but it didn't soak into my skin, into my persistently needy core. I closed my eyes and sighed, trailing slippery fingers over my breasts and down my stomach, giving into the need for touch, even if it might not end with relief.

I CHEWED at the corner of my thumb, mentally tallying my expenses, the new dent of MSA's fee upsetting the careful grip I had on my money. After the breakup with Brett, I'd applied for and been granted a fellowship with the university, which was just enough for my off-campus apartment. That spark of independence—the refusal to move back home into the cradle of my parents' affluence—had started a wave of me snipping financial ties. I had a TA position now, occasionally covering a lesson, and slogging through entry-level psych classes' paperwork. Library hours helped cover the cost of vet bills and cat food for my little side project at home.

There's always the trust, a soft voice offered in the back of my head. My aunt had left me and my sister a hearty inheritance, but with a few more years of interest, I'd have enough to launch my own sex therapy practice.

"How did it go?"

I looked up, closing out of my banking app, and smiled at Lyle. "Better than I expected. But the all-nighter has definitely messed up my sleep schedule. I was up until three again last night." And then could barely fall asleep till dawn.

Lyle tipped his head. "You could get a job bartending. Probably make better money."

I wet my lips as a vision—innocent and charged—of brushing against Elias behind his bar passed through my head.

"Too social for me," I said, laughing to pass off my brief breathlessness.

Lyle's eyes narrowed, and I jumped up from my chair, turning to the library cart behind me. It wouldn't distract him —he'd already caught what I would've rather hid—but it would be a polite way of asking him not to pry into why that suggestion thrilled me.

"I saved these for you," I said, grabbing a few books Lyle had texted about.

"My hero. Speaking of socializing, want to come work at the table?"

"The table" was a long, eight-seat study table—with no less than twelve outlets—that the gender and sexuality department had been holding in shifts for at least five years, always with two people working there, open to close, on any given day. I'd done a couple shifts there in my first two years, but now preferred the solitude I found behind the front desk.

"Not today," I said, my usual answer. "I'm here till eight tonight."

My phone lit up under my hand as Lyle shrugged and left me. Sunday night wasn't the most popular night at the university library, mostly occupied by the more studious underclassmen who still lived in the dorms.

I slid my hand away, wincing at the latest notification, an email from Professor Stanton. I'd logged my interviews from the weekend earlier today, and sure enough, found a passive-aggressive reminder that he wanted to sit in on one, "preferably at more accommodating hours."

I considered replying with an equally snarky email about accommodating the living hours of my subjects, especially when they were nocturnal, but it was safer to leave communication one-sided for now.

A new notification popped up before I set my phone down, this one considerably more welcome, and such a surprise that I stared at the red dot over my messages for a long stretch before opening the screen.

Emma: *How are you? We should get a drink soon, just the two of us.*

Had Brett fucked up? Did she need to talk? Was she okay?

You're catastrophizing, my therapist's voice soothed in my head.

I exhaled and answered. *I'd love that. I'm good. Studies are picking up, but I can make time. Let me know when and where.*

I waited for a minute, then hurriedly typed out a "How are you?" but minutes ticked by with no answer.

Still, she had reached out first this time. That was... progress.

The estrangement with Emma felt more like an accident—an embarrassing consequence of her and Brett's relationship. I'd never directly told her that I thought they made more sense, that I wasn't angry or hurt, but happy for her. It had felt too patronizing. Or vulnerable. I wasn't sure which.

My thumbs hovered over the screen, debating another message to leave unanswered, when fate intervened with a text from a new direction.

> We have volunteers available for a demonstration and interview. I can arrange a comfortable, private location. Weekends during the day are best for them.

My breath caught. A demonstration. It had been an idle suggestion, a goal I hadn't expected to be able to achieve. I wasn't even entirely sure how to pitch it to Stanton, and if he suggested attending that too, well...I would ask Elias to turn the offer down.

Wouldn't I?

> A naga and a minotaur, in case you're
> curious. Should be…robust. Feel free to
> swing by the bar to discuss.

I huffed out a laugh, then made sure no one was nearby to witness my flushed face and giddy, nervous trembling.

I wanted to run to the table and tell Lyle, but he would know how excited I was and all the myriad reasons for that excitement. Plus, everyone else would be there. I didn't mean to avoid the rest of our classmates, but they'd known me best when I was with Brett, and afterwards…

I was still learning who I was, now that I was living without a set of instructions.

> Don't be nervous. They do this sort of thing
> for fun.

My cheeks swelled with a grin.

> I'm free next Saturday.

Now I just needed to sort out the best way to keep Stanton out of the picture.

CHAPTER 7
Victoria

I PASSED the address twice before stopping on North Hoyne and counting every house number, turning slowly to the Victorian brick monstrosity at my back and squinting. Had Elias given me the correct street address? I'd assumed we'd be meeting at a hotel, and while this place was large enough, it looked more like a private residence.

I dug into my bag at my hip, searching for my phone to text Elias, when the front door—the front *doors* at the top of a high set of stone steps with two little Welsh dragons roaring in greeting at the base—cracked open, surprisingly quiet for how heavy they looked. I shrank, afraid I was about to be accused of...something, when a fluffy golden head peeked out.

"Lock the gate behind you," Elias called down.

Only years of social training kept me from gaping back at him. Questions could wait until I didn't have to shout them across a well-manicured lawn from the other side of a beautifully maintained wrought iron gate. It also refrained from any groans or creaks as I pushed it gently open, turning and latching the heavy tumbler lock behind me.

Elias shouldered the door open as I ascended the steps, glancing side to side every moment. Were we breaking into an abandoned mansion? No, of course not; it was too well kept. A history museum, perhaps?

"Elias…*where* are we?" I whispered.

He left me enough room to slide inside, my body brushing against his and then stumbling into a dim entry, my steps scuffing against dense carpet as I waited for my eyes to adjust.

"I didn't say? My home."

The thunk of the door closing covered the hitch of my breath at his response.

His *home*?

"That's not inappropriate for your study, is it?" Elias asked, but I was too busy marveling over his answer to consider the ramifications for the study.

This was his home? His, and no one else's? Or was it like a collectively shared Gilded Age mansion? Surely the latter.

"Cyril and Atlas have been here before, and I arranged a room that I think will serve our purposes nicely. Victoria?"

I was groping somewhat blindly around me, the floor tilting under my feet. A soft hand caught my elbow and guided me to the right, easing me down onto a cushioned bench.

"It's very hot today," Elias murmured in the wake of my continued stunned silence. "I'll get you some water. Wait here."

It *was* hot today, oppressively so, a last blaze of summer in September, climbing over into the triple digits in the city where the pavement baked and caused the air to shimmer with reflected heat. Elias was probably right that it contributed to my wobble. The other explanations—that I hadn't expected the mothman to own an exquisite mansion, that I'd stayed up too late thinking about what was happening today, that I'd been too nervous and excited to eat this morning—were better left undisclosed.

I caught my breath at last, adjusting to the low lighting of the art deco chandelier overhead, and satisfied my curiosity. The entryway was warm, my fingers brushing over the crushed velvet of the cushion I sat on, eyes drinking in the large, bucolic landscape of some English countryside across from me. There was a coat stand with a few tweed style jackets hanging from the arms and an old felt hat resting on top. I stood slowly, crossing closer, and spread one of the jackets open. It didn't have an open back for Elias's wings, and I highly doubted anyone else had arrived in a wool jacket on a day like today. The linings were silk, with old-fashioned labels carefully stitched below the collar and not a stain or tear to be seen, like vintage clothing that had never actually been worn.

Strange.

I turned and faced the hall, eyes widening at the enormous figure waiting past a few opened doors. A stuffed black bear, slightly more worn, obviously an acquired antique, and also topped with a hat, this one straw. Carefully propped in his hand was an ancient fishing pole, line running through the loops and a glittering, sharp, ornately painted tackle dangling, as if the bear might walk off to the lake at any moment.

Through one cracked door, I glimpsed a grand piano; through another, a sitting room that reminded me of the carefully curated mid-century modern style my mother had chosen as well.

Past the fishing bear were short halls splitting off in either direction, but directly ahead of me was a broad staircase leading up to a landing that separated the wings of the house. The long carpet I walked on was thick and spotless, the gleaming sconces running along the hall made of polished brass. The house was beautiful, and so...precise. It *did* look like a history museum actually, although one with a slightly tilted sense of humor, based on my bear friend.

Curiosity nipped at my heels, tempting me up the stairs or

around one of the corner hallways. I hadn't seen which way Elias had gone, but I wasn't sure I wanted to be found quite yet. The house was cool, and it begged to be explored.

Then light steps whispered closer from my left, and Elias appeared once more with ice water and lemon in a tall, cut crystal glass. He was dressed in loose pants—linen, I guessed, although there wasn't a wrinkle to be seen yet—and a white shirt that was only buttoned halfway up, a slightly darker gold fur exposed on his chest. I wanted to muss him, to tease him for the tweed jackets that were clearly hanging on a coatrack for effect rather than use, but I bit my tongue and accepted the cold glass with steady fingers.

"You didn't mention that we'd be meeting at your house, no," I said, raising a hand to continue without interruption. "But I don't think it's an issue in this case. Other than hotels or their homes, I can't think of a lot of options. The university certainly wouldn't give us access to space on campus."

Elias tipped his head, eyes scanning his home aimlessly. "There are some private clubs we can consider for the future, but I did my best to create an appropriate atmosphere. Would you like to see?"

I wanted to see *everything* in this home. Walking inside, discovering that Elias lived here, had created a vast unknown in his character I hadn't considered before, and now I wanted *all* the missing information. And also perhaps to stall a little longer.

"Are Cyril and Atlas here already?" I asked.

Elias sighed and nodded. "Mm, they're an eager pair. I've told them this is for academic purposes, but I'll warn you… they love an audience. Would you like to be alone with them, or should I stay?"

"Stay," I said, immediate and firm, my hands fisting tighter around the straps of my bag. If I were alone, I was afraid it would be too easy to…enjoy the experience. Hopefully, the awkwardness of someone else watching me watch the couple would keep me focused.

Elias nodded, and gestured back in the direction he'd come. "Shall we?"

I nodded, wetting my lips, but when he turned to lead the way, I found myself unable to follow. "I'm nervous," I blurted out in a whisper.

Elias stopped and turned back to me, frowning. "What aspects are making you nervous?"

I exhaled slowly, my shoulders easing. It was the right question. A problem to solve, a list to make. And although I'd had some regrets of how much I'd shared with him a week ago, it also made it easier to spill uncomfortable honesties once more.

"I'm concerned I'll be aroused."

Elias blinked, lips curving slightly. "Ah. I hadn't realized we shouldn't be," he said. "They would certainly be offended if we weren't."

I jerked slightly at that, a little thrill racing through me at the same time that a dozen more thoughts—about profession-alism, about whether or not what I was doing could be strictly considered academic—started churning in demand.

"I don't think arousal is an issue, unless it interferes in your ability to observe and record and ask questions," Elias mused. "Do you find that your arousal tends to overwhelm your intellect?"

"Unfortunately not," I said without thinking, then sipped water to keep myself from saying more. I should've eaten earlier. Maybe I hadn't quite recovered from the heat, or the shock, or—

"I find it difficult to quiet the analytical mind during sex as well," Elias said, which *did* quiet mine. "It's part of what I enjoy about sex work—it serves me better there than during personal intimacy."

"I'll still have questions," I said, relaxing slowly.

"They'll be delighted to answer them," Elias said, flexing his wings. "We'll just have to be mindful of when they get a bit…performative, rather than authentic. I'll be able to tell."

Because you have experience watching them have sex? I wondered. *Or having sex with them?* Neither question was relevant.

I inhaled deeply and released it with a soft nod. "All right. I'm ready."

"Good. Hopefully, they haven't started without us."

I thought Elias was joking, but when we arrived in the large room with an enormous king bed at the center, as if it were a stage, it was clear *something* was taking place. Except there was too much to see all at once—the velvet curtains draping down the walls, a hint of sunlight bleeding through from the far wall, the lighting that had been arranged on tracks, bulbs turned to the bed like spotlights, the low seating bordering the bed at every side. My face heated in understanding. Elias had made sure that I would have a thorough view, that we might move about the room, watching this pair.

And there they were, perched at the edge of the bed, a huge white minotaur with a dark snout and brown ears, nuzzling into the inky black hair of the elegant naga at his side. I'd never seen a naga in person, and I now had an obstructed eyeful. I wasn't sure what clothing someone who was half snake and half human in appearance might wear, and I still wouldn't know because Cyril was already naked, bronze brown chest gleaming, long indigo blue tail twisting like liquid over the edge of the bed, around his lover and—

Oh. Down into Cyril's trousers.

"I believe I told you that the interview would take place before the display," Elias greeted them dryly.

Atlas chuffed, ruffling Cyril's long hair, and turned to face us, ears tipping down in what somehow read as a minotaur's equivalent of a blush.

"We got bored," Cyril said simply, offering me a fanged smile. He had vivid green eyes with slitted pupils, high cheekbones, and slightly longer than human nostrils, but he was undeniably beautiful with an otherworldly grace.

Atlas reached down to his lap, and Cyril's more slender end of his tail slipped free of the partially undone waistband as the minotaur rose to his full and enormous height. It was a good thing Elias had outrageously high ceilings, because I was sure Atlas was at least eight feet tall. His arousal, swollen firmly against the tight fit of his pants, down into the left pant leg, was *generously* proportional.

I wondered if I could back out into the hall and steal another few minutes of being overwhelmed alone.

Atlas offered me a slight bow. "Cyril is incorrigible. And he wants you to know how excited he" —Cyril cleared his throat and arched a sharp brow— "*we* are to help you with your study."

Cyril leaned back on the heels of his hands, the many muscles of his abdomen tensing, and I realized with growing amusement that he was showing off. For me, or for Elias? Perhaps the whole room. To be fair, he was so beautiful he rightly deserved a larger audience. He leaned forward, rising up on his tail, and then I thought maybe he just needed to work his core that much for the sake of his own movement.

"I've always found intelligence stimulating," Cyril purred, offering me a heavy lidded glance.

"Quit flirting," Elias said, just a hint of a snap. "Her study is important to her."

Cyril just grinned and batted heavy lashes at Elias. "I prefer to call it 'admiration.' 'Study' makes me feel like an insect."

My eyes widened at the obvious insult to Elias, whose wings shivered at his back.

"Would you say you're posturing for dominance at the

moment?" I asked, stepping forward, gesturing between Cyril and Elias.

Cyril blinked at me and then released an airy laugh, curling his tail beneath him and settling into the cushion it provided. "My kind tends to flirt…aggressively. So, yes, a bit of that, and a bit just to see if I can rile the fae. He's too composed."

I nodded as Elias huffed and slipped behind me, sitting down on one of the benches he'd arranged.

"Would you say you flirt more with verbal sparring, or physical touch?" I asked, pulling my recorder from my bag.

Cyril swayed in my direction, head tilting invitingly. "Would you like to find out?"

"With a verbal answer, yes," I said.

Atlas stuffed his hands in his pockets, laughing silently, his broad shoulders shaking, and Cyril's eyes glinted at me, some internal debate waging for a moment before he sighed.

"Verbal sparring is the invitation. If it's accepted, I move quickly to physical. That's common amongst Nagavanshi."

"Is the physical competition aggressive as well?"

Atlas grunted but ducked his head and let Cyril answer. "Very. We like to trap, to test the strength of our partner. Coiling is common."

"Coiling?"

Cyril glanced at Atlas, who lifted his head, full mouth curving as he nodded. Cyril straightened, chest broadening, and snapped quickly upward, tail lashing out and wrapping itself around Atlas's waist, dragging him closer as Cyril swirled around, delicate tail end settling around the minotaur's ankle, Cyril's arms draped over Atlas's shoulders, his head tucked under a sharp horn, their cheeks pressed together. Atlas's arms tensed and swelled against Cyril's thick, scaled body, and his hips rocked forward, making the pair of them wobble in place.

"Is the goal to see if they can free themselves? Like a challenge?"

Cyril chuckled, and Atlas shook his head. "It's to see how long it takes for us to surrender," Atlas answered.

CHAPTER 8
Elias

I **CROSSED** my ankles and leaned to the left as Atlas grunted and bucked in Cyril's grip. Victoria was out of sight, hidden behind the writhing bodies on the bed, and if she didn't reappear in a moment it would be a challenge not to get up and follow her.

"Would you like a better view?" Cyril hissed, rolling his entire body, tail squeezing around Atlas's chest and legs, the minotaur's eyes rolling back in pleasure. Cyril's hands gripped Atlas's broad horns, drawing him into an arch, driving him forward with every deep grind. "Do you want to see my cock thrusting between his thick cheeks? It's quite a picture, I assure you."

A step tapped against the hardwood floor. I straightened, ears and antenna twitching uncontrollably.

"That's not necessary."

Was she breathless, or just trying to be unobtrusive?

And then a wisp of red appeared, and Victoria walked slowly around the bed, emerging from behind the lovers to face their sides, a respectful distance back from the bed but her eyes sharp. Her cheeks were blatantly flushed, and I itched now more than ever to join her, to scent her arousal, hover my wing at her side to see if her temperature had risen.

"You're keeping Atlas from coming?" she asked, bent slightly, a sudden focus at the minotaur's irritatingly impressive cock. It was too long and heavy to stand truly upright, but it made an arc in the air, tip slick and gleaming. Her head tilted, and I realized she was looking below to where the end of Cyril's tail had Atlas's weighty sac in a vise grip.

Cyril was quiet for a moment, swallowing a moan as Atlas rocked back into his thrusts. "It'd be a shame to waste him," Cyril rasped.

Victoria blinked at that, opened her mouth for another question, and then paused, watching the pair instead. Atlas huffed in deep breaths, his thrashing now in tempo with Cyril's sinuous motion. The naga's groan of pleasure was airy and quiet, and he nuzzled into Atlas's throat, the moment suddenly private, personal. Victoria took quiet steps away from them, watching the whole picture now, giving the couple the space to enjoy one another.

The interview had gone long, but neither Cyril nor Atlas made any complaint, and Victoria had long since stopped observing the clock in the corner near me. I'd scheduled them early in the day for this exact reason. Victoria's curiosity was insatiable, and they were a good pair to satisfy her—well, *that* part of her. Granted, Cyril approached answers like a form of foreplay, and stoic Atlas had an eager gleam in his eye when it came to performing.

"That's it," Atlas breathed, and then snarled as Cyril retaliated his soothing with a brutal grip on his balls. "Go on, my love. Give me what I want."

Cyril's arms lashed around Atlas's chest, and his tail grew restless, sliding up and down the silk of Atlas's fur. Scales shivered and gleamed, a soft *zzzzip* sounding as they brushed together, like glass pebbles being stirred by gentle fingers.

One of Atlas's arms squirmed free of Cyril's trap, hand reaching back and tangling into silky dark locks, thick neck stretching and flexing to offer Cyril's nibbles more room. They were beautiful together, a show I'd enjoyed and partaken of in the past, but my interest was now more eager for the slow, halting steps of the woman moving closer to my seat. Would she join me? Or continue to walk in circles around them?

Long, pale legs and freckled knees with the unsteady gait of a fawn, hips wider than slender shoulders, loose shirt hiding what I suspected would be modest breasts and an exquisite collarbone. I wasn't generally aroused by physical appearances, although I appreciated fine aesthetics, but I'd found myself fantasizing about little pieces of Victoria recently. Her hair tangling around me, the top of her head under my gaze, elegant fingers stroking my fur, and now these freckled knees would be tormenting me in my idle hours. She turned, and the backs of her knees were almost translucent, blue veins stark and pronounced under delicate skin I wanted to drag my claws over, trace the paths with my tongue.

Cyril released a rattling cry and then silenced abruptly, the snap of his jaw muffled beneath Atlas's appreciative groan. Victoria stumbled back two steps, just out of reach. If I thought it wouldn't startle her, I could lean forward and cup my hands around her hips, draw her back into me, settle her onto my lap for the rest of the show.

Victoria gasped at a sudden scuffle on the bed, and I tore my eyes from her.

Atlas untangled Cyril's now satisfied body from around his limbs, taking the naga by the shoulders and rising up onto his hooves, horns nearly scratching the ceiling. Cyril's smile was lazy at being bested, his mouth gleaming with Atlas's blood, mouth opening invitingly and long tongue flicking out, cleaning drips of glittering precum from Atlas's angry red shaft.

I didn't have to grab Victoria; she was paying too close attention to the couple as she stepped back, and I wet my lips as she almost mistook my lap for her seat. Rather than disturb her focus, I claimed the grip of her hips I'd been imagining—perfectly plush and fitted to my large hands—and guided her to the side, offering her the seat at my right.

"Now you'll see why I put up with Cyril's wicked mouth," Atlas teased, thick fingers tangling further into Cyril's hair, guiding his cock deeper between stretched lips.

Victoria's breath was uneven as she sat next to me, and she didn't notice as our arms brushed close. Slowly, I leaned in, breathing deeply and catching the whiff of her interest, musky and tart, ample enough to make my mouth water.

"Holy shit," Victoria murmured, eyes widening, and I glanced back to the bed, chuckling as Cyril's throat flexed and swelled, Atlas's cock disappearing inches at a time.

"One of my favorite things about the integration of species is finding all the fascinating ways unexpected pairs suit each other. Few can take all of Atlas or his kind," I said, keeping my voice soft and close to Victoria's ear.

"I did wonder," she answered. Her blouse rustled with the force of her breaths, and I glanced at the buttons. Was she small enough to not need to wear a bra? I could suck at her nipples as she watched Cyril gobbling down Atlas's enormous cock. Just a few loose buttons and— "His throat massages rather than needing to thrust. It's…gentler than I thought it would be," she whispered.

I cleared my throat, blinking, and refocused on the couple on the bed. If Victoria worried her arousal was unprofessional, she definitely wasn't about to let me seduce her in front of her study subjects. *Focus, Elias. The seduction can come later.*

"They're a mated pair," I said.

"Mating can be open? Or the flirting is just—"

"A bit of both. For some, mating makes it easier to have an open sexual relationship, I believe," I said, shrugging. "You're very secure in a mated pairing. There's no chance of another person fracturing that connection."

Victoria hummed as Atlas started to gently thrust, Cyril's sleepy, sated gaze growing clearer, his hands squeezing at the white globes of Atlas's ass, receiving a swat from the minotaur's tail in answer.

"Suck harder, my love, or you'll never see me satisfied," Atlas warned in a growl.

"It will take several orgasms before Cyril really drains him," I said.

Victoria's eyebrows rose, but she nodded, glancing between Atlas's spread legs. "I can imagine."

There was a pause of quiet, and then we both snorted. Victoria's hands lifted, scrubbing over her face, as if she was trying to distract herself from her interest. But her legs squeezed together, the hem of her shorts outlining the soft flesh of her thighs.

"Is this difficult for you?" I whispered.

Her hands lowered to her lap, and for the first time in over an hour, her eyes found mine. They were a little wild, pupils dilated, and her cheeks were flushed, a giddy kind of excitement brightening her expression.

"No...and yes," she answered, turning back as Atlas's grunts and moans grew more urgent.

I ignored the minotaur, leaning closer. "Tell me."

Her lips parted, lashes fluttering shut briefly as my breath teased a curl below her ear. "It's nice to feel aroused. That got difficult at one point. It's difficult not to have an outlet for it though."

Atlas's body bowed backwards, and he howled, covering the sound of my question. "Do you miss fucking?"

Victoria was quiet, almost as if she hadn't heard me, and Atlas wrestled Cyril down into the bed, straddling the naga in a kneeling position, lifting scaled hips up to his still erect cock. I relented, edging away, watching the pair. Cyril whimpered as Atlas's thumbs stretched open the swollen lips of his sheath, where his cock had retreated after finishing in Atlas's ass. Nagas were very versatile lovers, a fact which Cyril had bragged to Victoria and she now witnessed with stunned fascination. Atlas shuddered as the fat head of his cock squeezed into the tight sleeve.

"I can—" Atlas grunted and shook himself. "I can feel his little cock nudging against mine. We barely fit."

Cyril moaned, thrashing against the sheets, hands scrabbling for purchase as he rolled up as if to tuck Atlas deeper. "We always manage, darling." His tail whipped up, strangling around Atlas's throat, the minotaur bucking deeper with a shout.

Victoria's breath breezed into the furred collar around my neck, tickling at me, the air catching in my lungs.

"Yes. I miss it."

———

I SCOWLED at the empty room, searching it once more, as if I might find Victoria hiding in plain sight. There were still wisps of her scent, but they were thin and faint compared to the overwhelming perfume of Cyril and Atlas.

I'd walked the couple out after they'd made their goodbyes to a seemingly calm Victoria. She'd even managed not to blush as the naga flicked his tongue over her wrist during a gallant kiss on the hand. I'd left her here, in this room, with the soiled bed and her notes, and now it was all abandoned...

She'd run from me, from the charged moment. I planted my hands on my hips, wings flexing and chest puffing out, wondering if I was more irritated with myself for pushing her too far, or with her for skittering away.

Except her notes were here, her bag, her recorder.

So she was just...hiding somewhere. Perhaps even waiting for me to find her?

I turned on my heel, hands sliding down into my pockets. Perhaps she'd forgotten that most monsters were even more natural predators than humans. My race of fae might not have the scenting skills of a werewolf, but we had excellent hearing, and my antenna caught certain natural pheromones in the air, especially the ones Victoria would've been exuding.

I was halfway down the hall, tingling in anticipation of finding her, cornering her, catching those wild eyes with mine once more, when I heard the sound of water running and the squeak of a handle, the sound shutting off.

I leaned back against the wall across from the lavatory and waited. She didn't look surprised to see me as she stepped out, with little droplets clinging around her hairline. She'd splashed herself with cool water?

"We should talk," she murmured.

Two steps forward, now how many back? Since when had I ever been so impatient with a potential lover?

"Follow me," I offered, and I reached out my hand just to see if she would take it.

Her hand was cool and a little damp against mine, eyes sliding down to the floor, but her body remained close as I led her down the hall. I was tempted to take her back to the room we'd just been in—remind her of her arousal, of our bodies too close to one another on the bench—but instead, I chose a sunny room full of comfortable, casual furniture, a few books resting out on a table, the walls covered with old naturalist prints and pinned specimens. She slid away from me, my fingers loose around hers, expecting her retreat. She did so slowly and after a long pause.

"You regret accepting my offer earlier," I said.

She turned to face me, and I wanted to fist my hands at the return of her implacable calm, the unreadable woman back in place. She helped herself to a seat, curling her legs under her on a blue cushion that matched the color of the veins on her legs I'd been lusting after earlier.

"Was it an offer?" she asked.

I frowned and sat down in the matching armchair across

from her. "Not explicitly, but I intended the insinuation of one."

She nodded. "I intended the insinuation of accepting it, then—you're right."

My hands settled on the arms of the chair and I crossed one leg over the other. "But?"

But it would be unprofessional. But my work is important. But it was a result of my arousal and not a sincere interest in you.

Her answer didn't match any of my guesses.

"But I want to know how it would work between us," she said. I sat up, and her eyes softened before shying away. "I'm not rejecting the offer, Elias. I just need there to be…appropriate boundaries between sex with you, and working on the study with you."

"I can draw back from the study more," I said.

She smiled. "You're more interested in having sex with me than helping with the study?"

I opened my mouth to say yes, then thought over the question. Actually, I really enjoyed the subject of her study, and I enjoyed watching her work.

"I'm not sure I need you to draw back. I just need the…the Elias and Victoria working on that study to be different people than the you and me having sex together."

It was impossible, of course, but I could think of a couple solutions that might appease her. And I was selfish enough not to point out the flaw in her plan.

"And I need this to be about you getting off. Using me," she said, her voice growing thin, words halting and starting as color rose to her cheeks. Her eyes met mine, and they were bright again, eager. "I don't want you to try and make me come."

It took everything in me not to argue her point. I was *good* at what I did, and that was figuring out what got a person over the edge of their pleasure and then giving it to them. Repeatedly.

"Please, Elias," she said, gaze fixed to mine, breaths growing short.

Then again, maybe her request was about more than a pattern of frustrating connections with others. I leaned forward, resting my elbows on my knees.

"You want to be used?"

Her breath hitched, and she nodded in a small jerk.

I chewed over her answer in my thoughts. "Do you want to be forced?"

Her lips parted and she drew back, and then relaxed and shook her head. "N-no. I think it's… Not forced, but not about me or my pleasure. Like it's my role to make you come." She bit her lip and her brow furrowed. "Like it's all I'm good for."

Some degradation, but not force. A toy, perhaps, or… An inkling of an idea started to stir, and I glanced around the room.

Not here. Not *yet*. Just as I'd done for Atlas and Cyril's performance, I would have a stage to set and some roles to consider.

"Very well. Give me time to plan," I said.

Victoria's eyes widened once more. "Plan?"

I smiled, relaxing into my seat. "Trust me. This is what I do. And I promise you, I do it *very* well."

CHAPTER 9
Victoria

"THERE'S NOT much to support a thesis here."

I frowned, squinting over his right shoulder into the glare of sunlight from the window. "Of course not. I'm only a couple weeks in."

Phillip shrugged and held his hands up. "I'm just saying, as I've said before, you have too broad a scope."

"You're only looking at the anecdotal evidence of these interviews, which yes, I understand that this is only a handful of people—"

"Species."

"—but the larger survey is being distributed now, with *your approved* controls and variables. That's the greater evidence. This is meant as support and a means of enriching my research goals."

I caught my breath as Phillip sat back in his chair—a brown leather wheeled desk chair that was a little too familiar to me. I blinked and exhaled slowly, relieved to find that the tension in the room was my anger, not arousal.

"Do you really doubt I'm getting work done outside of these interviews?" I asked.

Phillip waved a hand. "No. The surveys were thorough. I know those took time. And they'll take time for results. But I worry that by the time you have those results, it will be too late for you to narrow your focus."

"And if I narrow it now and the evidence comes back in my original theory's favor, I'll have wasted weeks of opportunities," I countered. "It's a risk either way. I'd rather risk ambitiously."

Phillip's eyebrows bounced. "Would you, really?"

I bristled at the question, glancing at the clock once more. The first half of the meeting had gone smoothly, covering everything I'd done over the month, but I'd been itching for escape for fifteen minutes now.

"Forgive me," he said, sitting up. "It's just…you're different than you were. Which isn't relevant to your work. Very well. Consider a *possible* pivot, make an alternative plan, just as insurance."

I opened my mouth to object, but finding thinner threads in the pile I was working through wouldn't take that much extra effort to outline, not when everything was go so well already.

"I can do that," I said, reaching for my things. We still had ten minutes, but Phillip only watched me pack up rather than object to my rush.

"The freelance assistant is still working out for you?"

I bent over, hoping I wasn't blushing as I thought of Elias. "They are."

"Is he absent during interviews? I noticed there doesn't seem to be—"

"He doesn't interfere. And it just depends on what the subject is comfortable with. I don't think he's ever had cause to interrupt," I answered, lifting my bag strap over my head to rest it across my body.

Phillip nodded. "Your interviews are incredibly thorough. You never drop a detail. I look forward to seeing you in action."

A hint, but not a demanding one.

"Thank you for the meeting, Professor Stanton."

"I'll see you in class on Thursday."

I nodded as I turned for the door, trying not to be so obvious with my sigh of relief as I opened it. Phillip had a decent-sized office, not quite the narrow closet of some I'd been in, but it was filled with books and stacks of papers, crowding around me and making it hard to move. The scent, the light from the window, and of course the man himself were all oppressively familiar, tugging me back to the year when I'd stood with a match in one hand and a stick of dynamite in the other, just waiting to light the fuse on the order of my life.

I wove my way through the network of cubicles in the faculty offices, flicking fragments of an older version of me out of my thoughts. The sound of a giggle, a little shy and a bit forced. The nervous tic of twisting a lock of hair through my fingers. The memory of a warm hand brushing and retreating from my bare knee. The guiding pressure at the small of my back as I walked down the sidewalk of my old Chicago neighborhood.

There was no touch now. I didn't always know who I was now that I wasn't the Dempsey's eldest daughter, or Brett McAllister's girlfriend, or the nice redhead who kept her hand down in class and her skirt up in the professor's office, but I knew where the edges of my body were. I knew that every piece of me someone saw as they passed me in the hall, I had chosen that morning in the mirror. Intentionally or absently, I hadn't thought of anyone else.

I was myself, for myself.

———

Miss Dempsey,

This email may come as a surprise, but rest assured, I'm writing out of concern. Your recent work has been subpar and is taking a toll on your average. I know you take your studies seriously and am reaching out to offer you an opportunity to recover some of your slipping grades.

If you are interested in earning extra credit, please meet me at the N. Hoyne Ave address, second floor, right hall, last door on the left.

With respect,

Professor E.

"SHIT, VIC, ARE YOU ALL RIGHT?" Lyle asked, slapping me firmly on my back.

I brushed his arm away, covering my cough with my elbow, eyes watering and head shaking as my phone clattered to the table, thankfully face down. The last thing I needed was Lyle asking who Professor E. was, or why I was being offered the opportunity to earn extra credit at a private address.

At least my sudden choking spell—on an inconveniently timed gulp of water—would cover the reason for my face being so red.

Elias wanted to *role-play*?!

And of all the scenarios he could've chosen… Did fae read minds? For a moment, Lyle's voice faded under a ringing siren in my head as I tried to remember what I'd told Elias that night at the diner. I'd mentioned the affair, but…no, no, I was confident I hadn't said it was with my professor. This was a coincidence. A ridiculous one, but still, not intentional. Just as the dream of "lessons" I'd had afterwards had been a coincidence.

Hopefully.

"I'm fine," I rasped, shaking my head. "Swallowed wrong."

"Ugh, I hate when that happens. Everyone stares like you're dying, and it's the…" Lyle trailed off as I searched the taqueria, but it was late for lunch and early for dinner, and the only alarmed glances I received were from the staff behind the counter. "Sorry. I'll leave you to breathe," Lyle offered with a grin.

Teacher student, Elias? Really?

It was like a scenario out of a cheesy porno, the kind where a simpering girl in a too short skirt and too few shirt buttons—and dear god, *pigtails*—whines and pleads she'll do anything to raise her grade while a smirking—

I shuddered and closed my eyes, sadly put off my appetite for my nachos. I would have to email Elias back my disinterest, and maybe it would be an easier way of explaining I'd changed my mind altogether. Did he really think I was the type who would—

He doesn't. That's the point.

I paused, my hand covering my phone, staring into the swirling wood grain pattern on the table in front of me.

I'd told Elias we had to be different people in any situation we might have sex together. I'd been thinking of some basic compartmentalization, but this was creative. My lips twitched. Crude, and silly, and out of character.

A little filthy.

The shock of the offer, the resemblance to my fling with Stanton and the strange dream, was jarring, but I'd certainly never gone crawling to Phillip asking for extra credit.

And crawling toward Elias... A warm curl of interest brushed through me, stroking between my thighs.

It had an appeal. I wasn't sure I could simper, but I knew how to be demure. My mother had taught me that. I knew how to play a role.

My mouth watered at the thought of how I might be asked to earn the extra credit. It would be *for him*, just as I had asked. I would have to please him, gain his approval. "For my grades."

I snorted, and Lyle glanced at me.

"Better?" he asked, head tipped in curiosity.

Damn. I'd forgotten again about his sixth sense.

"Still breathing," I answered, sliding my phone into my pocket and reaching for my plate of nachos.

Professor E.

Thank you for this offer. I'll do whatever it takes.

Miss Dempsey

CHAPTER 10
Victoria

I BRUSHED my fingers through my curls, teeth picking at the skin of my bottom lip and staring at my own reflection. Elias's house was eerily quiet around me. He'd emailed me the gate code and where he'd hidden me a key. It felt a bit like I was breaking in, but there was a kind of relief in not seeing him right away. I'd brought a change of clothes with me, unable to brave the idea of walking around in Chicago in my…costume, even if no one would've glanced twice, and the solitude gave me the chance to change without facing him first.

I stepped back from the mirror, surveying myself. My recently thrifted pleated skirt would never have been short enough for the X-rated movie version of this scenario; it hit the appropriate height above the knee for any school dress code, and I'd buttoned my short sleeve blouse all the way up. But I'd taken off my bra and underwear.

Fuck. What was I *doing*?

It's just role-play, Vic. People do it all the time. Brett thought it was tacky, but it's perfectly normal and—

I pursed my lips and released a long breath. I had on sneakers and white knee socks. I just wasn't quite sure what to do with my hair.

Pigtails were a firm no. Two braids made me look like a child. A ponytail made a wild puff of curls behind my head. And I...I was already having a hard time wrapping my head around this. I twisted my hair back in the usual lazy way, grabbing a claw clip and fastening it in place, watching as strands worked their way free immediately, curling against the back of my neck and around my face. I looked more like a naughty librarian than a naughty schoolgirl, but I could still see *myself* in the mirror and I needed that right now.

He's not actually grading you. This won't matter, I reminded myself. And the minutes were ticking by fast.

"Can't be late to class," I murmured to my reflection, a slightly hysterical laugh rising up from my throat in answer. I shook my head, pulling the last detail of my costume out of my bag and tucking my folded clothes away, leaving them on the floor in the bathroom.

There was still no sign of Elias as I walked out into the hall, alone in the long space. The air flowing under my skirt and against my bare sex was a shock. I'd tried going without underwear a couple times with Brett when we were younger, wanting it to feel like an arousing invitation, maybe even trying to incite him into a semi-public quickie.

He'd told me it felt like an invitation to anyone, rather than just to him, and I hadn't repeated the offer.

Maybe this was too—

No. *I* wanted to try it. To see how Elias reacted. There was no real risk if he didn't like it.

I smoothed my hands over my skirt as I reached the stairs, climbing slowly, wondering anyone at bottom would've seen anything, had they been there. My face warmed, heat rising in my core.

It's cheap, Vicky.

So was role-playing as a student in need of extra credit. But apparently it also got me wet.

Elias had the doors of the rooms on the second floor

closed, and I itched to open them, but I knew from the last time I'd been in his home that it would take me too long to really enjoy everything I found. And he was waiting for me.

My palms were starting to sweat. I turned to the right hall, with only two doors on the left. We were at the back corner of the house, and I wondered if there'd be a view of his backyard, what it would look like.

The door was cracked open, a sunlit wood floor my only view from the hall. I paused, listening, and heard a scratch of chalk on a chalkboard, my lips curving up. How very retro of him. I wondered how long it had been since Elias had been in a classroom. It was all smart boards or whiteboards nowadays.

I knocked with two knuckles and waited.

"Come in, Miss Dempsey."

I shivered at the new firm snap of his voice and pushed the door open, frozen in place at the sight before me.

Nine desks, spread evenly in the room. The kind with chairs attached and little cubbies for your books. In *Elias's house.*

The windows had old vinyl pull-down shutters, and when I stepped in and glanced to the back wall, I let out a startled yip of a laugh. Inspirational posters. Thankfully, not the dangling kitten.

"Eli—"

"Miss Dempsey," he interrupted, and I startled, turning to the front once more, my mouth drying as he turned, golden wings tucking into his back.

Oh. Maybe I *did* have a bit of a kink for professors?

Elias was wearing perfectly tailored gray trousers, a brown leather belt, and a white button-down, although it was once again generously open over his chest. He was standing at the chalkboard, staring at me over a pair of tortoiseshell glasses. His gaze landed on my hand and the gift I'd been holding, and he offered me a perfectly indulgent smile.

"You brought me an apple."

I wanted to acknowledge what we were really doing—that I was playing a part, that this was theatrical. Had he always had a classroom taking up one of the rooms in his house? Or had he arranged this the same way he'd done with the staged bed downstairs for Atlas and Cyril's demonstration, for *me*?

"Take a seat, Miss Dempsey."

I wet my lips and then nodded, stopping briefly at the large, gently scuffed yellow oak desk. A tweed jacket with felt patched elbows was draped over the back of his chair. A jar of pencils. A few file folders. A cup of paperclips.

And a stack of little blue essay books.

There was no logical reason why my body clenched with arousal, feverish goose bumps racing over my skin, except for the sheer amount of *thought* he'd put into this moment.

I turned and faced the desks, three rows of three, not all of them a perfect match, like he'd collected them from different classrooms.

It'd only been a week since I'd asked him if we could get away with having sex. How had he done all this in that time?

I took the middle seat of the nine, my skirt long enough to keep a little modesty between me and the warm plastic. I read the words on the board. Biology 101. I pressed my lips between my teeth to keep from laughing as Elias shuffled materials on his desk, grabbing one blue book and one pencil.

My eyes widened.

"I think a short essay is the most appropriate penance, don't you?" Elias asked, head tilting and lips smiling. I hadn't really considered his age before—it wasn't that easy to read in his still unfamiliar features—but the gentle patronization in his tone dragged me back in years, and I had to fight down the trained habit of drawing myself up, cooling my expression to hold my own against an older man.

"I did say I'd do whatever it took," I said, shrugging. "I guess an essay isn't so bad."

"I suppose I could've asked you to email it, but I need you to take this seriously. I know the kind of work you're capable of, Miss Dempsey. I expect you to apply yourself."

He'd always been taller than me, but he towered over me as I sat in the desk, sunlight making him brilliant and almost blinding.

"Five hundred words. Take as much time as you need." The essay book rested on my desk with a rustle of pages, sharp pencil settling on top.

"Five hundred words on…"

Elias's claw looked sharp, but it moved flexibly as it tapped against the cover of the book. "It's in there. I'll be at my desk if you have any questions."

I set my hands on the desk, the ridges of the pencil rolling under my fingers as I drew it closer. It wouldn't come as much of a surprise to anyone to admit I was an eager student. I obviously wasn't in any rush to give up academia. Still, I wondered if Elias could've guessed how his thoroughness, right down to the yellow pencil with a freshly sharpened tip, would give me a small thrill. It was a fantasy I hadn't indulged in, realized to exacting detail.

I flipped the book open to the first page, and my sudden breath echoed in the room. Elias's steps back to his desk paused.

HOW I TOUCH MYSELF

I bit my lip, taking a moment to study Elias's small, even handwriting, letters blocked carefully along the top line.

Elias had turned to watch me and our eyes met, the heavy black of his lightened in the sunlight, a hint of a smile in the corner tilt of his gaze.

I leaned back in my seat, spreading my knees apart, letting one hand fall to my lap to hitch the hem of my skirt higher. A grin flashed over his features and then he sobered, a small *tsk*ing sound from his tongue and teeth. The warning made me shiver, my body freezing in place as he shook his head.

"Hand*written*, Miss Dempsey. There's no need for a demonstration...yet."

I hunched forward in my seat, drawing my knees back together and hiding my smile.

I like to start with my clothes on. It makes it feel more like a seduction...

———

I SHIFTED IN MY SEAT, a short sigh escaping, matching the airy breath as I turned another page. My skin was hot, and sweat beaded on my back, both from the sun shining through the windows and the steady pool of arousal that had been building the longer I thought about masturbating. I'd taken my hair down, the claw pulling uncomfortably at my scalp, but it just made me even more warm and I kept trying to twist it back away from my neck, only for it to slowly explode once more.

My tongue flicked out on my lips, and I scratched out "fondle" and replaced it with a more specific method. The clock above Elias was ticking loudly, and more than thirty minutes had passed. This was one of the most indirect methods of foreplay I'd ever experienced, and I found it agonizing.

And wonderful.

My hand landed in my lap, fisting and pressing over my throbbing sex.

Elias's throat cleared and I snatched my fist away, sitting up and turning another page, racing through the words once more, barely seeing them at all. It was enough.

"Done."

I sat up, resting my elbows on my desk. I flipped the book closed and my eyes lifted slowly to his, waiting.

"Bring it here. I'll grade you now," he said, pushing back his own seat, wings stretching.

I rose on weak, tired legs, blood rushing below my waist. The room seemed impossibly long as I walked, until suddenly I stood at the corner of his desk, holding out the essay book in one hand. Warm, soft fingers wrapped around my wrist, and I wondered if he could feel my pulse racing as he tugged me closer, between his body and the desk.

"Up."

My eyes widened and I rose up on my toes at the command, perching on the hard edge of the desk. A small gasp slipped free as he nudged my knees apart and stepped closer to stand between them. I gaped up at him, trying to remember to breathe, to predict what came next, and he snatched the blue book from my fingers, sitting back down in his chair and scooting it close, forcing my legs a little wider. The hem of my pleated skirt stretched and inched back higher on my thighs.

Elias flipped open the cover, and I tried to hold my breath, or to at least keep myself from heaving in eager breaths. His lips curved, and I watched his free hand raise and then hover above my left knee. My leg seemed to lighten, as if it wanted to lift and press itself into his touch like a cat stretching for a pet, but it didn't have to wait. Elias's hand settled, firmly pressing and stroking upwards, and I released a shuddering sigh at the velvety sensation.

"Lean forward, Miss Dempsey," he said, eyes sliding over the words on the page so slowly.

My hands gripped the edge of his desk, and I withheld my whimper at the loss of his hand on my thigh, only to release a short groan of relief as it lifted to grope my breast. There was no shyness, no hesitation. Elias clutched and rolled my flesh through my shirt, thumb swirling until it found my nipple, then brushing back and forth.

Just as I had written.

My eyes shut on the picture of him, sitting tall in the chair, shadowed from the sun, studying my essay as he put it to practice. Except—

My brow furrowed. Was he trying to use what I'd written to prove he could get me off? It was thoughtful, actually, a clever trick, but I knew the habits of my arousal, the pattern of pleasure I went through with another person, and I knew how easily I got in my own way.

"Eli—"

"Professor," he murmured, fingers sliding and pulling the buttons of my shirt open, then tugging the hem loose from where I'd tucked it into my skirt. "I can't give you an accurate grade without putting your thesis to the test, Miss Dempsey."

My hands slid back on the desk, giving him room even as I considered breaking the moment, calling us back from these characters to ourselves.

Elias stood up from the chair, arching over me, and I held my tongue as he pushed the collar of my shirt wide, over my shoulder, exposing one breast. I just wanted to feel—Ah!

My head fell back as his hand stroked over my bare skin. His touch was so soft, the coat of fur that covered him making it feel like he wore a velvet glove.

"It's a shame you can't suck on your own nipples when you masturbate," Elias whispered, close enough for his breath to rush over my throat.

I was torn between opening my eyes and reaching for him, drawing his mouth down in invitation, but he was studying the words I wrote, and I was already anticipating the rest of the essay.

"Let's see…where did I leave off?" Elias asked, slowly twisting the nipple poised between his fingers as I squirmed in place under the small touch. "Ahh, I'll need both hands for this. Can you hold the book, Miss Dempsey?"

I raised a quaking hand, and he slid the pages into place as my thighs spread wider for him, knees nearly touching the corners of the desk.

"A full hand cupping over your panties…" Elias recited, and I stiffened in expectation, the heat of his touch just hovering an inch from my skin. My eyes opened, and I found him staring down into my face. "But you aren't wearing any panties, Miss Dempsey. I'll have to take points off for that."

"I—I left them in the bathroom. I could go and—"

"Too late," Elias said sharply, and then that decadent hand was covering my sex, fingers delving into my folds, his claws dense but not harsh or scratching. He hummed as I moaned and arched into the pinch on my nipples, heels catching on drawer handles and trying to find enough purchase to lift my hips.

"'I like pressure.' How much, exactly? You could've been clearer here. Say when, Miss Dempsey."

I whimpered as Elias pressed and plucked but I had never found my own edge, and he was gripping me so tightly, pulling and twisting slightly on my nipples, claws digging in. I cried out even as I leaned into the touch.

"I see," he said, and it was distantly reassuring to hear the breathless note in his voice.

I rocked into his touch as it eased. My blood pounded and pierced into my breast as he released it, pushing the other shoulder of my shirt out of the way, trapping my arms close to my sides. His fingers brushed mine as he turned the page, and then his claws traced over my collarbone.

"Imagine if another professor were to walk in and see you like this," Elias said softly.

Unfortunately, that brought a sudden image of Phillip Stanton into my mind, and I stiffened, shoulders drawing forward and eyes skidding away.

Elias's fingers rubbed over my sex, and he released a strangely soothing hissing sound. "Never mind. We're alone, Miss Dempsey. I made sure."

"I…" I swallowed and shook my head as his fingers circled up to my clit. "I can't—"

He turned the page, ignoring my words, and then slowly eased a finger inside of me. My eyes widened at the slow pump, just the first knuckle, just as I'd written, and Elias's black stare pinned me in place.

"You're very wet. Were you wet before you sat on my desk?"

I nodded.

"Hmm, I suppose that interferes with the veracity of the essay as well. A few more points off."

I huffed out a laugh, but it strangled into a moan as he added a second finger. "That's not-not fair," I said, flushing at the whine in the words.

"Miss Dempsey, I've already offered you the opportunity of extra credit. It doesn't come with a guarantee of full marks," Elias said, smile hitching in the corner as his touch reached deeper, his thumb lifting to rub over my clit. "This angle is wrong, isn't it? I should have you in my lap."

I swayed forward, wanting that *now*, to crawl into his lap, have his arms around me, acting as my own touch. I didn't need to get off. It would be nice to be held.

"Circle your hips as you've written here, Miss Dempsey."

It was hard with my perch on the desk, but I lifted and rocked my hips into his fingers, drawing him deeper, gasping for air, savoring the heady warmth that built in answer. My body was tensing, too aware of his stare, of the expectation of what that building heat might turn into, and I tried to wrestle back the tension, to curve into familiar softness. Elias's touch slowed, the pinch on my breast softening, thumb passing lazily over my clit. My eyes were squeezed shut, cheek tucked toward my shoulder, breaths short and quick, and he stopped the pumping motion inside of me.

"Well, it's an adequate essay," Elias said, and my eyes blinked open. "But I'm not inclined to recover your grades for 'adequate,' Miss Dempsey."

He'd stopped.

His touch was lodged inside of me, the other hand on my naked breast, and he'd stopped. I found his stare once more, gasping as his fingers curled in my core before drawing free.

He stepped back, releasing me, and then sat down in his desk chair, eyes sliding down to my sex.

"How would you feel about an additional exam?" he asked, heavy lashes batting slowly before lifting to meet my gaze, his hand landing in his lap and the two slick fingers that had been inside of me squeezing over a thick ridge of arousal. "This one would be oral."

CHAPTER 11
Elias

SHE'D BEEN SO CLOSE! I wanted to shout. Closer perhaps than even she realized. And then she'd started to tense and shrink.

She relaxed now, a broad smile stretching over her lips, that rare glitter of laughter teasing me in her gaze. "Oh, Professor, *anything* to get my grade back up," she said, tilting her head coquettishly.

She didn't need to be coy. I'd been hard ever since I'd had her bowed in my grasp, crying out in the pleasure of being possessed with a brutal grip on her pussy. I wasn't normally interested in rough sex, but this was something different, something I wanted to study and dissect. But to do so, I needed Victoria's trust, and we weren't there yet.

She slid off the desk, shrugging the shoulders of her shirt back up but leaving the buttons undone, just the edge of one dark peach nipple visible.

"What's the grading criteria for this exam exactly?" she asked, still smiling.

This was what Khell and Sunny referred to as "playing." Their sexual escapades, regardless of intensity or tone, always seemed to have an element of joy to them, according to the orc. Victoria had entered this staged classroom, nervous and reserved. It had been backing out of touching her that had opened this new ease. Which meant it had been the right choice, no matter *how badly* I'd wanted to take her apart, unraveling her tension and proving her wrong. She could orgasm. *She would.*

I could be patient.

"Just do as I say, Miss Dempsey. You want to please me, don't you?"

Victoria's eyes lit up, cheeks flushing. "Of course, Professor." Her hand covered mine as she lowered to her knees, pressing down as if she were bracing herself against my hard cock. I grunted, bucking into the touch.

Apparently, I liked pressure too. Or I was simply triumphant in the moment. Her hand studied me through the fabric of my trousers, gaze bouncing between my eyes and my lap as she mapped my cock in gentle squeezes and strokes.

"Have you ever seen a moth fae's cock before, Miss Dempsey?" I asked, knowing perfectly well she wouldn't have. I was the only one of my kind in the city. Chicago's endless winters didn't suit our wings, but I liked the challenge.

"No, Professor," she murmured, leaning in and breathing deeply. I held my breath, eyes wide as Victoria's lashes fluttered shut, her cheek landing next to her hand, rubbing over my crotch, face turning to nuzzle. A low sound thrummed in my chest as she scooted closer. Was this part of this story we were weaving, or was it a revelation about the reserved and cool woman I'd be learning? I lifted my hips once more, and her lips curled and then parted. Her breath sank through the fabric, moist and hot against the base of my cock, making it twitch in protest against the zipper.

"Don't stop," I rasped, reaching for my belt.

"Let me," she said, the tease of her mouth muffled through fabric until she opened wider and stretched her teeth over my balls, faintly scraping, firm and perfectly dulled.

I cursed, and her hands raised, batting mine away, deft and practiced with the belt. She was heating my skin through the wool, pressing her nose side to side, stroking me, all too dull, all wonderfully dense. Riotous red curls framed pale hands, deft and quick as they pulled a button loose, teasing and scratching over the zipper. A damp touch, fiercely hot, burned through my pants and against my length, and I realized she was tonguing me through the fabric.

"Don't waste your tongue on wool, Miss Dempsey," I hissed, shifting, trying to climb my way out of my trousers, to get closer to her.

"Are you grading for efficiency or effect?" Victoria asked, her voice bright and clear, her head lifting enough to share a glance glittering with humor.

No one had ever accused me of being an *efficient* lover, and outside of mating cycles, I'd never felt much urgency to get off. I was impatient now. Not for the end, just…for more.

"Obedience," I rumbled, my own smile appearing as Victoria's pupils dilated in answer, and she leaned closer, one hand gripping around my shaft. "Take me out, Miss Dempsey."

The zipper was loud as she tugged it down, our breaths both stuttering as I lifted my hips and she helped pull fabric out of the way. I groaned as I was released, falling back into my seat, head tilting and eyes shutting.

Victoria's breath was abrupt, and I shuddered as my core-mata unfurled from around the base of my cock. There was a pause of quiet, and I gathered myself to explain my anatomy to her, when something brushed against the fine strands extending from the sensitive tendrils.

"They look like the antenna on your head," Victoria murmured, and I grunted as she stroked the back of her knuckles through the threads. "They…smell good?"

I lifted my head and stared down, a strange warmth

unfurling through me at the sight of her, partially obscured by the feather-like structures of my groin.

"They sense and emit pheromones," I said, my voice uneven and thick with arousal.

"Are they as fragile as they look?" she asked, one fingertip running up the thicker tendril at the heart of one corema. It twitched and fluttered against her touch, and her smile was dazzling, distracting.

"Not quite so fragile, but they like to touch more than they require handling. That feels wonderful," I added quickly, not wanting to discourage her from her delicate exploring. "Should I have warned you?"

Her shrug and the shake of her head was easy, relaxed—she was more focused on playing with the three swaying lengths in front of her. I felt somewhat sorry for my cock, as a matter of fact, eagerly extended towards her throat, waiting for its own gentle petting. Victoria's eyes slid to the right as one corema waved its strands, searching the air until it found her curls, brushing over them. She laughed softly, turning her face, eyes falling shut as fine threads found her skin and mapped her face. I shuddered, closing my own eyes, wondering if I ought to better explain their purpose, what they shared with me. Victoria's scent, her arousal, the added pleasure and heat provided to my body as my coremata approved of this partner.

"Touch me, Vic—Miss Dempsey," I rasped.

She hummed, and then her hand enclosed my shaft, my body jumping into the touch briefly before surrendering back into the chair, legs spreading wider for her.

Her fingers were firm and confident around my cock, and I gasped as she tugged, drawing me down in my seat, bringing me close enough to her lips for me to feel the breaths puffing from her nose. Soft curls tickled against my inner thighs and the crease of my hips, the ends of her hair combing into my fur. I could taste her at the back of my throat as my coremata had time to explore her, grazing over her hair, but also her forehead, her cheeks, one playing at the lobe of her ear.

Salt and sweet musk, a hint of the chemicals in her hair products, and something deliciously like evening primrose. And then all my focus snapped tight as the tip of a hot tongue lapped against the long seam at the tip of my cock.

"Mm. You taste good too," Victoria murmured.

I opened my mouth to tell her that the flavor would get richer and more potent as I neared my mating cycles, partly just to keep my head present and away from the shockingly sharp arousal that threatened a too soon finish. But before I could speak, Victoria's hand cradled my length against her cheek, and her mouth opened along my base, tongue swirling and stealing every coherent thought I might have managed.

Her skin is soft, my coremata informed me as they brushed over her face and throat, drawing out a chuckle against my aching cock.

Her tongue is like fire, my cock declared, more directly.

Jealous, my fingers dove into her curls, tangling and greedily gathering thick locks into my fist. The underside was cool and heavy silk, soothing my palms. I groaned, staring down at Victoria through slitted eyes as she stroked the flat of her tongue up the ridges of my cock. Her eyes crossed slightly as she reached the tip, and I was sure I had a ridiculous smile on my face as she glanced up, leaning her head back into the cup of my palms.

"Guide me, Professor. Show me how you like it."

It was strange to think I might be a novice at anything sexual, but I wasn't usually the one receiving attention. Of course I'd had my cock sucked before, but generally at the bequest of my partner.

How do I make my *pleasure about her in a way she will accept?* It was the puzzle I'd been working over the entire week, as I built this room and planned the encounter.

"Trying to wheedle answers out of me when you're the one earning the grade?" I asked, arching an eyebrow. Victoria's cheeks flushed. "You don't fool me, Miss Dempsey. I believe you know your way around this particular problem."

For a moment I wondered if the words had offended her, the open, girlish expression vanishing. But what replaced it was wicked determination and a promise of retribution. Victoria faced my arousal once more, all innocent exploration and teasing at an end.

She dove forward, mouth open and tongue laving voraciously up and around my length, slick and swirling. It was a struggle to keep my focus on her rather than arch into the starving welcome of her lips. It was useless to keep from crying out, and her cheeks brightened further, as if I'd paid her a compliment.

"Very good," I hissed out, bucking as her hands went to work, squeezing and pulling at my base and sac. "I knew you would excel at this."

Victoria's breath hitched, caressing against my painfully stiff length and then she rose up on her knees, wrapping her lips around the head of my cock, nuzzling her tongue into my slit, tension snapping up my spine as she hummed a soft, pleading sound. My fingers tightened, fisting ropes of red silk, and my hips lifted, begging her mouth to make a home for my need.

"Fuck. Victoria!"

She sucked precum from the source, filthy sounds echoing in my ears, and then opened wider, stroking slowly down my shaft with wet lips and a greedy tongue.

"What a...a gifted mouth you have," I rasped, struggling to find words to offer her, rewarded for them with a moan that vibrated down to my balls. "If I had-had known the effort you'd apply to extra credit...uhhhhnn..."

Was I...using her face? Fuck, I was. Not roughly, but with gentle nudges that she followed *so* eagerly, hungry sucking and soft whimpers wrapped around my cock. And then she shifted, rising up slightly, the hand on my balls disappearing between us. She returned to licking me, gasping to catch her breath, eyes flicking up to glance at me through her lashes.

"A for effort?" she teased, her hand dipping under the hem of her skirt.

I slid one hand free of her hair, grasping around her arm, stopping her from touching herself, staring down at the shadows between us.

I wet my lips, and her eyes tracked the movement. Would she let me kiss her? She wanted to be kissed, but that didn't mean the same thing. I would wait, make her *crave* it. "Oh, Miss Dempsey, I think you know what I require for you to get your A."

"I told you I would do whatever it took," she murmured, just a hint of a plea in her voice.

I wanted to take us both down to the floor, strip bare, and slide into her. I wanted to sit on my heels with her spread around my hips and watch her fall over the edge, wetting my cock. I could have that later, when she was ready. For now…

"Face down on my desk, Miss Dempsey."

Victoria's eyes lit up, and I consoled myself with the knowledge that I was getting this right in one way. I could always give my clients what they wanted. Generally, I gave them what they didn't even realize they wanted.

Victoria isn't a client, I reminded myself as she rose on wobbling legs and then turned immediately around, bending and draping herself over the desk, ass high and fiery curls spilling like ink over the far edge. Her skirt was just short enough to offer the scantest glimpse of slick red lips and wisps of bright gold and orange curls. Her breaths were harsh, anticipating, fingers white knuckled around the edge of the desk. I rose from my chair, stepping closer, pausing before my cock could prod at the hem of her skirt.

Her thighs were full, soft, pliable under my grip, a tiny

whimper crying as I touched her, stroked up. Her ass was generous, pleated skirt rucking up around my wrists, and then higher, up to her waist and over her back as I revealed her, like raising the curtain on a stage.

"Elias."

It was a whisper, a break in our roles, and her face turned away, hidden by her mass of hair. I swatted at her ass, a bright clap of sound and an appealing bounce of flesh, and she cried out.

"Professor!" she corrected, and then moaned as my thumbs slid down, stroking over the lips of her sex. Her voice choked as I spread her open, a glossy hole, a trickle of arousal. "Oh, god. Please, I—" Her head shook, unable to continue.

I rummaged in the right-hand drawer, pulling out the condoms I'd tucked away.

"Thank you," Victoria whispered as I tore open the packet and sheathed myself.

I grunted an answer. She didn't owe me thanks. This was a selfish act, just as she wanted. She didn't even realize how much.

She was the perfect height.

Victoria lifted her head from the edge of the desk as I poised myself at her entrance, a small, expectant sound rising in her throat. It turned into another whimper as I sleeved myself in her and then a long, low moan, body shuddering as I pressed forward and never stopped.

My own breath was short. The condom may have dulled the feel of her, all her lovely, wet, welcoming flesh, but it couldn't hide her heat, the way she squeezed tighter and tighter with every inch. And there was no hiding the view of her aroused, swollen flesh swallowing me down, my core-mata greedily stroking and petting over her ass where a pale imprint of where I'd gripped her marked into her skin.

"A perfect fit. I knew you would be" I breathed, my eyes

falling shut. I shook my head and tried to recall my role. "Such a lovely, eager cunt. Exactly what I would expect from my star pupil."

Victoria's laugh was husky and uneven, and I should've expected her retaliation, but I was too busy snuggling my hips to her ass. I liked to be inside a lover, close and deep, liked to wait there until—

She began to move, and my eyes flashed open. She was up on her elbows now, whining slightly as she rocked back into me, fucking herself on my cock.

"Ohhh, very good, Miss Dempsey," I murmured, wishing I had thought to put a mirror at the other end of the room. "Yes, that's it, that's—" I couldn't finish the thought as she arched her back and rose up onto her toes, taking me deeper, moving into the impact.

"Ahh, yes, yes," she hissed, bouncing herself against me, head bowing forward, rougher and more demanding than the pace I would've set.

I leaned forward, bracing my hands on either side of her waist, and her breath hitched but she didn't stop. "Determined to prove yourself, aren't you?"

She whimpered and nodded.

"You want to be the best?"

"Yes!" she gasped, and the desk shook slightly with the force of her movements. I slid one hand to cup around her hips, to keep her from bruising herself.

"Work harder," I breathed.

And Victoria shook and moaned, arms sagging and body falling back into me, the fur of my skin softening the sound of our collision, a muffled wet slap against my groin.

"That's it, very good," I said, more as a throwaway for her obedience, a slip of the tongue. Victoria whined and shivered right down to her core, fluttering around me. My eyebrows rose and I licked my lips, watching her. "What a pretty little cunt, taking me so well."

She clenched, stiffened, and then doubled her efforts.

"Oh, yes, Miss Dempsey, I like when you squeeze me tight. Such a good little slut for her grade," I murmured, marveling as she nearly collapsed with a sob of pleasure.

"Please," she whispered, so faint I almost didn't hear the word.

I reached my hand at her hip down to her sex, and she tensed until I spoke again. "So wonderfully wet, just the way I like."

And like magic, she was lost again, moaning and thrashing, fucking herself on my cock, fucking *me* with a desperation that made me want to gather her up in my arms.

And I would one day. When she was ready. For now…

"Perfect wet, tight cunt. What an eager little slut, working so hard for me. Fuck, Miss Dempsey, you are exactly what I needed today."

Victoria's cries were soft, begging, a tender contrast to the hunger of her body. She was so open, revealing secrets—secret *needs*.

"Yes, I needed your mouth and your tongue, but most of all I needed this pussy, all snug and slick and clutching on my cock…"

I poured filth out for her, bending slowly over her body until she could barely move, whispering the words into her ear. I brushed her hair back over her shoulder, found her eyes wild and searching, and then they squeezed shut, blocking me out. She was fluttering and then frowning, dragged toward climax and then spooking herself away again.

I knew what she needed.

I clasped my hand over the back of her neck, and she gasped, eyes flashing over me—a skittish creature glancing back in my direction. I rose up, bracing against her, pinning her in place, rewarded with a tight clench around my length. She was so close, and so confused, and so frightened of herself.

"You take me so well, but now it's time to earn your A," I purred, the sound ragged.

"Yes," she sighed out, body relaxing into surrender.

I rarely fucked for my own relief. It came, easily enough, but only when I'd satisfied my partner. It was not *selfish* of me to hold Victoria to the desk and fuck her hard, not when what I wanted was to torture her slowly for hours, watching her flash closer to the edge and back again, over and over, until her body could no longer withstand the battle.

My hips clapped against her ass, snapping in a quick, rough, greedy rhythm she would recognize. She relaxed, eyes going soft, hips lifting to take me, and I grunted in appreciation.

My own preferences aside, she was delicious and I *was* close.

I would give her what she wanted.

"Fuck yes. Oh, you good little slut, perfect cunt, yes, take it—"

She moaned, suddenly languid, arching into me, and I came with a snarl, not stopping, not slowing, only pushing harder against her, pressing her into the desk, growling my release into her ear and purging myself into the condom. She hummed, a faint shuddering around my cock, but remained limp over the desk as the release caught up to me and my body faltered, my grip easing.

"How did I do, Professor?"

I leaned forward, resting my head against her back, catching my breath. "A plus Miss Dempsey," I said. *But you'll do better next time.*

CHAPTER 12
Victoria

I NEARLY CAME.

Elias's hands were gentling, soothing over my shoulders and the back of my legs as he slowly pulled out of me.

I didn't want to move yet, the wood of the desk still cool under my cheek, my body still thrumming, mind reeling.

"Do you mind a bit of a cuddle after?"

I blinked at the question, the sound of an elastic snap— Elias tying off the condom—and then considered my answer.

"That sounds nice," I admitted, surprised to be telling the truth.

I braced my hands on the desk to move, then stiffened as a stronger than predicted pair of arms easily hefted me up, rearranging me as the room spun. We settled with me on Elias's lap, the pair of us leaning back in the chair.

He sighed, relaxing under me, head tilting away, eyes shut, but his hands were busy smoothing my skirt and hair. I remained still for a moment, still dazed by what had happened, how *fucking incredibly good* it had been, and also by the picture of Elias at ease in front of me. My arms found their way around his shoulders and he hummed, smiling slightly. I softened into him, and he stroked my hip over my skirt.

"Thank you," we said at the same time.

One of his eyes opened. "It was good?" he asked.

I nearly fucking came, I almost said, but I didn't want him to spoil the moment by offering to try and finish me off. I knew some women found it frustrating to get that close and then not orgasm, but in all honesty, it had been a couple years since I'd been so far outside my own head with someone else, and that was its own thrill.

"It was exactly what I wanted," I said, and then hoped I wasn't crossing a boundary by drawing him closer.

I wasn't. Elias let out a pleased sound, something low and almost as hungry as his growls as he came, and then our mouths met. I grinned at first, realizing we hadn't kissed before now, and his lips pulled at my lower one, soft and plush and perfect. And then it was too easy, too good—a kiss so familiar I wondered if I'd forgotten one we already shared. Elias's mouth glided and caressed and enclosed over mine, warm and almost caramel in flavor.

My breasts ached and my core throbbed and I moaned into the kiss, his tongue licking in, more tentative than his cock had been as he'd first entered me, teasing and flicking before meeting mine for long strokes. His hands roamed over my back and hip, and he lifted me when I shifted, moving me to straddle over his lap, legs dangling down on either side.

When I was young, when Brett and I were in high school, we had kissed like this and I'd loved it. I'd loved grinding on his lap, getting close to coming, the build slow and sometimes futile depending on what we'd been wearing, how much it muffled the sensation. At some point, when it had been a long relationship, and Brett's friends and my friends were all starting to have sex, sex between us had seemed like a necessary step to take. Afterwards, we'd kissed and humped and fondled less, like knowing the destination had made a longer trip there not worth as much.

Elias chuckled as I started to squirm on his lap, but he didn't stop kissing me, petting up and down my back. He'd already come, I supposed. He didn't need to rush there again. And then he pulled away slightly, pressing a kiss to my lobe.

"You did this for me?" I asked, and he blinked before I gestured over my shoulder to the room.

"Oh, yes. For us. For fun." He shrugged.

"Like the room we used with Atlas and Cyril," I said. He had shades of amber in his fur, and glints of white gold, all shifting warm tones that belonged in some kind of fantastical treasure chest.

Elias nodded, and I suspected he was studying me as much as I had him. I'd meant for this to be impersonal. To end when he finished. And then he'd let me kiss him.

"Would you like a tour?" he asked.

———

"THE DESK IS A GOTHIC REVIVAL, marked 1848. I found it wallowing in a basement in Logan Square during an estate sale. It *is* hideous," Elias said, tipping his head and glaring at the piece of furniture, his arms crossed over his chest.

Hours had passed. My head was spinning. After I'd cleaned up and changed, we had wandered from room to room, Elias eagerly describing the dragon's hoard of antiques and art he'd so meticulously arranged throughout his house. A house that now seemed more like a cross between a museum and a stage dressed for a performance.

The room we stood in now was an early Victorian styled office, complete with an inkwell on the indeed gaudily carved desk and an enormous ten-point buck head looming out over the mantle. There was a tea set waiting on a low table between two stuffed armchairs by the fireplace, and brandy in the cut crystal bottles on the sideboard. "Not era accurate, unfortunately," Elias admitted in a cheeky whisper.

I turned slowly in place, still absorbing the full scope. Not simply the wealth it took to amass this collection—he had a pop art pantry off the kitchen that included a set of Andy Warhol polaroids of bananas—but the time, the thought. And the…*who*.

Who would do this? Every room was its own character in a disjointed novel of a home, and the author was…

Watching me, I realized. The room—no, *I* had been quiet too long, and Elias was now standing, staring back at me, posture too straight and chin a little high.

I opened my mouth to offer some kind of platitude. How beautiful the room was? No, beauty wasn't the point of any of the rooms, even when they were beautiful, like the sunroom where Elias had pulled covers off of watered silk chaises as massive monstera fronds hung over our heads like umbrellas.

"This is fascinating," I said, because that was true. Elias's snorted dismissively, but he looked slightly less aloof. "You don't really…live in any of these rooms, do you?"

There was no sign of him. No mail on the desk in his "office," and no actual bananas in the banana pantry.

Elias shook his head. "It's the process of arranging them that I enjoy. I like to create environments."

"They're all incredible. The classroom was—"

"I only had a week," he said quickly. "I just put it together from what was on hand in the basement, really."

My eyebrows rose. "In the basement?"

He shrugged and waved his hands around the room. "I go through phases, rearranging a room. But I don't get rid of my pieces."

"You're a collector," I said.

"I suppose." His hands slid into his pockets. "I'm certainly an acquirer."

I crossed past him to a bookshelf full of leather and fabric spines, gilt titles faded. I didn't doubt for a moment that there was a single book printed later than the eighteen hundreds. Elias was…meticulous.

"Do your clients for the Agency come here?" I asked.

"No. But sometimes, I take things to the Agency if I think they'll suit an appointment," he said. "Are you…bothered by my hobby?"

I startled and spun to face him. "No! No, not at all. But I am trying to puzzle you out, I think."

Surprisingly, Elias smiled at that. "Fair enough." Which probably meant he was trying to puzzle me out too. His hand reached out in offering to me. "Come, let me show you the rococo parlor. It's ghastly. I haven't decided what to do next with it."

His hand was warm and smooth, and I suddenly itched to be pressed up against him once more, combing my fingers through his hair, peeling off his tidy button-down shirt. He was so soft in the places I'd touched or the parts that had touched me so far, and I wanted to feel him everywhere, learn all his textures.

"I can improve on the classroom if we'd like to use it again. Or change it altogether. Whatever you prefer," Elias said, his clasp on my hand firm and guiding.

I considered the offer. Playing teacher student with Elias had been fun, but it made me wonder what other roles he might invent for us. It was like visiting the bar and finding a drink waiting on the counter for me, something delicious and unfamiliar and designed just for me.

"I think I like when you choose," I said softly.

Elias's hand just squeezed gently around mine.

"OH, there you are, Vicky. We thought you'd never show up."

I should've known this was a trap, I thought, my hands clenched around my messenger bag strap as I stood in front of the restaurant booth where my mother, father, and an as yet unknown man too close to my own age for comfort waited. If Elias hadn't fucked me silly earlier, leaving me quite light and cheerful, I might've seen her text this afternoon for what it was.

The man slid out of the booth, smiling nervously, but my mother refused to budge and let my father out.

"Ben Stone," the stranger greeted, offering his hand. He was tall, lanky, and to be honest, fairly cute. And I was too well trained to be rude, even if this was clearly a setup.

Because of course my mother wouldn't simply offer to take me out to my favorite restaurant on an otherwise meaningless evening. Not without motive.

"Victoria Dempsey," I offered, shaking his hand, giving into a cursory, skittish sweep of study.

Dark hair, with a bit of gray in the mix. Well dressed, but not quite up to Mom's usual standard, and wearing thick framed glasses that at least hinted at a personal sense of style. Ben Stone had Clark Kent vibes, but without Superman's beefy build.

"Ben's the son of an old college friend. He just moved to Chicago and I promised I would give him a little orientation, but really, you know the city better these days," my mother rattled as Ben took his seat once more, leaving me the spot next to him. "I figured the bribe of dinner would lure you out."

Ben's expression was slightly stricken and awkward at that. *He* hadn't realized the scheme, at least.

"No bribe necessary, of course," I said smoothly. The bribe was necessary. If she'd given him my number or vice versa, I would absolutely have ignored or deflected any attempts at connection.

A fucking setup. I should've known. I should've been on my guard. I was suddenly surprised she hadn't attempted something sooner. She must've really believed I was mourning the loss of Brett before now.

Resisting the urge to sigh, drawing up the smile that had

been instilled in me that came easier than my own honest expressions, I settled down into the booth. "So what brings you to Chicago?"

I hoped my mother could read the irritation in my glance. I was going to order an outrageous amount of food and take it all home in boxes and feast on fine dining for the rest of the week. It would be her penance.

"Work, of course," Ben admitted with a sheepish shrug and a charming smile. "But I've always loved Chicago."

"He's at the museum, darling, isn't that fascinating? Oh, we'll have to call that waiter back to get you a drink, Vicky. Where did he go?"

I braced myself for the evening ahead.

CHAPTER 13
Elias

I SCOWLED DOWN at my phone, staring at the three text messages below as if they were a code I might solve.

> Professor Stanton is attending the interview tomorrow.
>
> You don't have to come.
>
> If you don't want to, that is.

The first felt like a warning. The second, a dismissal. The third, a retraction of said dismissal.

I didn't particularly like any of the three messages, or their potential meanings.

"What's got you so scowly?"

I lifted my head to glare at the disruption and blinked when I found Natalie sitting across from me at my bar.

"What are you doing here?" I asked, glancing around the room.

Her eyebrows rose. "You are so fucking rude. This is a public bar, yeah?"

My wings rustled at my back, and I waved my hand through the air. "I didn't...I didn't mean it like that. I just wasn't expecting any of you tonight."

"*You* being..." Natalie leaned forward, resting her elbows on the bar top.

I huffed and searched the bar for Theo, her werewolf husband. "You know...our...the..."

"Your...friends?" Natalie suggested slowly, eyes glinting with humor.

I stared back at her, jaw fixed as my tongue played over the word in my mouth for a moment. I'd had friends in the past, but those connections always seemed to fade over time. Had I found myself making new ones? It hadn't occurred to me to try, but perhaps that was what Rafe and Khell and the others were becoming after all.

"What do you want to drink?" I asked.

Natalie relaxed and smiled. "Why don't you ever offer to surprise me, like everyone else?"

"Because you would gleefully heckle my efforts. But, if you insist..."

Natalie brightened further at that, probably a confirmation of my suspicion. She nodded. "Please. Also, Sunny and Hannah should be here soon. We instructed the guys to stay home. Girls' night. Plus you now."

I turned away, determined not to investigate why that declaration pleased me.

"I suppose I do really prefer beer," Natalie mused at my back. "But it's the thought that counts, you know. I assumed you just didn't like me."

"I am ambivalent about all of you," I lied. I did like Natalie, mostly because she struck me as someone who didn't impress very easily. And if I couldn't impress her, I wasn't going to humiliate myself by trying.

"Well, that was so obvious, now I *know* you do like me," she muttered.

"Of course he likes you. What's not to like?"

I glanced over my shoulder and nodded at Sunny, who beamed and waved in answer. Behind her, the tall, slim shadow of Hannah shot me a wary look and slid onto the seat on Natalie's other side.

I usually made Sunny something custom—she was easy to please—and I had yet to solve the mystery of Hannah. Tonight, I decided to triple an order for Natalie, setting three half full beers on the bar and three shots.

"Don't touch those yet," I warned, and then dug in a drawer for a lighter. "For the record, this is illegal."

"Girls' night," Natalie hissed in approval.

I topped all of the shots with 151 and then lit them on fire. Hannah's eyes brightened and she laughed, and Sunny released a minor squawk of surprise. Together, they lifted the shots, blowing out the fire and then dropping them into their beers and chugging quickly. Over the rim of the glass, Natalie waggled her eyebrows at me, and I found myself laughing.

"Flaming Dr. Peppers," she announced, then politely tucked a quick belch behind her hand. "Classic. Better than usual. Did you make the liquor yourself?"

"Of course."

"Well, that was a way to start the night," Hannah mused, but she smiled at me, which I accepted as a rare victory. "Mocktails from here on out for me."

I nodded, and Sunny giggled and bounced. "Well, *I* am going to get trashed. Khell's picking me up at one."

"No road head," Natalie said, pointing firmly at her best friend, who rolled her eyes.

"Khell will just pull over," Sunny said breezily. "And then *I'll* get road head too."

"Maybe a little more alcohol," Hannah said, holding my gaze with wide eyes.

"Drinks and snacks, coming up," I offered. "Which of your ne'er-do-wells' tabs should I put it on?"

"Khell's," Hannah said at the same moment Sunny said, "Rafe's."

"Mama's paying," Natalie said, smoothly sliding over her credit card.

And because I was not running a charity for my friends—which, yes, they were that—I accepted the card and sent a warning to my kitchens to keep the fryers hot.

———

EVEN STAYING out of the trio's way, keeping my ear on the rest of the room, I learned more about my friend's sexual prowess than I might've cared to. Well, no, I didn't really mind.

And really, good for Theo. I'd underestimated him.

It was a shame Victoria wasn't here. She might've had some academic uses for this gossip.

Khell arrived promptly at one and accepted the cheerful heckling of the girls as he scooped Sunny up off the stool and carted her out the door. Hannah and Natalie both waved their goodbyes, but I was surprised to see they kept their seats rather than heading out for the night too.

"—just wonder if he'll feel differently when the supper club takes off and gets interrupted with our touring schedule."

I lifted my eyes up at Hannah's words, her half smile tilted in Natalie's direction. Natalie shrugged in response.

"You'll figure it out when that happens. Rafe's right that the scarcity is part of a supper club's appeal."

"It could lead to really big opportunities for him. And they're already scheduling us for a festival circuit," Hannah said with a grimace.

Natalie's smile was sly. "Hey, some of those festivals are here in Chicago, at least."

"True," Hannah said, eyes lightening.

"The rest of the band is eager to get back on the road?" I asked, giving up any pretense of not listening in.

"Actually…well, no. Kiernan is glad to be home too. He wants to write a new album. The label wants to milk this one for as much as they can." Hannah sipped at her mocktail. "I think Mikey and Kelsey could go either way. We were all glad for the break though."

"If Rafe quits overthinking, he could easily have two dinner club events before you have to leave again," I said.

Hannah grinned at me. "I'll tell him you said so." I shrugged, unconcerned with the idea of Rafe's blustering. "How's the study going?"

"Very well, I think," I said. "I haven't told Victoria yet, but I have rather more volunteers for demonstrations than I suspect she needs. Or has time for."

"I'm very offended that humans are being left out," Natalie said, without an actual hint of offense. Her smile widened. "But Theo is relieved. And I understand why she doesn't need human comparisons."

I lifted my chin in thought. "There may be something to explore with human and monster relationships specifically. Perhaps for a second study."

"Planning a new professional venture as a research assistant already?" Hannah asked me, her chin propped on her hand, something coy in her tone.

"I make a very concentrated effort not to overstep my place in helping Victoria," I said, my own tone a little too tight.

Hannah's smile softened. "Of course. I'm only teasing."

Which, it occurred to me, Hannah had never really done before. I relaxed and nodded to her, but my thoughts were turning in a new direction, and I glanced back and forth between the two women, wondering if my curiosity might lead me to overstep after all.

"What?" Natalie asked, pointing at me, her brow furrowing. "You've got a funny look."

Hannah huffed a laugh as I bristled. "You do look on the brink of something."

"I have a…hypothetical question…related to the study that I'm curious about," I said.

"Isn't that for Victoria to discuss then?" Hannah asked.

Given the hypothetical *was* Victoria, I shook my head. "I don't want to accidentally…influence her own lines of inquiry."

"Hit us," Natalie said with a careless wave of her hand.

I wet my lips and then set about pouring myself my own drink. "There's an open booth. Let's go there. Nora can handle the bar." The bar was crowded, but it was also nearing closing, and mostly we were dealing with people finishing their drinks and winding down for the night.

Hannah and Natalie hurried to claim the booth, and I followed them out a moment later, finding them whispering with their heads bowed as I approached.

"This is exciting," Natalie declared, her eyes a little glassy from drinking. "I hope you know I love giving my opinion on things that aren't my business."

I refrained from answering and settled into the booth, carefully spreading and draping my wings at my sides.

"It *is* okay that you're asking us, isn't it?" Hannah pressed me.

It probably wasn't, but… "I don't see why not," I said. I just had to frame it carefully. "There was a case…an interview, with an individual that finds achieving orgasm challenging."

Both women sat back in their seats, Natalie with surprise, but Hannah was wary.

"This isn't really relevant to the study. I suppose this is something I've been mulling over myself," I continued. "They, the individual, claim that it is more satisfying for them to have that aspect of sex ignored."

"They enjoy sex?" Natalie clarified with a raised finger.

I nodded. "Yes. But not when it's focused on their pleasure."

"Okay…" Hannah said slowly, head tilting. "So…what's your question, exactly?"

I placed my hands on the table top, frowning upon finding it sticky. "Well, I suppose…should their partner really *not* try to offer that to them? It's not *impossible* for them to achieve an orgasm, but the process seems to be tangled up in some kind of mental or…" I floundered for a moment and shrugged slightly. "Emotional impediment?"

Natalie slumped. "I mean…if the partner knows they *can* get them to orgasm…"

"The partner is hypothetical," I said quickly.

"It's *all* hypothetical," Hannah said, eyes narrowed.

"Well, yes. But in this case, let's say yes, the hypothetical partner is absolutely certain he-they can—"

Mercifully, Natalie interrupted my bumbling. "It's a hypothetical of '*can't*' achieve orgasm, and not one of 'doesn't want to?'"

My head jerked back. "Why would they not want to?"

"Hypothetically," Hannah muttered under her breath.

Natalie shrugged. "Some internalized sense of sexual shame."

Victoria's broken pleas, the eager thrust of her body, the sight of her back arching to take me deeper all flashed through my mind. Her ease in the aftermath, relaxed and pleased and smiling.

"I can't say for sure. They said they can't."

Natalie's expression twisted, and she shrugged. "I think I'm leaning that…yeah, hypothetically, go ahead and prove them wrong."

Even though it was the answer I wanted to hear, it gave me an uncomfortable twist in my chest. I turned to Hannah and found her expression too sober, too *knowing*.

"Really good sex is about trust. Taking someone at their

word, not trying to prove them wrong or yourself right. Just observing their boundaries, even if they're smaller than you'd like, would matter the most to that individual," Hannah said softly.

Disappointment was strangely a relief in the moment.

"Ohhh, yeah," Natalie murmured, nodding. "She's right."

"The partner would have to decide if he—"

"They," I said quickly—too quickly, probably.

"—could be satisfied with that. At least until there was enough trust to discuss the boundary."

"You're right, of course," I said.

Hannah relaxed back in her seat and offered me a smile. "It's certainly an interesting hypothetical."

———

NWU'S CAMPUS was a perfect setting for the fall, far enough out of the crowd of the city to have broad green lawns and a quintessential autumnal range of changing trees. Classic graystone buildings with green ivy crawling around mullioned windows set an ideal scene for academia. It was too easy to imagine Victoria walking over the curving sidewalks, arms full of books and crossbody drumming against her hip. Or there, sitting in the shade of a grand old oak as she typed a paper, or in the crowded halls of the old Gothic buildings, stuffed with seated amphitheaters for lectures.

It'd been a week since I'd seen her. A week since we'd fucked on the desk in the little schoolroom I'd set up just for that occasion. Since she'd shivered and clasped my cock inside of her.

I was undoubtedly *too* eager to see her again. Especially when I knew we'd be meeting with not only an interview subject, but also under the supervision of her professor. I should've declined the meeting altogether. It was clear that Victoria wasn't quite sure whether or not she wanted me to come, and I wouldn't be needed. Not when I did my utmost to be unobtrusive to her interviews.

Was it curiosity over her reticence that drew me today, or just the basic urge to see her, even in such a stifling setting?

A startled squeak stopped me in the hallway, and I blinked at the young woman who'd nearly collided into me. She was tall and quite pretty, with large dark eyes and a smooth sheet of black hair. A hand rested on her shoulder, and I followed the arm up to the man at her side, handsome, older, and distinctly academic. The girl's eyes widened as she stared up at me, her lips slightly parted in some human combination of shock and awe.

Glancing around the hall, it was clear that the majority population of NWU was human, and what other species I spotted easily blended in with the crowd. Even then, this young woman would never have seen my like. I stared back at her and watched her shake herself and stare down at the floor, realizing her own rude gawking.

"Sorry—"

"You must be Elias," the man said, his hand retreating from her shoulder as the other lifted in my direction. "Phillip Stanton."

Now it was my turn to be startled. I'd been imagining someone…older and less good-looking as Victoria's thesis advisor. Why, exactly, I didn't know.

Personal preference, perhaps, a dry tone mocked at the back of my thoughts.

I shook the man's hand as he gently ushered the girl away from us. "I'll see you in class next week, Swathi." He turned back to me. "We're just here, actually. I offered my office, but I suppose it would've been a bit cozy for all four of us," Stanton said with an almost pointed glance at my wings.

He gestured to a door I'd already passed, apparently too lost in my own thoughts, and we both did our best surreptitious study of one another as we wove through a pour of students to reach the door. I was subtler. I had the advantage of my gaze being unreadable.

Phillip Stanton was busy looking me over as we stepped into a comfortable study room, but I caught Victoria's flush as we entered together, the nervous bounce of her gaze between us before she calmed and called up that frustratingly smooth facade she often wore. She was standing with Dana, our selkie interviewee, who offered me a quick smile and nod of acknowledgement.

"Oh good, we're all here," Victoria murmured, with a final flick of her eyes in my direction.

The room had a large dark mahogany table at the center, with a matching set of weathered wood and leather chairs surrounding it, and Victoria pulled out the seat at the head of the table for Dana before taking the one at the corner next to her. The back wall had three slightly outdated computers available, and the rest of the room was bare. Stanton closed the door behind our entrance, and the roar of the hallways muffled to a gentle white noise.

Stanton was sliding around the table toward Victoria without a beat of pause, her shoulders stiffening and spine straightening. I felt a foreign urge to drag him back by his collar, to toss him out of the room, and it was such a strange and unusual sensation that it made me want to wallow and explore in it.

Was this jealousy?

How fascinating.

I settled at the far corner of the table and wondered if Victoria looked relieved or regretful. She made it too difficult to tell.

"I'll take notes," I offered, drawing out an old notebook and inkwell pen.

CHAPTER 14
Victoria

I TRIED NOT to scramble around the table as Elias packed up his things.

"I should head for the bar," he said, and it was the first thing he'd said in the two hours he'd been camped at the far end of the table.

"I'll walk with you," I rushed out, too determined to care how desperate I sounded.

Elias paused, holding the door open for me, and I inched just out of Stanton's reach, his hand raised out of the corner of my eye.

"I was hoping we'd take the time to discuss—" he started, eyebrows raised.

"We do meet tomorrow," I reminded him, barely looking over my shoulder. "And I need to get to my library shift."

For a moment, it seemed like he might push the issue, but I continued on my path to Elias, sure that he was holding my stare. Even with those bottomless black eyes of his, his gaze felt like a beacon to aim toward. The safe call of a lighthouse in the dark.

"Very well. Tomorrow then."

I might pay for that tomorrow. Phillip had been a bit of a

pest during the interview, not *quite* undermining me but coming close. That, or he had a very inconvenient sore throat, because he kept clearing it meaningfully as I asked questions.

Elias was silent as I reached him, and we slid out into the flow of traffic in the hall together, our sides not quite touching. We reached the stairs, a crowd of students rising up against us, and someone jostled me into Elias. The back of my hand brushed his and I twisted my palm, clasping his hand in mine, my chest tight until he wove our fingers together.

"Why does he make you uncomfortable?" Elias murmured, ducking his head just enough to keep his voice low.

We shouldn't have been holding hands. There wasn't any justifiable reason for it, except that I wanted the touch. I'd never even really liked holding hands before. And even now, with Elias, it was slightly awkward. But the truth was that what I really wanted was to be wrapped around him somewhere private, and if I couldn't have *that*, then I wanted *this*, clammy and unfamiliar as it was.

"The affair," I answered, my eyes squinting as we stepped outside into the glaring sun as it lowered itself into the trees.

"Oh. *Oh*. That is…" Elias made a strange sound at the back of his throat as he led us down the steps. "Awkward… considering…"

I laughed, and my vision eased enough to see Elias's antennae curving down, his shoulders creeping up. I interpreted it as sheepish.

"Yes," I agreed, finding myself grinning. "I nearly refused you."

He coughed, but I had a feeling it was covering up a laugh. With the crowds dispersing around us, our hands unlinked slowly, and we turned to face one another, safely out of the way on a patch of green lawn. In another few weeks, the grass would be thinned out from all the student traffic.

"It wasn't remotely the same," I said softly, wondering why I was trying to reassure Elias.

He nodded and shrugged. "All the same…we'll try something different next time. Unless you want—"

I shook my head quickly. "It was perfect, but not for that reason," I said, grimacing and looking around us.

We were talking in half confessions, and it wasn't really making anything clearer. But there was no one familiar around, and certainly no one listening.

"The most arousing part was how much thought you put into it, and how much you listened to what I asked you for," I admitted.

Elias was generally too hard to read, but I caught his surprise, the bright lift of his antennae, and the way we leaned into one another slightly. His hands wrapped around my wrists, gentle but commanding too, and warmth rushed through me, my eyelids growing heavy with the weight of heat in my core.

"I can't wait for next weekend. I need you to tell me when you're free next. Email it. I'll take care of the rest," Elias said, his voice low.

I can't wait…

My breathing was labored as I nodded, strangely dizzy and hot. There was a tree behind me, and if Elias had told me he was going to fuck me against it in that moment, I would've said, "yes, sir."

"Now. You can tell me this is none of my business, but I'm going to ask anyway," Elias continued, his tone clipped tightly enough to rouse me from my stupor of lust. "Is Stanton harassing you at all currently?"

I sucked in a breath, a refusal sharp on my tongue, and then forced myself to relax and think. "No. There's tension, but I think it has more to do with us ignoring our history, or trying to work around it."

Elias's stare was hard on my face, but he considered my answer for a long moment. "I couldn't tell if he was being exacting or obnoxiously disruptive."

My lips quirked and I ducked my head, staring at the gold pelted fingers wrapped around my wrists. "Both, but I don't think he's punishing me through the study or anything like that."

Elias nodded slowly. "Your work is too good to be impeded."

Don't swoon, Victoria, I warned myself. "What are we going to do next?" I asked, my voice embarrassingly breathy.

"Bar, library," Elias said, pointing at us each in turn.

"You know what I meant," I said, and my breath caught as our hips brushed. When had we stepped so close to one another?

Elias's wings flared out at his back, and I imagined he was shielding us from view. "You'll see," he said. My lips pursed in irritation—categorically *not* a pout—and Elias's grip on my wrist suddenly tightened, snapping me against his chest, his soft fur collar and hair so smooth against my cheek as he hissed in my ear, "Don't look at me like that, or I'll put you over my knee right here and show everyone what a cock hungry little whore you are."

I staggered, gasping for air as he released me, his stride smooth and long, carrying himself away too fast for me to go crawling after him, begging him to follow through on the threat. "Email me," he shot over his shoulder.

———

HOW DOES *Thursday the 5th suit your schedule for our next meeting?*

- Vic

———

I'VE BEEN *hard since I emptied into you. I need a better offer than next week.*

- E

"Okay, who the hell are you fucking?"

I startled, my head jerking up from my phone to gape at Lyle across the table from me. "No one— What?"

Lyle's eyebrows rose. "I've known you for years. You've never been this horny. Not even when I was inside of you."

"Lyle," I hissed, searching around the library, but everyone was deep in the stacks and he hadn't spoken very loudly.

Lyle smirked. "Is it one of your interview subjects?"

I sighed, shaking my head as I lowered it down into the crease of the book I'd been failing to focus on ever since opening Elias's email. "No. Why? There isn't— Are people talking?"

"No! No, no, nothing like that," Lyle said, gentling his tone to reassure me. "I just think other species are better in bed than humans and figured you were reaping the benefits."

I looked up from my book. "Why do you say that? Or think that? Can you—"

Lyle lifted his chin and stared down his nose at me. "I'm not participating in your study. It's not..." He mouthed the name, "Stanton?"

"God no," I huffed, falling back into my chair. "You know this isn't any of your business, right?"

"Did you meet someone at Nightlight?" Lyle asked, head tipping.

I laughed. "Lyle, no, st—"

But it was too late. Lyle's lips parted in shock and he leaned forward, slapping his hands to the table and catching the attention of a few students browsing the shelves.

"It's *him*," Lyle breathed.

And even though that was too vague a statement to really confirm or deny, I flushed warm. I'd given something away as

Lyle had said "Nightlight," probably. Not in my face, but some flicker of arousal at the mention of Elias's bar, the thought of him.

We were both silent for a long stretch, staring at one another, my eyes narrowed in warning, Lyle's wide in some kind of surprise or fascination or delight.

"I'm going to ask this, and I want you to remember that it's me, not your family or Brett or any of those types, and that there's no judgment—"

"Lyle, you're pushing it," I said flatly.

"Did you pay?" he whispered, leaning in close.

I sighed and shook my head, mostly in annoyance, but it worked as an answer to his question too I suppose.

"Okaaaay," Lyle said slowly, and for some reason he looked even more excited. His voice lowered. "Did you get off?"

My heart skipped nervously in my chest. Nearly. I nearly had. And somehow, that might've been better than if I magically had at the first provocation. "I told him I didn't want him to try."

Lyle nodded. He and I had broached that issue together when we'd briefly tried to have a fling, but as passion had quickly fizzled into friendship, our interest in one another sexually had amicably waned. "It was good though," he noted, already aware of the fact.

"Really, really good," I breathed out, and Lyle softened, his smile huge but genuine. "It's not related to the study at all."

He shrugged. "I'm not sure it matters, but I figured as much."

I sagged into the chair a little deeper. "We role-played," I whispered.

"Mmm, kinky," Lyle said, nodding appreciatively. "You know he's kind of like the equivalent of a reclusive socialite to other species?"

"How can you be both a recluse and socialite?" I asked.

Lyle waved his hand. "He has status. Influence. That he rarely uses."

I opened my mouth to tell Lyle about Elias's house, all the carefully arranged rooms that reminded me of the miniatures at the art institute, and then shut my mouth again. Somehow, that seemed like a more private detail than what we got up to while fucking.

"It's not very personal," I said, which didn't feel quite true. Elias knew as much about me now as Lyle did, actually, and Lyle was my best friend.

"As long as you're having a good time," Lyle said, and then grinned. "And you tell me the occasional fun detail."

I snorted and tried to return to my work, but my phone was burning against my palm, Elias's short email demanding a response.

"I need to go check my work schedule real quick," I murmured, sliding up from my seat and heading for the desk. Lyle's smile was smug and too knowing, but it was pointless trying to be subtle around him anyway.

It was too late to call off or swap work nights with any of the other library staff, but I didn't have to come in until four tomorrow and I didn't have any classes during the day. I opened my phone and found another message from Elias, this time a text.

> I'm going to use my fist instead of your cunt
> if I can't have you tonight.

My body answered the threat with a surprising clench in my core and a flare of heat that rose all the way up into my cheeks.

> I can be at your house by 9pm.

> No makeup. I'll provide everything, including
> the clothes. Expect a long night.

Any hints?

I spent the next three hours waiting for an answer that never came.

CHAPTER 15
Victoria

MY STEPS PAUSED as Elias opened the door to the room, my breath catching in my throat. It was *gaudy*. All shades of gold and chocolate brown and pink and red, dressed in lace and velvet and fringe, like the entire concept of St. Valentine's Day had exploded over every surface.

"Come," Elias urged, tugging gently on my hand, drawing me into the room.

The floor was covered in thick woven carpets, while an enormous canopy bed loomed and filled the space on my left. In front of us was a large dark armoire and a small vanity set at its side, with a mirror corroded by age. An oil lamp burned on its surface.

"Undress and put your clothes out of sight. There are stockings, drawers, and a chemise. I don't want you in a corset or anything like that," Elias said with a lazy wave of his hand. "But maybe pin up your curls. I'd like to muss them. And use the rouge. Especially on your nipples."

My eyes widened at that, and a startled, garbled laugh escaped me.

"Is this a…a brothel?" I asked.

Elias grinned. "The nervousness is good. I want to be your first tonight."

My heartbeat stuttered at the words. It'd been a long time since I'd lost my virginity, and the idea of pretending otherwise was unsettling.

Unsettling and somehow exciting?

"My first," I repeated in a murmur.

Elias nodded and tipped his head thoughtfully. "I imagine I won the privilege at auction. What do you think?"

I didn't have a clue. My head had started spinning at his demanding text messages, then simply careened right off my shoulders and out the door at the sight of the frankly atrociously decorated room.

Elias stepped in front of me, wings spreading as much as they were able in the stiflingly crowded space. His hands settled on my hips, and his dark gaze caught mine.

"I don't want to give too much away, but I really think you're going to enjoy this idea."

I swallowed and wet my lips, nodding slowly.

"My *first* first time, or just first time umm…paid?" I asked.

"First first," Elias said, voice lowering and growing thick. "A lovely, untouched, un*trained* flower for me to pluck."

Tell me what you like, though.

It's all good, baby. I like you touching me.

But I want to know.

Vicky, it's fine. I like it.

"Okay," I rasped, looking around once more, anywhere but at that potent black stare above me.

Soft claws stroked up my throat, guiding my chin higher. A slight furrow creased between Elias's eyes. "Is this all right, Victoria?"

I nodded, but he remained watchful until I answered, "Your ideas overwhelm me. I like it."

Satisfied, Elias smiled slightly and stepped away toward the door. "It's going to be a long night," he warned.

My breath was ragged as the door clicked shut behind him, and I swung in a circle, taking in every overwrought detail. The ruffled curtains draped to the floor, the bed topped with an outrageous number of ruched and fringed pillows. The red scarf over a tall lamp bathing the room in lusty shades. I reached for the doors of the armoire, and there was just enough space for me to open it while standing at the foot of the bed. My costume waited for me—delicate white undergarments, black silk stockings, and ruffled garters in white lace and pink ribbons. A burnt velvet robe hung from a hook on the inside of one of the doors, but Elias hadn't mentioned it in his instructions, so I left it there and pulled the rest out, laying it over the bed.

My fingers trembled as I reached for the buttons of my shirt, and I could almost imagine Elias at my back, watching me undress for him. Maybe he was watching. Maybe I should have offered. I stripped myself bare and shivered, my toes curling into the thick wool rug as I carefully folded and tucked my clothing into the wardrobe.

The bedding was soft underneath me as I sat on the edge, lifting one stocking and running it through my hands. There were creases and a little discoloration, as if Elias had found a pair of vintage stockings, still in the package, and purchased them for this occasion. Had he been thinking of me at the time, or was it just a product of his habit as a collector?

I dressed slowly, carefully, terrified of snagging the silk, failing to tie the garters tightly enough twice before finally getting them right. I blushed as I found the loose split at the crotch of the white silk drawers, open for a lady's ease but also convenient for a man's use, in this case. I pulled them up over my hips, and my skin pebbled at the gentle flow of air that licked between my legs. The chemise slid on over my head, leaving the tiny pearl buttons fastened down the front. Aside from the opening on the drawers, it was a surprisingly modest outfit, but the cool drape of the silk over my skin left me feeling decidedly naked.

I crossed to the vanity and found a small tin with a single

shade of rosy red pigment, a bowl of black bobby pins, and an even smaller pot of black kohl. It'd been too long since I'd attempted makeup of my own, but I sat down on the stool, squeaking at the cold surface against a sliver of my bare sex, and fiddled with the delicate brushes laid out over the vanity like a set of surgeon's tools. I wasn't brave enough to attempt anything interesting with the kohl, aside from a few small brushes of it against my lashes, but I rubbed my fingers over the rouge, pinching my own cheeks until I looked flushed and then dabbing it into a small pout at the very bow of my lips. The effect, though small, was enough. I looked younger somehow, girlish and innocent and dressed up like a doll.

My hair twisted around my fists, and I stuffed it full of pins into a slightly lopsided bun at the top of my head. It would come undone easily, but that seemed to be Elias's aim.

Finally, I paused, staring at the girl in the mirror, a crea-ture from another time in more ways than one. I looked closer to the version of myself I'd been a decade ago, and also like a stranger, a woman from another era. Slowly, I inched up the chemise, staring at my own bare breasts. I was more liberal here with the rouge than I had been on my face, finger painting them into bright little puckered cherries, my breath catching as I stroked circles around them and they tightened with arousal.

A knock tapped lightly on the door, an impatient throat clearing on the other side.

"Just a minute," I called, my voice too high and breathless.

I wiped my fingers clean on a cloth that waited on the vanity, then dropped the chemise. The fabric was thin enough that the rosy marks shone through, sharp tips beading in welcome.

I spun the stool to face the door. "Come in."

I hadn't been the only one getting into costume since Elias left me. He stepped into the room and took my breath away, long black trousers gleaming, brass buttons on his waistcoat catching the light, gold and onyx cufflinks flashing. He was wearing a beautiful black tailcoat, and a shining top hat sat crookedly on his head, one antenna sitting at a jaunty angle like a feather.

My eyes widened as my lips twitched.

"Well. Stand up. Let me have a look at the pretty piece I spent a fortune on," Elias rumbled.

I rose up immediately, smoothing the drawers and then raising my arms from my sides slightly to offer him a spin, the carpet coarse against my bare feet.

"Mmm, very fine indeed," Elias purred.

It was just a part of the game, but the words made me warm with pleasure.

"Let me help you with your coat, sir," I said, trying hard not to laugh at the ease of falling into this role. It should've been even more absurd than playing a schoolgirl, and yet somehow it was more fun, the real Victoria falling away to make way for this fictional little coquette.

"There's a snap at the back of the collar," Elias said, and I paused in my approach, the rasp of his voice out of character. I nodded, realizing that was the real him guiding me, somewhat bashfully, in how to undress him.

His hands came to my shoulders as I unbuttoned his coat, thumbs rubbing away some of the chill from being so underdressed.

"Are you pleased with your purchase?" I asked.

"That will depend on how well you take instruction, my dear."

I shivered at that promise and ducked my head, teasing my fingers under the short hem of his coat, against the high waist of the trousers. Elias bowed slightly at the waist, offering me an easier reach to his collar. I lifted my arms up around his shoulders, arching slightly, and smiled when his gaze seemed to point directly to my painted nipples under the white silk.

"I'm eager to learn," I whispered into his ear.

Without warning, one of Elias's hands slid between my thighs, up into the opening of the drawers, stroking over my sex. I muffled a cry and fisted the collar of his coat as he rubbed at me gently.

"Oh, yes, you are, aren't you? That is good. I prefer my indulgences sweet rather than sour."

My knees bent, body trying to fall into those questing fingers, but I managed to unlatch the two halves of the coat collar, the heavy fabric falling suddenly from Elias's shoulders. He pulled away, tugging at the cuffs himself, and I staggered in place for a moment.

"Sit on the bed, darling. Spread your legs and show me that fresh little pussy of yours," Elias said, the casual roll of the explicit words leaving me dizzy.

I'd never really cared about dirty talk, mostly found it embarrassing, false. But this *was* false. We were playacting, and yet it made everything come easier.

I hopped up onto the bed, leaning back on my palms and spreading my legs open so the split drawers offered a framed view of my sex, russet curls peeking out.

Elias folded his coat and draped it over the stool by the vanity, his figure long and lean in front of me. His wings shielded his back from view, but I realized he must get his shirts and coats tailored like halter tops to accommodate his wings, and the thought made me smile.

Elias dropped to his knees in front of my spread legs, and my smile faltered.

"What are you—Oh!" I gasped as he grasped my knees, pinning them open and then thrust his face against my sex, nuzzling there. "Eli—sir!"

"Nothing like a good clean cunny, untouched. Mmm," Elias purred, mouth burrowing against my pussy as I tried to squirm back. His fingers wrapped around the back of my knees, making me squeak, and he yanked me closer to his face, groaning into my cunt, licking there.

"Elias!" I cried, even as I bucked against his nose, rubbing myself over his open mouth, my head falling back.

He eased back, and I whined. "I thought I'd teach you to fondle me and suck me first, but I've decided I'll have to be a bit rough to start. Which means you need a bit of prepping, darling. And there's nothing that makes a honeypot sweeter than a good tongue-lashing."

I barked out a laugh, but it turned into a moan as Elias set to doing exactly that, his long tongue whipping back and forth over my sex. "Fuck. Fuck, put it—put it in again, sir," I pleaded, then shouted and collapsed back on the bed as he obeyed, thick, slick tongue delving into me.

Christ, it felt so good, swirling and petting inside of me like eager fingers. Nothing had felt this good since—I couldn't remember, not while I stared up at the carved roof of a vintage bed, humping Elias's face like my life depended on it, like I might just—

I growled as he pulled away, starting to lift my head to tell him to *get back* to whatever it was he'd just been doing when two long fingers speared inside of me, making me scream and arch, thrashing on the velvet coverlet.

"Now, now, don't be greedy, darling. It's me that's paid for you, remember?" Elias purred, hot breath ghosting over my clit. My skin sizzled over my body, and all at once, the wispy under-garments were stifling. I reached for the hem of the chemise, lifting it to clutch at my own breasts but only making it as high as my ribs. "Oh no you don't," Elias snapped, grasping both my wrists in one hand. "You're my present to unwrap, you little slut."

I gaped at the words, my face hot as I choked on any possible reply. His thumb brushed over my clit in a brief cursory touch, but I quaked at the contact, freezing stiff as my core fluttered and flooded with arousal.

Elias chuckled darkly, and his fingers dragged out of me with agonizing patience, like he was trying not to stimulate me first. My breath was ragged, and I softened once more as he stood in front of me, one hand raised as he sucked his fingers clean with a noisy thoroughness that made me blush, the other hand quickly unfastening the front placket of his trousers and untying the briefs below.

A glitter of gold fanned out from the opening, and I smiled at the playful appearance of Elias's tendril-like core-mata. They'd been a surprise last time, but an amusingly pleasant one. A moment later, with a tug at the hips of his trousers, Elias's long, thick shaft slapped free, bobbing in the air. My mouth filled with saliva as I recalled the strangely rich flavor, and I tried sitting up, only to catch the shake of Elias's head.

"Just remember, my dear, it only hurts the first time," Elias said, and then he reached down, scooping up one of my knees and pressing it back to spread me open.

He guided his cock into place and met my gaze.

"Sir, I—Ah!" I screamed as he thrust in fully, all at once. The stretch was sudden and shocking, but it didn't hurt. I was slick and ready for him. Instead, the immediate pressure and possession made me clench harder around Elias, throwing me close to the edge once more. I clawed at his chest, and he bent over me with a long groan, pinning me in place, his stillness almost as powerful as the single deep thrust.

"That's it, darling. You'll be all right," Elias murmured into my ear as I twitched and settled beneath him, my body adjusting into an eager, wet welcome of him inside of me. "There, now. Yes, what a good, tight little cunny you have. I know it hurts, but you're such a good girl."

I whimpered as if his words were true, although it was a whine of pleasure, *need*, rather than the opposite.

"It…it doesn't hurt." I relaxed the claw of my fingers into

softer strokes, petting Elias's chest through the layers of clothing he still wore.

He lifted slightly, smiling at me, and tipped his head. "Oh, doesn't it?"

I shook my head and felt a pin catch against the bedding, slipping free. "No, sir. You feel good." I nudged my hips into his as proof, batting my lashes.

Elias's smile softened. "You feel good too, darling. So good, in fact, I need to—" I yelped as he snapped his hips back and into me once more, roughly, just as he'd said. He groaned, eyelids sliding closed, head lifting. "Oh, yes, little girl. You feel good. I'll leave you sore after all, I'm afraid."

I opened my mouth to reassure him, but Elias reared up, thrusting hard once more, drawing a cry from my throat and fucking me across an inch of the bed, my hair pulling from the pins.

"Mmm. Pretty little whore," he rasped, and I flushed from head to toe, my hands flying to cover my face, to cover the strange shamed joy of the taunt.

Soft claws grazed over my chest, catching the collar of the chemise, and I shouted as he bucked again, brutal and quick, tearing the thin silk open nearly to the waist, shoving the ripped material aside to reveal my breasts.

"Hold your legs open," Elias ordered. I shook as I caught my legs behind my knees, squeezing my eyes shut, knowing the picture I made, loving it. I sobbed as his hand gripped my breasts, pinching and pulling over my nipples as he started a steady, rude rhythm inside of me. "A little tart all painted and primped for the first time. For *me*."

"Yes," I breathed, the word ragged with the force of Elias's fucking.

"I'm going to teach you how to take a man in hand, little whore. How to suck and nurse on cock. But oh, I'm going to fill this little pussy so you'll be dripping with me for days, darling."

I twisted, trying to hide my face in the sheets, but Elias gripped my chin and my eyes flew open to meet his.

"No, darling. You'll watch me. You'll remember my face. The first man to ever teach this sweet cunt what it was worth."

"Oh god, El—Sir!"

Elias groaned, and his hands joined mine around my knees, spreading me until my thighs burned. His head fell back to expose the soft fur mane around his throat, and his wings stretched wide, monstrous red and rust and gold eyes staring down at me until lust and terror mingled and burned through.

"Oh, Victoria, you are tight," Elias squeezed out, his body shuddering over mine.

I was getting tighter, rocking back and forth over that edge that had evaded me for so long. Hot stinging tears rose to my eyes, and I wiped them quickly against my shoulder, not wanting Elias to mistake them.

I didn't care if I came. I didn't care if I didn't. I was just grateful for the shocking storm that came right before the fall, the way our breaths grew loud and echoed in my ears, the way my blood seemed to boil and race through my veins, the irregular clench and drum in my core that skittered away when I tried to focus on it.

So I watched Elias instead, watched the moment his eyes spread wide in surprise, his throat flexing as he bellowed his pleasure, his body jerking and stuttering forward, hands slipping free of me to brace his fall toward the bed.

"*Fuck,*" he snarled, the word drawn out on a groan, shoulders trembling.

I released my own legs and wrapped them around his hips, savoring the weak moan from his lips. He collapsed, and I trapped him there, my arms around his neck, my face buried in his fragrant mane, Elias twitching helplessly atop me.

My body thrummed in triumph and denial, frustration sweet as the near but uncooperative crash settled down once more, tamed by the weight of the man who'd just taken his own relief.

He sighed and tried to move away, but I tightened my grip around him, a grunt of over sensitized pleasure in my ear.

"I had a whole plan," Elias muttered, but he stroked his nose around my ear gently.

I laughed. "What happened to it?"

His hands stroked down my sides. "Got too into character, I suppose. You were close."

The words were light, more an observation than anything too pointed, but I was shy of answering, afraid of where it might lead.

"Do you want me to try next time?" he asked, leaning back enough to catch my gaze.

I shook my head quickly. "I don't know how to explain it, but I like how much you just want to fuck me and get yourself off. It feels…incredible."

Elias watched me for a moment and then nodded, shifting out of me and to the side but keeping us tangled together. "I can't argue that."

"Are we…done?" I asked. *Please say no.*

He huffed. "Not nearly." He had to sit up and rearrange himself to rest back on his wings, but it didn't seem to bother him to do so, and he raised his arms up to rest his head in his palms. "Undress me and then fondle and suck me until I'm hard again. I'll tell you when you do something I really like."

I scrambled up, shrugging out of the torn top.

"Oh, yes. Off with the drawers too," Elias nodded, watching me, the warm light of the room brightening his dark eyes. "I want a good view of all of you. My darling little whore."

CHAPTER 16
Elias

VICTORIA HAD SO MANY TELLS. The way color striped across her cheeks. The compulsive wetting of her lips. The frequent hitches of breath.

My favorite of all was when she would dig her fingers into her thighs, thumbs pressing into the soft flesh that met between her legs, nearly to her own sex.

I checked to be sure that the orcish couple we were watching was busy—thoroughly, their backs to us as Lenata had Eck'am pinned to the mattress, nearly an inch away from mounting his cock—and then dropped my hand into Victoria's lap, curving my fingers down between her thighs to cup her sex through her jeans, not enough for her to enjoy the pressure, just to tease.

"We could do that later," I whispered, nodding to the orcs.

Granted, Victoria probably couldn't best me while wrestling, but it wasn't like I'd make it hard for her.

Her hand covered mine, and just for a brief second she pressed my fingers harder into her sex.

"I can't today," she whispered.

I was surprised by the bitter flavor of disappointment at her answer, and then a moment later thrilled. Disappointment was a good indicator of advancing *feelings*, surely. And she had only said "today."

"Tomorrow night." I pressed my lips together, frowning at the eager bite in my tone.

Victoria softened, sliding forward on the bench and pushing herself into my touch as Lenata sank down on Eck'am's thrusting cock and stav. "Yes," she breathed as the couple moaned.

We had another interview and demonstration the night after. My schedule was filling up with Victoria and her research, and yet I was still trying to stuff her into the gaps, impatient to see her, to touch her, to unravel the tight knot she kept her pleasure trapped in and claim it for myself.

Victoria's breath hitched and her hand squeezed over mine, tugging on it slightly. I'd gripped her tighter without realizing, and I wondered for a moment if she was close again. If I could keep rubbing, squeezing and she would come here and now, quietly, in front of the fucking orcs and at my side, under my hand.

I wanted to be patient. I *could* be patient.

She would ask me, *beg* me not to stop one day. Soon, I was sure.

I stroked her through her jeans, a final press over the seam that was surely digging against her clit, and then pulled my hand away.

———

ELIAS: *If you want time off, you're going to have to earn it. My office. ASAP.*

Victoria: Do you mean at the bar?

Elias: I can't get away, and I need to use your pretty pussy before I burst.

Victoria: Yes, boss. omw

———

A SOFT KNOCK rapped against the door of my office, barely audible beneath the music in the bar. Music I'd inched up slowly over the past hour, wanting to make sure there was cover for any sound that might come out of this room tonight.

"What?" I asked, and the snap in my tone was too easy to conjure as I stuffed the gilded summons scented with violets underneath a stack of paperwork.

A strange and giddy thrill burst in my chest as the door cracked open and a flirtatious red curl peeked around the edge, banishing the thoughts of responsibilities and lineage from my mind. Victoria's face followed, her eyes bright and cheeks already flushed.

"You asked to see me."

"Well. Get in here."

Her lips twitched and her head ducked shyly, body sliding into the barely opened door. My office was small, but generally I kept it clear of clutter—just a comfortable chair to work in, my laptop, and the necessary files of paperwork and receipts. Tonight I'd dragged in spare boxes of booze to stack against the walls until the room was tight and hard to move around, my desk covered in odds and ends, including framed photos of a dog I didn't own and a house I'd never seen before.

Victoria was wearing a dress. I'd never seen her in a dress before, and there was something odd about the sight. She pinched the hip of the skirt and tugged at it, fussing with the seam of the waist. She didn't like dresses. So why wear one?

I arched my brow as I spun my chair to face her, our knees knocking together in the process.

"Lift your hem," I said.

Victoria wet her lips and gathered fabric up in her fist. "I need to ask for Friday off."

"You want to ask for the busiest night of the week off, with all of two days' notice?" I fought my smile as she stopped with the fluttering black hem around her knees. What was this dress for, anyway? Potential funerals? Donor galas at the university? "Higher."

She sucked a breath and scooped the fabric over her arm, raising her skirt to her waist, revealing everything. And nothing. She'd come to me without panties on again. That was becoming a theme, which intrigued me. It meant *she* liked it. And was she already wet? It looked to be the case.

"I can make up the hours for everyone else," she said. She had short, practical black boots on. The curling hair covering her pussy was a deeper shade of red, auburn, almost brown, but it caught the shitty lighting of my office and glinted like rubies where she was damp. "I just need to know what I have to do to make it up to you."

"Is the door locked?" I asked, rolling the chair closer, stopping as I ran a wheel into the toe of her boot.

She nodded, her loose, wild hair bouncing. "When I shut the door."

"Put your foot up on that box," I said, nodding to the box of moderately cheap vodka I'd tucked away just inside the door.

Victoria wet her lips again, pupils growing wider, and lifted her leg, turning it out and balancing her foot on the box, giving me a better view of her sex, of the dark purple pink lips that clashed with the red of her hair.

"Take out one of your tits," I said, opening the waist of my pants, my cock swelling with relief, coremata flaring open so I could grip and pull on myself.

Victoria's breath was coming harshly now, and she had to squirm and wrestle down one shoulder of her dress, tugging the cup of a well-worn gray bra aside. I groaned as I squeezed myself, my mouth watering at the sight of the darkened nipple. She'd fucking rouged it again?

"What did you do?" I whispered, glancing up at her, dropping the act for the moment.

"Tinted lip gloss," she said, groping and molding her breast in her hand. "Pomegranate flavor."

I moaned, and Victoria laughed and scooted her other leg open for me as I surged forward, suckling on the nipple she'd offered—waxy and sweet and so eagerly tight for my mouth.

"Can I be rough with you?" I murmured, nuzzling into the soft skin over her chest. There was a healing mark on the underside of her breast, where I'd sucked hard the last time we'd fucked.

"Please," she answered in a gasp.

I stood, the chair rolling back to knock against the desk, and reached up to the shelf above Victoria's head, grabbing a condom and lube. Her eyes widened, and she burst out in a laugh.

"Right by the door? That's so skeezy," she said, lips stretched in a bright grin.

"And exploiting my employees in exchange for time off isn't?" I answered.

Her smile softened. I cast a shadow over her, but not enough of one to darken the glitter in her eyes. "I like your dedication to the details." She reached for the lube, and I hurried to roll on the condom, leaning forward, pinning her to the door as she stroked me slick, reaching down to her own sex to wipe the excess lube there.

"Wanna know the truth?" I asked, grabbing her thigh, lifting it so only her toes touched the box.

"Mmm?"

"I knew the first time you let me touch you that there were no lengths I wouldn't go to to do it again," I rasped.

I bent my knees, staring down into Victoria's wide eyes, knowing she was wondering if that was part of the game, the act, or if I was telling her the truth. Knowing that she would never find the answer in my shrouded gaze. I found her opening, gave a cursory thumb stroke to her clit, and then thrust inside.

"Ahh, *fuck!*"

I growled, my arm circling Victoria's waist, surprised by the sudden pulse of satisfaction, the near pound of my own release. Not yet, damnit. My arm tightened, one hand braced on the wall.

"Wrap your leg around me," I ground out.

Victoria whimpered, her cunt so tight it was like she was trying to squeeze me back out, but she jumped slightly, and I rose up as she hiked her leg around my hip, one foot balancing on the liquor box and the other bracing into my ass.

"Did you wear this dress to make it easy for me to fuck you?" I asked.

"Kind of, yes, and to make it easier if we had to stop suddenly," she breathed, squirming, trying to adjust to my sudden intrusion.

I purred, rolling my hips, using the arm around her waist to lift and lower Victoria on my cock. I leaned back, and her head hit the wall, lips parted on a silent moan.

"You think I would stop fucking you just 'cause someone else walked in?"

Victoria shuddered, eyes falling shut as her core clasped around me. She liked that. I wondered if I could talk her into the two of us doing a demonstration of our own someday. Atlas and Cyril would certainly volunteer to watch.

"You think everyone doesn't already know what you came in here to do? That you let me use you as my personal fuck toy?"

Victoria's arm flung around my shoulder, her face burying itself in my mane, breath hot and damp into my throat.

"They're all jealous," I hissed in her ear, thrusting roughly, a muffled clap of my furred hips hitting her flesh. "Jealous that I get to fuck this perfect" —*slap*— "wet" —*slap*— "greedy" —*slap*— "insatiable pussy."

"Elias," Victoria whined.

I grabbed her other thigh, bouncing her on my cock, and she yelped, held up, trapped between the wall and my body. I squeezed her ass and then stroked up the back of her thighs.

"Grab the doorframe and the shelf, Victoria."

Her hands groped through the air until she had a weak grasp behind her. It was good enough. I wouldn't let her fall.

I gripped the back of her knees and hiked them higher. She liked this vulnerable pose, pinned open and unable to move. I wondered if she'd like being tied up too, but that would have to be another role for us to play.

"I'm going to use your pussy till you milk me dry," I said, and her eyes flashed open to hold my gaze. "You can say it's for a night off, but we both know the truth. You just wanna be my little cock whore. If I offered to pay you to sit in here all day, naked and ready for me, you'd say yes, wouldn't you?"

Victoria panted as I started a slow push and retreat inside of her, her head nodding as she stared in a shocked kind of wonder up at me.

"Mmhm, you'd let me use you whenever I wanted, as hard as I wanted. Would you let me fuck you raw too?"

She sobbed, hiding her face once more, and I picked up my pace, clapping into her, wanting to whisper the truth into her ear—I'd let her do the same. Fuck, I'd wrap a bow around my cock and glue a vibrator to my tongue if I thought Victoria would let me try and get her off properly. But she still fell in and out of her head, tensed when she started to get close, locked up at the offer.

Soon, I promised myself.

In the meantime, I'd prove over and over that I could give her exactly what she asked for.

Not that it was exactly a hardship.

My own breaths were ragged, the squeeze of Victoria's cunt around my cock growing tighter by the second. She was barely holding herself up against the wall, and my knees were growing weak.

"Take the condom off."

I faltered at the words, shaking my head and staring down at Victoria. Her eyes were almost entirely black with arousal, face red and lips bitten. Why hadn't I kissed her yet?

I bowed my head to do so, and she arched away.

"Fuck me raw, Elias," she rasped. "I'm on birth control, and I tested clean."

The thought of it—of the wetness that splashed against my hips coating my cock, the velvet interior of her pussy sucking and kissing all over my length—made me snap, electricity in my veins and crackling down my spine. I threw my head back with a strangled roar and came with a violence that sent the pair of us dripping down the wall, my hips chasing pleasure with an uneven gait.

Victoria hummed against my ear, a breathy laugh, and twined her arms around my shoulder as I sank to my knees. One of the legs of the rolling chair rested below my ass, and my heels tangled with the base, turning at uncomfortable angles.

And I didn't care a bit, because Victoria was soft and smiling, legs and arms wrapped around me, the heat of her still enveloping my throbbing, sated shaft.

"Sorry, didn't realize that would tip you over," she said, combing her fingers through my fur.

I grunted, dropping my forehead to her shoulder, not caring that I was sitting like crumpled origami, as long as she kept touching me like that, comfortable and familiar.

Her nose brushed back and forth against my temple, and I froze in place as her lips pressed to the spot. "You really are so good," she whispered.

I could be even better, I wanted to say, but she continued talking and I liked the melting tone in her voice.

"It's like you know what I want without me having to

ask," she said, kissing there again, a strange, tight fever blooming in my chest. "It is making me a little greedy. I think about all the things that… Never mind."

I lifted my head, hiding my wince as I shifted us on the floor, kicking the chair as much out of the way as I could. Perhaps cluttering up the room hadn't been such a brilliant idea.

"When you ask, I will listen," I said.

Her eyes were bright, her cheeks still flushed, and her core teased around my shrinking length. Damn. Did she even realize that she was still close? Didn't it frustrate her not to reach the fall?

"I think…at some point, I just started to feel like what I asked for wasn't supposed to be in a healthy relationship," she admitted, sagging back against the wall.

I slid out of her, twisting to grab a tissue and dispose of the condom. I gathered her back up in my arms after, leaning against the boxes and shelves, and she snuggled willingly. She was used to the way I liked to hold her after I'd finished —even seemed to enjoy the closeness.

"Communication is part of a healthy relationship. Taking another's desires and limits into account is part of a healthy relationship. Tell me something you wanted that you got talked out of."

Victoria chewed at her lip, absently adjusting her dress back into place to cover her breast. "I… Sometimes I…" She frowned and took a deep breath, and I reached up, untangling the riot of her hair and twisting it around my fist. When I tightened my grip, Victoria sighed and met my gaze. "I told Brett I wanted him to fuck me while I was sleeping, rather than wake me up. And I… It wasn't just about not wanting to be woken up. I just like the idea of being used in that way. I suggested it a few times, and he said that if I didn't want to have sex with him, then I should just say so. He didn't really listen when I tried to explain."

"Somnophilia is a well-established sexual interest," I said, shrugging. "We'll have to arrange a sleepover."

Victoria froze in my lap, eyes wide, and then suddenly her mouth was on mine, hungry and clumsy, licking and biting. I wrapped my free arm around her back and softened my hand in her hair, tilting her head to settle the kiss into a deep, smooth stroke of lips and tongue. She moaned and rocked on my lap, hands petting and squeezing at my chest. With a twist of her hips she was straddled over my lap, wet sex rubbing over my now bare cock. I groaned into her mouth and pulled away slowly.

"Did you mean what you said about losing the condom?" I asked.

She nodded. "I'm not sleeping with anyone else. Oh…are you? For MSA?"

I tried not to read into it so that she didn't look nervous at the suggestion. Rafe and Hannah had been falling in love while he was still working with other clients, and Hannah had found it easy enough to compartmentalize the fact at the time.

I shook my head. "I haven't been interested in any cases but yours in ages."

She smiled at that, and I glanced down at our lap, gently adjusting her skirt so I could see where her pussy touched my cock. It was still mostly soft, but it wouldn't take much encouragement for it to grow hard again.

"Want to know a secret?" I whispered.

Victoria nodded immediately, her hands fisted in my shirt. I gripped her hips and rolled her wet sex over my lap as I leaned in close.

"I love frottage," I said, nipping at her ear, keeping her in motion on my lap. "There's something innocent about it, and that makes it feel even filthier."

Victoria moaned and grasped my face, turning it to her and fucking her tongue into my mouth. She took over the motion, riding on my lap, slow and heavy, matching the circling of her hips to the stroke of our tongues. I groaned, hands squeezing her waist, and then leaned closer, wrapping her in a tight hug as she moved, as we kissed.

It was almost better than the sex.

I lost track of time, Victoria's hands sliding through my hair, my own massaging her back, heat building and retreating and building again. She moaned as I massaged her ass, then skidded up under her dress to stroke her bare skin, never pushing, never asking.

Victoria shivered and whimpered, tensing in one moment, sighing and softening the next. I forced myself to slow, to pull softer kisses from her lips, waiting to see what she would take for herself. But she slowed to a stop, panting slightly, her breaths mingling with mine. My cock was hard and soaked with our arousal.

I could've sworn she looked a little disappointed as I leaned back. The expression smoothed too quickly, a shy smile rising in its place.

"Take me inside of you, Victoria," I whispered.

The disappointment vanished, lit up by hunger, and I scooted down against the floor, staring avidly as she rose up on her knees and then sank, her wet, swollen sex swallowing me one inch at a time.

CHAPTER 17
Victoria

THE BAR HAD FALLEN silent outside Elias's office door, and I was going to regret this late night when I had to show up to class tomorrow morning, but at the moment I was too caught up in the strange, private little world of a cluttered office and the golden fae cradling me against his chest.

His hand played between my legs, more like an absent thought than any real intention, but it was just shy of irritating. Too soft and yet too stimulating at the same time. Generally I enjoyed sex, and even masturbation, without *needing* to get off, used to getting by taking whatever pleasure that came. But tonight had been long and drawn out, and I'd been so close so many times that I now felt like an exposed live wire, crackling and ready to spark.

I covered his hand and slid it up to my stomach, fingertips tracing damp lines on my skin.

"No more right now," I said. I needed to calm down, at the very least. Actually, I needed to go home. If only I wanted to.

I was sore. Elias had been more demanding tonight, and after making me ride him to a groaning finish, he'd put me on my hands and knees and fucked me all over again, never flagging in arousal.

"Sorry. My mating season is starting," he said softly, kissing my forehead. "I'm not normally quite so pushy."

I snorted at that, and he laughed.

"I mean, as myself, I'm not," he said.

Which was a disquieting reminder that we hadn't really been playing roles for the past hour or so.

"What's a mating season?" I asked, adjusting my dress to cover me as I rolled. We were on the hard floor, but I couldn't bring myself to care and Elias apparently didn't either, his feet propped up on a box against the wall.

His chest rose and fell beneath me as he sucked in a deep breath. "The usual—heightened sex drive, increased pheromone production, more extreme awareness in the senses," he said, gesturing up to his antennae and then down to the coremata that were flicking over my clothed stomach.

My eyebrows rose. "What do your coremata sense?" And why hadn't I asked earlier, considering they had been playing all over my pussy and ass every time we'd had sex?

"They're something between…a tongue and the subconscious process of human scent receptors, I suppose," Elias mused, shifting more comfortably and reaching down to tuck the tendrils away. "That's a bit inadequate. There aren't always reasonable comparisons between species, you know."

It was enough to leave me blushing at least, but Elias wasn't studying me for once. "And your antennae?"

"Those are much more subtle. They detect arousal, fertility, cortisol, fear—"

"So both sexual and predatory," I pointed out.

Elias sniffed primly. "It's nothing you aren't doing. We moth fae just do it at a more expansive and informed level. I can tell the difference between *your* scents, and the scents added to all your" —he flapped a hand in the air— "products."

"During the mating season?"

"All the time. During the mating season…well, I can sense all of that, and I can…manipulate a response a bit as well."

Eyes wide, I pressed my hands to Elias's chest and levered up into sitting, my back against the leg of his desk. He looked as though he might've been pouting for a moment.

"I didn't do it tonight, if that's what you're about to ask," he muttered.

I shook my head. "No, that's not— This is fascinating, Elias! *How* can you manipulate all of that? With the antennae?"

He laughed and sat up, scooting back against the wall and wearing a smile. "No, there are glands around my throat and groin, especially beneath my mane. It is a predator quality, I suppose, but I don't believe it works so well as to overpower the other person's will. I suppose…if you naturally were disgusted by me and I wanted to fuck you, I would have to get close enough for you to scent me. Ideally have your face right up in my fur. You might be surprised to feel some arousal, but it wouldn't outweigh your disgust."

"But if I was attracted already, and we hugged and I put my face in your mane—"

"This is at the height of the mating season, mind you. That's still a couple weeks away," Elias interrupted.

"Elias, I'm not accusing you of seducing me via your pheromones. I'm *curious*."

He sighed and nodded. "If you and I are around each other in a couple weeks, we'll fuck. Ideally, quite a lot."

"Like tonight?" I asked, head tipping.

Elias puffed a breath. "Like tonight on repeat for several days. Until I've so thoroughly depleted myself that I can no longer rise to the occasion. Which I suppose doesn't give you enough information. We'd fuck for days on end, with very little or no refractory period."

My mouth was dry, but another part of me was making up for that in wetness. "That's not— Can that even—?"

Elias's smile was silky, eyelids drooping slightly. "I mentioned I loved frottage. I also enjoy soaking. Oral, thigh fucking, handjobs. And keep in mind, my libido is heightened. Someone once got me off with a feather. It's all about being creative."

And already, my mind was eagerly adding suggestions. Did Elias like toys? Brett had never wanted to masturbate for me when he would rather have sex, but after we'd broken up, I'd realized that it was one of my favorite forms of porn to watch. Would Elias let me use a fleshlight to get him off?

"H-how often does this happen?"

"Thankfully, just once a year. It's not as though I lack interest the rest of the time, and anymore than that would take it from being a fun, lusty holiday into a chore," he mused.

"Have you spent it with Cyril and Atlas in the past?" I asked, remembering their eager flirting.

Elias smiled. "Not the entirety. To be honest, I don't always want company for the majority of it. That's a great deal of time to spend with other people."

A sudden rough laugh escaped me, and I slouched more comfortably against the desk. "Fair."

Elias blinked slowly, watching me. My own tongue was tied, and the silence shifted from easy to charged, the obvious question hanging between us.

"Victoria," he purred softly, and I tried and failed not to squirm on the hard floor. "Do you want to be my pretty toy?"

I gasped, and even though I was more well fucked than I had been in years, my cunt gave a needy throb.

Elias bent one leg and leaned forward, propping his chin on his knee. "Do you want to spend days in my bed, being used and fucked and soaked? I promise to be gentle."

"I don't want you to be gentle the whole time," I blurted out too easily.

This was absurd. We'd already left impersonal behind

tonight, and it had only been a few hours. Days of sex? Since when had I ever wanted it more than twice in one night?

It's not about what I want. It's about what he needs. Me, a dark voice whispered in my head.

Elias grinned and shrugged, his wings scratching softly against the wall. "When, I need to be then. Let me use you. My cock's grown very fond of you, and I don't think anyone else would do, truth be told. I'd just be craving your cunt the whole time."

I exhaled and the air rattled out of me, bitter with the jealous thought of him going to anyone else now. "I'll need dates. I have cats."

Elias blinked and brightened. "Do you really? I hadn't imagined that. How interesting. But of course, we can schedule our reckless debauchery."

I rose up on my knees and Elias sat up, spreading his legs in invitation. I nodded, and his black eyes gleamed. "All right. I want to be your sex toy for your mating season."

Elias purred as I scooted closer, stopping with my knees between his thighs. His hands wrapped around my hips, his fingers digging into my ass.

"You'll let me use you day or night?" he asked.

I nodded again.

His voice lowered and he leaned in, whispering into my throat, "What about when you're so, so tired, and you fall asleep lying next to me, darling?"

I shivered, my eyes sliding shut. "Especially then."

I groaned as his long tongue stroked up the side of my throat, swirling over my pulse.

"Do you want me to be careful? I have ways to block the scent glands that—"

"No," I breathed out, shaking my head, brushing my cheeks against his dense, velvety hair. "I don't care. I want—I want to be out of my mind with wanting you."

Elias moaned and his hand flew up, fisting my curls and

drawing my mouth down to his. I groaned and parted for him, sucking on his tongue, throwing one of my legs to sit and grind on his thigh, heat and ache and a lightning thrill jolting up my spine as we kissed.

I'd told my therapist once that around the time of the affair, I'd felt like I was on the brink of exploding, that I'd been searching for a spark or a match to set my whole world on fire. The reality of the breakup with Brett was quiet, although it had left an impressive wreckage for me to sort through for at least a year after. And that feeling of barely contained energy, dangerous potential vibrating inside of me, had passed with every week.

It was back now. I didn't know if I was racing toward another reckoning, another collapse of my life…

Or another metamorphosis.

———

I PAUSED inside the entrance of the bar, taking in the heavy, dark wallpaper, lush greenery, and excess of patterns. Spanish funk music played over the stereos, just loud enough for the beat to be warm and inviting. It was fairly early still, and there was only one woman sitting on the brief barstool. Waiting for me.

Initially, when Emma had suggested drinks—with an actual confirmed date and time for once—I'd been tempted to offer up Nightlight as a location. After the other night and the agreement between me and Elias about his mating season, I was relieved to do this elsewhere. It would be too nerve-wracking to talk to my sister properly for the first time in over a year, with my new…whatever Elias was watching over us.

Emma waved shyly, and I hurried to join her, scanning the back of the bar, noting a few labels Elias carried but plenty of others he didn't bother with. His bar had more in-house recipes anyway.

Quit thinking about him, my thoughts snapped.

Emma was standing, and I realized too late she was reaching for a hug. The gesture stuttered as I gaped, and then we both tried again, awkward laughter adding sad punctuation to how estranged we'd managed to become.

But she felt familiar in my arms, a little taller than me, and she leaned in the way she had when we'd been close, bending and hunching to tuck her chin over my shoulder as I rose up on my tiptoes. I squeezed her tighter before she could pull away.

"I've missed you," I said, then released her, blinking rapidly at the burn in my eyes.

"I've missed you too," Emma said, breathless and keeping her face turned away as she climbed back up onto the barstool.

It took us too long to settle, passing minutes by examining the cocktail menu, asking harmless questions about her work or my study, stirring our drinks and making innocuous observations about the weather or Chicago traffic.

Finally, after a quarter of an hour, Emma took a sharp, deep breath, and I braced myself against the bar top, waiting for her to land the punch.

"We set a date."

I exhaled in a rush, a smile rising easily on my lips. "Congratulations!"

Her eyes were wide, flicking in my direction. I resisted the urge to roll my eyes, relaxing back slightly and sipping on my drink. It tasted good, and I'd taken a photo of the list of ingredients to show to Elias. He could make it better.

"You have a venue?"

"The Rookery."

I nodded, smiling. My mother had pushed for a wedding at the La Salle Library, our families both being deeply loyal to the idea of a classic Chicago venue.

"I asked to elope to Paris," Emma whispered, laughing.

"Do both," I suggested, nudging my shoulder to hers. "Just don't tell Mom and Kathy. It'll take the pressure off for the big event. What's the date?"

"March third."

"So soon!"

She huffed and nodded, and I wondered if I imagined the spark of panic in her eyes. "A cancellation popped up, and we were next on the waiting list."

"Well, that's amazing!"

Emma's smile wobbled as she turned to me, eyes welling and glittering with the reflection of the hanging colored lanterns above us. "I don't think I can do this."

I froze in my seat. Oh, god. Poor Brett. Not once, but twice. And by sisters?

"Not if I don't know for sure that you're okay—"

I nearly collapsed, and I was surprised to find it was relief cascading through me. "Oh, Emma—"

"No, it's just—I know Mom said you'd need time and space—"

I barked out a laugh.

"—and I get why it would be a shock—"

"Emma," I pleaded, reaching for her hands, grateful that no one else had sat at the bar yet and the bartender was being fairly discreet while dissecting a pineapple in the far corner.

"—and I really do love him, but I can't handle the idea of *every* holiday being so awkward and just—"

"Emma, stop." I squeezed her hands in mine, and she choked on her words, meeting my gaze. Her eyes were darker than mine, but so lovely. Emma had always seemed so comfortable in the mold our mother had shaped for us, and I hoped that was true, that she wasn't suffocating inside the way I had been.

"Em, I didn't need time or space or whatever it was Mom claimed. Splitting up from Brett *was* the time and space I needed. And to be perfectly honest, I wasn't that surprised when the two of you connected."

"Oh, god," Emma groaned.

"I always knew you had a crush on him."

"Vic, I swear, I never—"

"Emma, it's *fine*. It doesn't matter if he pursued you. It doesn't matter if you jumped out of a cake naked the day after I left his apartment. Okay?"

She blushed, but huffed and tossed her hair over her shoulder, scented like a meadow, the strawberry blonde shade shimmering to pure pink under the lanterns, falling once more to a perfect, straight curtain.

"Sometimes, it feels like I'm just the replacement for you," she murmured. I opened my mouth, back straight, ready to chew Brett to pieces, before she continued in a rush, "That's just from Mom and Kathy. Don't worry. It's just…you know they got so attached to the idea of the families being connected. And when Kathy found out Brett and I were dating, she wasn't just happy for us, she was *relieved*."

"Kathy hated me, but she loved Mom. She's probably ecstatic that Brett upgraded," I teased Emma. It was easier than I'd expected it to be to make jokes now. This was the only closure I'd really needed. Just knowing my sister and I were okay. "But Brett—"

"It's not like he compares us or anything. He's very careful to make sure I know that he loves me and that's nothing to do with anything that came before, good or bad," Emma said carefully, but her voice was soft and her smile was sincere. She lifted a mango garnish from the inside of her glass and nibbled in thought. "If Mom knows you and I are good, she'll want you to be in the wedding party."

"Don't you dare," I hissed.

Emma grinned. "I was thinking about a pastel rainbow for my bridesmaids."

"Emma, I really want to be at your wedding, but if you make me a bridesmaid, I *will* leave the country."

She giggled, with just a hint of wicked intention, and for a moment I had to resist the urge to give her a strangling hug.

And then I realized it would be better to succumb.

CHAPTER 18
Victoria

"ARE you using incubus powers on him?" I asked, scowling as Lyle nuzzled his nose against the supposedly feral kitten who'd been visiting since the summer.

Lyle snorted, and the kitten batted him once on the nose and then butted his head against Lyle's chin. "Maybe," Lyle said, waggling his eyebrows. "Or maybe he just likes me better."

I huffed, glaring at the leggy little traitor as he squirmed and climbed onto Lyle's shoulder, settling around my friend's neck and starting a steady, motoring purr.

"I guess I own a cat now?" Lyle asked, wearing that familiar stricken expression of having your heart captured by the tiny paws of a feline.

"I guess you do," I said. "You can take him into the apartment with you. Hube and Sera won't care, and I've seen him use the litter box out here since I got him fixed. Thanks again for doing this."

Lyle grinned. "You know I'll be annoying you endlessly with questions when you get back from the fuck fest. Anyway, Frank's got his girlfriend for the weekend and *doesn't* want to have a threesome, so it's better if I absent myself."

I mustered a smile and tried to think of anything else I could share with Lyle. Had I given enough instructions about connecting to my Wi-Fi? What about the TV remote? Watching cats and apartment-sitting wasn't especially complicated, but maybe there were a few more details I could scrounge up. It was easier than getting onto my feet and heading for Elias's.

"Are you nervous?" Lyle asked, scratching the kitten with one hand and an orange stray I'd named Buster with another.

"I think so," I said, since it was mostly pointless lying to Lyle.

"It's not like you guys weren't already fucking at a rather ambitious level," he pointed out, catching a laugh from me.

"It's just… It feels a little official. Like we went from being casual fucks, to fuck buddies, to—"

"Lovers," Lyle said simply. "In the most profane sense of the word."

I shot him a glare. He wasn't making this easier. "I've only had one real relationship and one other longer term sexual partner. And those were tangled together in the same fucked-up timeline."

"Do you want to avoid a relationship, sexual or otherwise?" Lyle asked.

No. The answer came easily. A major part of my studies was reconciling myself with what I wanted sexually, searching for a better way of feeling satisfied in my sexual relationships. Before this, it had all been theoretical. Something about what I was doing with Elias felt a little bit like an experiment—could I put into practice what I wanted in a relationship?—and on the other hand, it was becoming…too significant, and personal.

"I'm anticipating too far into the future," I said, and Lyle nodded.

"Aside from, you know, the excessive kinky sex, it sounds like you're dipping your toes in slowly. Just take things one boink at a time," he said, winking. "And stay hydrated."

I sighed and stood, reaching down for my backpack and the half gallon water bottle I'd filled and hoisting them into the air. "I'll do my best."

———

I HADN'T SEEN or heard from Elias much since the night in his office. He told me he'd take the week leading up to my visit off from work, and I suspected he'd been busy dealing with whatever his mating season required of him. What word I had received had been incendiary texts, promising all kinds of filthy, delicious treatment for our weekend. The last message had been comparatively mild.

> If I let you make it through the door, it'll be a miracle.

I hadn't realized how seriously he'd meant it.

"Oh god, Elias!"

He snarled at my back, my body pressed to the wall just inside the front entry, one foot still over the jam. My shorts were caught on my spread knees, and Elias's claws hung to the top of the doorframe as he straightened, cock driving higher into me. I was fairly sure we were out of sight from anyone on the road, considering how far back his house was set, but he wasn't exactly being quiet either.

"Just—just let me close the door," I rasped, bucking back into him, swallowing a whine at the shockingly tight fit.

He huffed, and then one hand grabbed my thigh, pulling my leg in. With an awkward buck of his hips and a tug of his arms around me, he jerked us sideways. The hem of my blouse caught as the door swung shut, dropping me into the dark entry.

"Hands on the wall." Elias nudged my ankles together, making the fit of his cock inside of me unbearably, wonderfully tight. My hands groped up the glossy wallpaper and my eyes slid shut. Elias groaned and thrust, hardly able to move inside of me. "You're just lucky I had enough self-restraint not to track you down at home, Victoria."

I shivered at the change in his voice, all the usual smooth glide and stroke turned to dark growl.

"I thought about hunting you down last night. Claiming what's mine."

His hands settled on my hips, around the underwear I was fairly certain he'd torn in his haste, and he pulled out in an agonizing drag, every inch of him sharply present.

"Do you know what is mine, Victoria?" he whispered, licking around the shell of my ear.

I shook my head, gasping for breath.

He growled again, and I shouted with him as he thrust deep. "This." Another retreat, and another brutal thrust. "Tight." Thrust. "Wet." Thrust. "Pussy."

I moaned, my knees hitting the wall, sinking me deeper onto Elias's length.

"Say it," he groaned, rocking against me.

"Elias!"

"Say it, Victoria." He scooted us closer, until my head fell back against his chest and my breasts were smashed to the wall.

"This pussy is yours," I breathed out.

Elias purred with pleasure, drawing out, giving me a chance to catch a breath, before slamming in once more. I quivered and choked, my head bouncing against his fur, a rich, creamy scent wafting into my nose and making me dizzy. I turned my face, remembering what he'd said about his pheromones, and rubbed my cheek into his mane.

Elias laughed, low and ragged. "Oh yes, she's all mine, and she wants it so bad. Don't you, toy?"

"Yes."

He rumbled. "Then you'll have it."

An arm braced at the nape of my neck, pressing my cheek to the wall, and I shouted as his hips snapped to mine, unapologetically rough and quick.

"Fuck, I needed you," Elias whispered. I panted, my breath fogging over the smooth wallpaper with every beat of his length inside of me. "Every time I came this week, it was to the thought of you. I can't—I don't—*Victoria*."

I squeaked as he crowded me close and deep, so tight to the wall I couldn't breathe, hot flashes of release bursting inside of me, wet and shocking. It'd been a long time since I'd had sex without a condom, and I forgot how much I liked it, how it made me clench a little more, like a kind of victory in the other person's surrender.

Elias moaned in my ear, easing back and circling my waist with his arms to keep me close. He staggered away from the wall, yanking my shirt loose from the door, keeping me on his cock. My toes scraped over the floor, legs tangled in shoes and shorts and torn underwear. My water bottle and back-pack were abandoned by the door, and I let out a half-hearted mumble of objection.

"Don't move," he grunted, carrying me with uneven steps past the fishing bear, pausing once to bend us both over and give another emptying thrust inside of me, a little of his cum sliding out to drip down my thighs.

We made it to the stairs in starts and stops, where Elias pulled out of me with a groan before collapsing down on a step near the bottom. His fur looked damp from sweat, and his cock was still arching eagerly toward his stomach, dark and swollen and still slick with release.

"You weren't exaggerating," I said, toeing off my shoes, privately thrilled by the mess seeping out of me.

His head was draped back on another stair, arms and

wings spread akimbo, and he opened one eye, humming in interest as he looked me over.

"Take off your shorts. I want you to rub that dripping pussy all over my cock and balls," he said.

I swayed in place for a moment, Elias's words keeping the earth moving under me so I wasn't able to find an even keel, and then I did as he ordered.

———

IT TOOK over an hour to make it up the stairs between all of Elias's hungry pawing and demands for me to suck him, ride him, and once to just let him rest and catch a little sleep.

"I haven't gotten any since yesterday morning, I think," he'd rasped, cradling me over his half hard cock, stretching out over the hallway carpet. I'd lost my shirt somewhere on the last flight, but Elias was warm enough to snuggle against.

When he woke, he'd groaned, scooped me up in his arms, and hauled us both to a plain looking door and up a flight of stairs into what I'd assumed might be the attic.

It probably had been an attic at one point. Now it was a loft apartment, complete with a kitchen in one corner, an enormous platformed tub tucked behind a half wall, a brief, small living room area around a standing fireplace and two bookshelves, and finally, a massive bed surrounded by the bay windows that faced the corner of the street.

There was no theme, no staging, and it compromised between modern and vintage styles. *This* was Elias's home.

He kicked the door shut behind us and carried me as far as the large and comfortable looking couch before putting me face down over the back and into the dense cushions.

"Elias?" I asked, laughing and preparing for him to press back inside of me. He hadn't since the front door, and as rough as he'd been, I wasn't feeling sore yet.

Instead, I heard his knees thump behind me, and soft breath rushed over my ass.

"Wait—" I choked out, stiffening.

"I need this," he growled, and the words had an effect like magic on me, making me go limp once more, hiding my hot face in the soft bouclé of the couch.

I thrashed slightly as he spread me open, and then I buried a moan deep into the cushions as a scorching hot, wet tongue stroked around my labia.

"You're my toy now, Victoria," Elias whispered into me. "I'll take whatever I want from you. Including this."

I hauled air into my lungs in desperate gasps. Elias's tongue explored me with a thoroughness that matched the thoughtful, erudite nature I'd grown to know in him. He mapped me with delicate little laps in small creases, long strokes at a perfect pressure over my lips, and across the back of my thighs.

"I like the way we taste together," he whispered, and I sagged further, giving up and accepting this treatment. My muscles softened, and he groaned in approval, pressing his face embarrassingly deep into my ass and sex, and still I remained unwound.

I'm his toy.

The meaning felt clearer now. I could be an empty vessel for Elias to use, at least until he called to me for action. The sounds I made, the muffled whimpers and heady sighs, were just answers to the way his long tongue burrowed inside of me, his nose nuzzling at my cheeks.

He stroked up my right thigh with his hand, his thumb coming to circle around my clit, and I shook at the small earthquake it sent through me. His tongue retreated, and he nipped at my ass.

"I just want you to drip into my mouth a little more," he explained gently, knowing I usually might object.

I couldn't now. I was his to use.

It was…liberating.

The back of the couch dug into my ribs and my breath was hot and stifled against the cushions, my head growing heavy from the inversion for so long, and none of it mattered. I wasn't anything but Elias's toy. I didn't have to *be* anything else.

Elias's slow, circular rubbing coiled inside of me, tightening, heating, and I gasped as the warm, tickling pool of arousal gathered inside of me. His groan as it slipped down into his open, waiting mouth vibrated into my core, my legs twitching and a brief spark crackling in my core.

His hand flattened, soothing over my clit and folds and opening as he backed away, and I swallowed my whine, ragdolling over the couch once more.

"Perfect," Elias said, and then he pressed his rigid length back inside of me.

———

"RAFE MADE ME A CASSEROLE. He says I have to reheat it in the oven rather than the microwave, but…"

"Mmm."

Elias straightened slightly, glancing at me over his wings, sadly folding them to his back and hiding the beautiful reveal of his ass once more.

"Microwave is fine," I said. "We probably don't have much time, right?"

Elias grinned, flashing a hint of fang. "Now she's getting it."

Just in case, I clasped the open collar of the silk robe Elias had dressed me in a little tighter around my throat and tried to look as unsexual as possible on the kitchen counter where he'd deposited me.

"Don't worry, I can restrain myself for an hour. Or most of

one." He turned back to his fridge and hefted out a glass container of food.

"Is your mating season meant to be for finding a mate?" I asked, thinking of Rafe and Hannah.

Elias set the dish down with a thunk. "No. Fae don't mate in that way, actually. I suppose it's more of a breeding season. Would you like to know a secret I find somewhat funny?"

I relaxed back against the cupboard behind me and nodded. Elias's apartment—in his house, which was still a wild concept for me to wrap my head around—was turning rosy and orange from the setting sun outside. This was the most intimate experience I'd had in years, and in spite of my nerves earlier while talking with Lyle, I found it fairly easy and natural.

But maybe that was partly due to the fact that I'd already been fucked silly several times.

"Fae males have a very low sperm count."

I blinked and shook the cobwebs loose from my brain.

Elias smiled smugly. "It's true, and for some reason, the fae population has decided to take extreme offense to that fact being pointed out or recorded in any academic or medical journal. All of the old fae tradition, like the wild hunt and frolicking about the maypole—obvious phallic reference— were nods to our fertile seasons. But we have those to make up for the somewhat lackluster results."

"Fae are rare because of low male fertility," I summarized, and he nodded.

"There's no female breeding season, either. Before we joined the other species in integration, they just had to put up with us losing our minds once a year. Fae unions are growing thin now that the female population has more prolific options."

"I read a study that said in two generations, there will be dozens of entirely new species," I said, watching Elias arrange slabs of some kind of unidentifiable but no less delicious looking food onto plates.

"Mmm, yes. The old guard who objected to integration are saying it'll be a chimerical mess, but it's not as though half the so-called monster species that exist weren't already born of genetic blends. Humans will be next," he said, punctuating the statement with a press of the button on his microwave.

"Next?"

Elias shrugged. "More and more humans mate with monsters each year. I imagine at some point, there will be some kind of uncomfortable and inappropriate conversation about preserving species as they are. It will fail. We all seem to be irresistible to one another in the end."

I leaned my head back against the cupboard. "How old are you?"

"A lady doesn't confess her age," Elias answered with a coy bat of his thick gold lashes. He was naked head to toe, standing in front of a whirring microwave, and a giggle burst out of me at the picture of him.

"Were both your parents moth fae?" I asked.

He nodded. "It was a wild hunt union. My mother was eager for a child, so she mated with every available male moth fae she could find over the festivities. And here I am," he said with a flourish, then swapped out the plates to heat, setting the steaming one down at my side. "The forks are in the drawer under you."

I shifted, following his directions while my brain processed what he'd just told me. "Did you ever meet your father?"

"I met a few likely candidates over the years. Truth be told, considering it had long been common practice to swap fae children for human babies, my mother's attachment to me was devotion enough by our standards," Elias said with a wry smile. "She passed away before integration, but I think she would've been absolutely livid at the idea."

Considering monsters had been living with humans for a century already, that told me enough about Elias's age to go about eating my casserole in a daze.

"She wouldn't have approved of integration?" I asked.

"She might not have said she disapproved, but she certainly wouldn't have taken part," Elias murmured, his gaze growing distant and a furrow appearing between his brows. "I haven't thought of her in quite some time, you know. She'd be shocked to see me now, to see me in a place like Nightlight."

A place where all the species gathered together. In a city where he was the only one of his kind. I wondered how many moth fae were even left in the world. I opened my mouth to ask more questions about Elias's past, when he changed the subject.

"Did Rafe tell you about his supper club?"

I shook my head. "This food is really good."

"Casseroles aren't on the menu, but I agree. He has a flare for flavor," Elias said.

We ate in silence for a moment, Elias with his hip cocked against the counter, mindlessly shoveling food into his mouth. I realized I was witnessing him more at ease than I ever had before, almost as if I wasn't here to observe him.

"You're a lot more clearheaded than when I arrived," I said, wondering if he'd arranged for me to come at the end, when everything was winding down.

He smirked. "I'm compartmentalizing arousal. You needed a breather, and we both needed fuel to continue. But now I'm thinking about sex again and…" He gestured down to where his cock was starting to swell, then laughed as I blushed. "Eat up, Victoria. And then take off the robe and let me watch you stretch before we begin again."

I tried not to choke on the next bite.

CHAPTER 19
Elias

A WHIMPER. A sigh. A weak roll of her hips, grinding us together. A soft sob in my ear and fingers digging into my back, only to release and soothe in halfhearted circles. Poor Victoria.

"Are you tired, darling?" I asked, my own voice raspy from the growls and purrs that had been nearly constant since she'd arrived at the house.

I combed my fingers through the tangled strands of fire spread over my white pillow, and Victoria's bleary eyes blinked up at me. I already knew the answer. It was well after three in the morning. My lover was wrung out with exhaustion, delirious with the arousal that my pheromones left her drowning in, and more openly frustrated with the edge she seemed to be riding.

"Don't stop, just finish and—"

I bent, gently folding her lips between mine, tracing my tongue around the seam, teasing into her as I rocked against her, content to stay buried. A soft sound at the back of her throat made me purr, and her feet scrambled against the sheets before falling limp once more.

"Just fall asleep," I offered, pulling away to kiss the high peaks of her cheekbones, the bridge of her nose, a line across her forehead.

"But—"

"Sleep, and I'll enjoy your lovely little body while you rest," I whispered, brushing my mouth over hers.

Her core clenched around my length, and I resisted the urge to buck. She was nice and soaked, but she needed a break from all the friction and I wanted to linger.

Victoria hummed and softened beneath me, her arms sliding from my back down to splay open at her side. I balanced on one arm above her and reached for her hand, bringing her palm up and licking over it in a spiral. Her brow furrowed, lips parting on a silent moan, and I nudged her knees a little wider, making room for me to nest down on top of her.

"You'll keep going?" she asked, sleepy words slurring together.

I nodded, but she could barely keep her eyes open. "If you want me to." I kissed the center of her palm, then drew her index and middle finger into my mouth to suck, fighting my grin as she squirmed beneath me.

"Mmm, yes. I want you to."

I lowered her hand gently to her side once more, petted her up over her hip and waist and back down to her thigh. "There now, just rest."

I swayed against her with easy, shallow rolls that made her breath hitch, growing more and more gradual until I was still and her breaths were deep and even, eyes shut and lips parted.

Sleeping. Relaxed.

All mine.

I swallowed my groan and resisted the urge to rut, surprised by the sudden greed and triumph over her surrender, of having a woman so willingly pass her body into my possession.

Now was not the time to lose control.

I shifted slowly, watching Victoria's face, the subtle tangle and then softening of her brow as I curled my knees under me, the restless arch of her spine as I sat up, keeping her speared on my cock. She lay sprawled beneath, beautiful and vulnerable. Mine to do with as I pleased. Which was one very specific thing at the moment.

I reached down, gently gripping her breast in one hand, squeezing and rolling, a small murmur of approval sounding in her throat. I stroked my other hand up and down her hip, carefully massaging at the join of her thigh, down into the crease that led like an arrow to where she was spread over my length. My coremata danced over her skin, relieved not to be squished between us, able to taste and touch and sense. She was blazing with heat, glossy skin cooling.

I brushed my coremata aside and set my thumb over her clit, just pressing for a moment. Victoria's soft sounds grew high, and her hips rolled up and into me. I tightened my grip on her breast to a pinch of her nipple, and her lips shut, swallowing a moan.

And she remained sleeping.

My breath rattled out of my chest, and I started to circle my thumb over her clit. I considered waking her, begging her to let me get her off. I *knew* how close she got when we had sex, and if I was only allowed to try a little—

Or perhaps I didn't realize.

She'd already been so close.

It only took two brief circles, two soft pinches.

Victoria arched with a sleepy cry, and I choked on air as her cunt squeezed and fluttered around my length. She thrashed slightly in sleep, rocking urgently, riding out the pleasure.

I nearly howled with victory.

Victoria's hips kicked against me and then settled, her

lashes fluttering, at the brink of waking. Would she realize what she had done? What I had done?

I pulled out before I could succumb and follow her into bliss, then hurried off the edge of the bed.

"Eli-Elias?" A soft mumble, the whisper of a hand reaching over the sheets.

"Are you mine, Victoria?" I asked, opening the bedside drawer to find the stash of toys I'd placed there earlier.

"Yes," she answered, so easily. "What are you doing?"

"I want you to suck my cock while I play with you."

"Mmkay." Victoria's thighs pressed together, and I watched the understanding wash over her face, her eyes growing wide. She would still feel it—the warmth, the soft throb of release that followed an orgasm, the wet rush.

She started to roll toward me, and I dropped the toys on the bed, catching her shoulders and pressing her back down. "No, on your back, like this," I said, and then I tugged her toward the side of the bed. Her head would rest over the edge. "I want to use toys on you, is that all right?"

Her brow furrowed as she blinked up at me, glancing at my cock now gleaming with her release. I had made Victoria come. I would again.

"Elias, I—O-okay."

It took every better quality in me to ask, "Okay?"

She relaxed back, her shoulders heavy in my hands, hair sliding over the edge of the bed to gaze at the carpet. "Mmh-mm." And then she opened her mouth and licked the tip of me, gasping at the taste of us mingling together.

I hurried to act before she could make me lose myself. I'd purchased this toy specifically for her, specifically to make it so impossible for her to remain in her head. I grabbed the tangle of cords, taking a suction cup and rubbing it between her legs as she started to lick over my length, cleaning herself off of me.

"What is—? Oh!" She paused as I rested the damp cup

over one breast and then repeated the process with the other. A soft laugh escaped. "Is that going to do what I think it's going to do?"

"Almost," I answered, taking the final piece, a little U-shaped vibrator, and fitting one side inside of her, the other resting over her clit.

She stiffened, and I leaned back, staring down at her, the Y shape of the toy's cords creating an almost harness like effect on her body.

"Victoria, I'm about to face fuck you. Is it so bad to make you feel good at the same time?"

She blinked and then eased, shaking her head with a sheepish smile. "I suppose not."

I bent, catching her lips with mine, stealing some of her flavor for myself. Damn. I was going to eat her out before the end of this weekend, and I would use every dirty trick I knew to get her gushing on my tongue.

But first—

"Thank you," I murmured, one hand reaching for the remote.

"You're welco—Ah!"

The buzz was loud, mingling with Victoria's suddenly harsh breaths, and she shook, reaching down between her legs. I grabbed her wrists, not waiting to see if she would try and pull the vibrator out or hold it against her core.

"Oh fuck, Elias, I—"

I pulled her hands to my ass, and she moaned as I aimed my cock for her open lips, sucking at me eagerly.

"Slap if you need me to stop," I said.

Her fingers dug in, clutching, and I shuddered for a moment, then pressed on another button, groaning as Victoria's whine vibrated up my shaft, the suction cups kissing and pulling at her nipples.

"That's it, darling. Swallow me down. I know how deep you can take me," I coaxed, only really partially focused, careful not to thrust too deeply. Not that I needed to. Victoria was loud on my cock, trying to distract herself from the heavy sensation of the vibrator on her pussy and the air pulse suction on her tits.

Her heels dug into the mattress, hips jerking side to side, like she was trying to throw the vibrator out of herself. I leaned forward, one hand bracing against the bed as Victoria sucked and licked hungrily over my cock. I reached the other hand out to cover the vibrator, keeping it in place, and groaned at the shout that surrounded and shook over my hard length.

She choked as I turned the intensity up, then whined as I eased my hips back to give her room to breathe.

"Uhn, fuck, I—" I looked down the length of her, bent my head and tongued her belly button, and Victoria took a grateful pull on my cock as I nudged and thrust carefully against her throat.

"You're going to come for me," I rasped, and her nails gripped into the flesh of my ass. "Oh, yes. You want it so bad. And I've been so obedient for you, following your little rule for weeks."

Victoria sobbed, her hips inches off the bed, humping the air, rubbing against my hand. I dipped two fingers in alongside the vibrator.

"Not tonight," I growled.

Victoria screamed as she came for me again, body bowing high off the bed, coughing as she took too much of my length. I pulled back quickly, watching her thrash on the mattress, eyes wide and face flushed, fucking nothing, quaking from head to toe. The remote had slid under her waist and I grabbed it quickly, turning down the volume as her gasps grew ragged and tears formed at the corners of her eyes.

She moaned and the sound rattled, a low, crooning note of sorrow in her throat. I was still hard, dripping, near the edge of my own release, but I reached for her, relieved when she grasped onto me with desperate strength and let me bundle her close. The buzz and thrum of the toy stopped, and Victoria shuddered as I pulled the pieces away from her fevered flesh.

"Are you all right?" I asked.

She was crying, gasping, but she wrapped her arms around my shoulders and tried to drag me on top of her.

"I-I *need* you," she managed. "Please, Elias, I—"

I covered her mouth with mine and hurried to obey.

CHAPTER 20
Victoria

I WAS STILL CLENCHING on nothing, and the slow glide of Elias inside of me made the anxious edge soften, a moan mingling with my sobs. I clutched at him, my hands at his shoulders, my lips at his, my cunt squeezing his length.

"Fuck me," I gasped, knowing my face was a mess, that I was begging for sex while weeping, that I'd just come with a partner for the first time in over five years.

Elias's hands soothed over my cheeks as he started to rock, soft fur absorbing my tears, his mouth gentle over mine.

"I have you," he whispered, his movements as slow as they had been when he'd told me to sleep.

I'd woken up feeling like I'd just had a wet dream, baffled and tired and amazed. "You got me off while I was sleeping," I said, although it was partly a question.

"I did," he said, and I found myself moving with him, slow and patient, every nudge against each other sweet with recent relief.

"How?" I whispered, and he blinked. "Show me."

Elias kissed my brow, and more tears rolled down my cheek. I tried to tangle myself closer as he pulled back.

He laughed. "I have to be able to touch you, darling."

I forced myself to let him go, gasping as he reached between, fingers gentle over my overstimulated clit.

"Like this," he said, circling his thumb. Then he shifted, arching his back, bending his head to suckle at one of my breasts. "All the things I've been wanting to do from the start. You tremble so beautifully when you come."

I let out a sob and Elias purred, tracing a line of wet kisses up between my breasts and across my throat to nibble at my ear.

"Don't tense," he said, still circling his thumb. "You don't have to come again if you don't want to."

Which started a whole new round of crying, of clinging to him. If I'd cried like this during sex with Brett—or god forbid, Stanton—they would've stopped immediately, probably taken it personally.

Elias kissed me, licking into my mouth, cradling me in one arm, never stopping his easy motion inside of me.

"I do want to," I squeezed out, and his forehead rested against mine, nodding with me.

"I know. I know you do. Just let me touch you."

So I did, my arms around his back, soft fur under my fingers. His coremata tickled against my stomach, thumb steady and slow over my clit. And kisses. Swallowing my sighs and shaking sobs, licking into my ear, sucking at my pulse, laving over my breasts.

Pressure built slowly and Elias purred in approval, glancing up from my chest to laugh as I started to tense.

"You always put up such a fight," he teased me, and the comment startled me back into relaxing. "That's it. It won't hurt, you know," he said, smiling.

There were a couple of lamps lit around the room, just enough glow to see him clearly. The glitter of his eyes was consuming, and when his stare snared mine it was easy to fall into, to surrender under that gaze.

"Oh, yes, there it is," Elias said, dark and satisfied, right before a familiar heat started to bubble in my core, echoing in my chest. His thumb pressed harder, distracting me from my surprise. "Fuck, you feel so good, Victoria. Such a good little toy, squeezing so tight on my cock. Yes, yes, that's it."

The moan rose up before I knew I was at the crest, and it sharpened into a cry as Elias grew rougher, more urgent, his face sharpening with a wild edge.

"Come on my cock, darling. Yes, just like that. Your pretty wet cunt is sucking so hard, draining me dry."

I laughed at the crude words, choking on the joy and shock of the orgasm, marveling at the sensation, familiar and yet sweeter, stronger than I remembered. And then I gave in, eyes falling shut and body arching into the shaking relief that burned through every thought and every other sensation but the sound of Elias's shout in my ear.

———

IT WAS late afternoon the next day before Elias's need abated and we had enough rest and food to have an actual conversation about what happened. The sun was shining through the bay windows, and we were bathing in the light, Elias's cheek resting on my bare breast, one arm and leg draped over my body.

"I know it wasn't a magic curse to break, or something silly like that," Elias murmured. I hummed in agreement. "I won't expect to get you off every time, and I won't put that pressure on the experience."

I turned my face, an antennae tickling my nose, those potent caramel pheromones making a gentle heat stir, but Elias was right and it was easy to set aside for the moment. "Thank you," I said, burying my face in his hair to kiss the crown of his head.

He stretched as I leaned back, scooting up the bed until we were nose to nose. "However," he started, and I let out an easy laugh. I'd come with him more in one night than I had in years. I'd also *not* come a few times, and Elias hadn't batted an eyelash either way. "However, I do feel fairly confident that with your permission, I am resourceful enough to manage the job," he said, grinning.

"I'll keep that in mind," I said, reaching up to play with his hair the way I'd been longing to since the beginning, so thick and velvety soft.

He sighed at the touch, arching his neck and leaning his head back into my hands. The flex of his throat was beautiful too, catching the warm light of the afternoon, every hair a thread of gold.

"Elias?"

His head was shifting between my palms, pressing one side and then another into my rubbing fingers. "Hmm?"

"Why do you…live up here?"

His eyes opened and then slid shut once more. "You mean in my attic?" he asked, and I pursed my lips at the way his languid tone had been lost at my question.

"I suppose so, yes."

He sighed and shifted away, and if it hadn't been for how tired my body was, I would've tried to wrap my legs around his hips to keep him close. But he only moved to my side, his arms tugging me to his chest, almost like a teddy bear, and one of his golden wings draped over us like a blanket.

"The house had been neglected for decades, went into foreclosure, and still stood abandoned. It was going to be demolished. But I could tell how beautiful she'd been once. It seemed a shame that she should be buried."

"You bought her."

"I did. For a while, it seemed like even that wouldn't save her. She'd been alone too long. We couldn't risk fixing the roof without the walls coming down, and it would've been a waste to do anything inside with all the leaks as they were."

"You like a challenge," I said.

His mouth grazed over my forehead, right at the line of my hair, breath teasing against the new strands. "I do."

"This was a long time ago," I noted. It had to have been, as there was no sign of ruin now.

"Quit fishing for my age," Elias murmured, and I huffed a laugh, pressing my face into the soft fur of his throat. He was half hard, cock nuzzled against the crease of my hip. "I don't need a huge house. But she needs someone to take care of her. Without any expectation."

"Are houses meant to stand so…empty?" I asked.

Elias shifted slightly at the question. "I could sell her and move, but what if the next owner let her fall to pieces again?" he reasoned.

I stroked one hand down his chest, nails combing lines through his fur, and breathed his scent deep into my lungs, letting it fog my thoughts and build heat in my belly. His coremata tangled around my fingers and joined me as I took his length in a gentle grip. He groaned, bucking into my hand.

"Elias: bartender and business owner, rescuer of old manors, and deliverer of orgasms," I teased.

He grinned and leaned back enough to catch my eye. "Would you like another?"

"Not yet," I said, surprised to find that might not have been entirely true. I squeezed him in my hand, studying the way he swelled and his coremata quivered. "Are there any rooms you've left the same the whole time?"

His tongue flicked out, wetting his lips, and his body shifted in subtle movements, his cock thrusting inside its soft sleeve, fucking into my hand. "A couple."

"Which ones?" I asked, starting to turn my wrist, twisting my fingers over the weeping flared head of his cock.

"Victoria," he groaned, brow furrowed and lips damp and parted on uneven pants. "Is this important?"

"You interest me," I said, shrugging and, incidentally, pulling on his length.

"Ughhn. The-the east wing second-floor lavatory, and…" His throat flexed on a swallow, and he thrust more urgently into my hand now. I loosened my grip, and he ground out, "And the third-floor linen closet."

I laughed. "A bathroom and a linen closet? That's what you were satisfied with?"

"Victoria, please," he hissed, hands scratching softly over my back, his body hunching to kiss and lick and bite over my shoulders and throat as he fucked my hand. "Please."

"What do your friends think of your house? Do you entertain them in all your little puzzle piece rooms, or up here?"

"Huh—uhnn." He glanced at me blankly, and then his eyes fell shut once more, pace slowing down to savor my hand as it tightened around him.

"Your friends—Rafe, Hannah, you know," I prompted.

"They haven't been here," he rushed out, back arching now, head thrown back. "Oh, I—Fuck! Don't *stop*," he snapped out.

"Haven't been up here?" I asked, fingers loose and hand only resting against him as he tried to rub and nudge me back into action.

"Haven't been to the house. No one's been to the house. Except you. And the demonstrators."

I blinked. He didn't even use their names.

"Victoria," he whined.

"Well, I think you should invite them," I said, sitting up, wrestling back his hands as they tried to grab and pull me closer. He surrendered when he realized I was moving down the bed, and his wings tucked against his back so he could roll over and make room for me.

"Fine. Fine, we'll have a dinner party and— Oh, thank fuck, ahhh!"

I fought my smile as I wrapped my lips around the tip of Elias's cock and sucked.

"Oh, Victoria," he purred, all the frantic temper softening once more. "Has anyone told you that you really are remarkable at giving head?"

Damn him. When had he learned so much about me? Long, fingers stroked into my hair, gathering it up so he could watch as I pulled him deeper, my lips relaxed and tongue pressing up to cradle him to the roof of my mouth.

"Mmm, yesss. Such a cum hungry little slut."

I moaned, and Elias's echo of the sound was ragged, his hips lifting and cock thrusting deeper.

"The vibrator is just by your ankle, darling," Elias breathed. "Use it while you suck me. I like the way it makes you whine."

A part of me, the sometimes too present part that liked to dissect and study, which kept my brain buzzing when I wanted it off, took notes now on all the things Elias had been collecting about my arousal.

I liked compliments when they related to how I could make him feel. Liked degradation delivered sweetly. That if he framed my pleasure on how it would please *him*, it didn't make the still anxious part of me balk at the suggestion.

I wanted equal ammunition against him, some semblance of control. But it wasn't control that got me off.

I did as he asked, pressing the simple wand vibrator against my clit and letting the needy sounds rise up in my throat, surround him, *satisfy* him.

"Uhn, yes, that's it. Oh, you suck so hard when you get horny, darling. That's it. Take more of me, I know you can. Here, let me show you. Mmm, yes, gag a little, it's all right. What a good student you are…"

The soft and strong brush of his coremata wrapped around my throat, the scent of the fur under my nose hazing my busy thoughts. I let Elias's words weave their spell, dragging us to cataclysm together.

CHAPTER 21
Elias

IS THIS LOVE?

Victoria was stretched out on the cushioned seat of the bay window, perfectly nude and sunning herself like an orange tabby cat. She looked *right* there, a bright glow of peachy pale skin and vibrant flame hair, like a splash of well-considered color to accent the otherwise drab corner of my home I'd left mostly untouched.

It must be love, I decided.

After all, it made sense. The spark upon first meeting, the slow seduction, the challenge Victoria presented, and finally, the triumph.

The culmination was perhaps a little underwhelming, or my friends were prone to exaggeration. Still, I'd done it. I'd fallen in love. Goal accomplished.

Now what? a voice hissed in the back of my thoughts.

Victoria's head rolled, and her eyes fluttered open, her gaze not searching but wandering through the apartment. I suppose I hadn't given her much opportunity to study the space over the past few days. Oh, we'd surfaced for food and breathing room, paused to sleep, migrated to my shower to refresh, but I'd given her more physical space for the past six hours, and my pheromones were probably all processed out by now. I'd even showered alone to wash their residue out of my fur for a bit.

I crossed her vision, heading toward my kitchen area. "How are you feeling?"

"Like I'm in a dopamine fog," she murmured, her voice raspy from pleasured cries.

A feathery thrill traced up my spine at the sound of her, and I smiled as I pulled down a glass from the cupboard. There, that was better. More like what I'd expected from a romance.

"Is there a crash? I can't… Well, I was going to say 'remember,' but it's not like I have a precedent for *this*."

She was moving, groaning as she sat up on the bench, slim torso and shoulders gilded by sunlight.

"A crash?" I asked, filling two glasses with ice water for us, then taking a bowl of precut strawberries out of the fridge.

"I know about dopamine versus prolactin, of course. I suppose I mean…is it worse after your mating season? After the prolonged repetition of orgasm?"

I blinked at my nice cherry cupboards. This was not the conversation I'd expected. I was thinking about love, and Victoria was thinking about…

"Explain," I said, turning and crossing to my small table.

Victoria stood by the bed, slipping the robe I'd lent her onto her shoulders. "Orgasms release extremely high levels of dopamine. The body regulates that with prolactin—as it rises, dopamine lowers. It's responsible for that sense of satiation, but also the lethargy." She crossed to the table, accepting the glass of water and drinking quickly, her thirst suddenly striking her.

"The *human* body," I said.

Her eyebrows rose, and she set the glass down with a gasp. "Oh! I hadn't considered that. Do you think it's relevant to the study? Has anyone published about biochemistry across different species?"

"I'll investigate," I said, drawing her attention back. "Why did you ask about a crash?"

Victoria popped two pieces of strawberry in her mouth and shrugged as she chewed. "Too much dopamine can lead the body into a state of stress and anxiety. Too much prolactin would be the equivalent of a depression. They're meant to balance one another, but for some people, one weighs over another. And I don't know what happens in...in a situation where there's been a great deal of both."

She blushed, and I was fascinated, studying her more closely. Her eyes were unusually bright. Victoria was an observer, studying *me* or her interview subject with a quiet patience. This was a wilder, more excitable version of that woman. I thought of the way she'd wept in my arms when I'd first broken through her orgasm. I'd assumed it was just an emotional response, like extreme relief.

"Do you remember a pattern for yourself? Highs or lows after orgasm?" I asked, watching as she gobbled strawberries. I picked up her glass and left the table to refill it.

"I suppose...I suppose lows," she admitted after a moment of quiet. "Brett would fall asleep and I would lie awake, thinking and feeling so...alone."

Brett. I stiffened. Somehow, having a name for the man who'd come before me made me...angry? *How strange.*

I carried the full glass back to the table, but I didn't return to my own seat. Victoria smiled as I lifted her and then settled us once more, with her in my lap and my arms around her waist and hips.

"I don't know all about the chemical responses, but I know that aftercare is incredibly important, especially in sexual experiences that feel extreme," I said.

Victoria hummed and tipped her head. "Serotonin, probably. Dopamine is a reward response. Serotonin is contentment. It lasts longer."

"What would you have wanted after sex? What could he have offered you that might've made a difference?"

Victoria stilled, strawberry poised at her bottom lip. It was an erotic picture, but I could see the bricks starting to stack in her mind. She'd cracked open in my arms this weekend and was suddenly aware of the fact.

"You know I enjoy touch, like this," I said, stroking a hand up her back, distracting her from her defenses. "But, for instance, I've had clients that wanted physical space and conversation. I would make them tea. A massage is a common request—I'm trained, of course."

"Of course," Victoria said, smiling.

"One liked me to read to them. They'd bring whatever book they were in the middle of."

Her eyes were shining, tears welling, and the bricks were gone once more.

"I know asking for what you want troubles you," I said softly.

Victoria huffed out a watery laugh and nodded. "Yes."

"Let's see, what else? A bath is very popular, with or without me. I can—"

"Can you braid hair?" Victoria asked softly, blinking away tears.

"Elaborately," I said, flaring out the word just to make her smile.

"Would… Could we do a few of those?"

"We could do all of them," I said. She shook her head, laughing. "Which ones?"

"Tea would be nice. A bath too…" She hesitated, but I was patient. "Would you wash my hair and then braid it?"

I stood up, and Victoria barked out a full belly laugh as she found herself scooped up in my arms. "Of course. Let's get the water started while you pick out which flavor of tea you'd like."

———

VICTORIA HUMMED as I tucked a curl behind her ear and into the thick mass of twisted braids. It was still dark out, but dawn would come soon, and then it would be time for her to leave.

She was meant to leave the night before, but I'd whispered "stay" in her ear while we'd lain on the bed, and she'd told me to find her phone so she could text her friend to make sure he didn't mind an extra night.

I wondered if I could repeat the word once more, if it was like a magic spell.

"I've been thinking about your biochemistry problem," I said instead.

Victoria's lips curved up at the corner.

"You shouldn't go cold turkey, right?"

We hadn't had sex after our conversation and the bath the day before. My mating season had slipped away, and I had no doubt that Victoria was sore.

"I can't yet, Elias," she said, confirming the very thought.

"Not now," I said, kissing her brow, noting the way she relaxed and leaned into me. "Only maybe...not so...by appointment?"

Her eyelashes tangled into the fur on my chest, and she leaned back. I could see her in the dark, and I suspected she didn't realize what a good view I had of her puzzling frown.

"Did it feel like an appointment before?" she asked.

"Not like a job," I said quickly. "I just... What if I called you up one afternoon and said, 'Hey, what are you doing tonight?'"

She smirked. "Booty call."

"Booty calls happen after midnight. And they're mainly texts now."

"Ah, so this would be a more sophisticated version," she teased.

I rustled on the bed, feeling an itchy, annoyed pleasure at being poked at this way. "Victoria—"

"Elias, we've already crossed the boundary we set at the beginning," she said with a sigh. A hard, intangible blow struck me in the stomach, and I braced for her refusal. "Of course we can see one another without making it an act. I'd like that."

Love, I observed as relief swamped me like a wave, was the symptom of extreme responses to small gestures. I hid my relief by covering Victoria's lips with mine.

"Tomorrow night?" I asked, and then scowled at the burst of nerves in my chest. It was only a question! But every millisecond Victoria didn't answer seemed to call on another flare of anxiety. "Doesn't have to be for sex. Dinner. Or we could…watch a movie."

I didn't own a television, but that was easily remedied.

"Mmm." Victoria stretched against me, huffing and dropping her cheek back on my chest. I should've been letting her sleep. "I suppose a little shot of dopamine tomorrow would be good. You know, to regulate."

I huffed and analyzed my own response to her answer. Sex it was then. Was I disappointed or pleased?

This was the problem with fae not taking mates, like many other species. My markers for love were based on watching Khell and Rafe, who had more or less moved in with their partners upon the discovery of their mating bonds. But as confident as I was of my own feelings, I was fairly sure the suggestion of cohabitation at this point would result in Victoria making a quick excuse to leave my bed. Or at least a very uncomfortable and romantically discouraging conversation.

It struck me, suddenly obvious, that even though I was in love with Victoria, she probably wasn't in love with me.

This would require planning.

———

BRRRR. *Brrrr.*

I paused the film on a scene of the couple embracing in the rain, frowning as I dug my phone out of my pocket. Research had promised that this film was a romantic masterpiece, but like all the others I had watched in my pursuit of understanding love, I failed to see Victoria and myself in the story.

I glanced at my phone screen, and my scowl deepened as *Unknown Caller* flickered into an unfamiliar name, then *Wade County Library*, then a series of indecipherable symbols.

I considered refusing the call, knowing not exactly but roughly where it was coming from. But it had been over a decade since I'd heard from the other side of the fae veil.

"Elias Goldwing speaking."

A soft melody crackled over the long-distance—across realms of reality—phone call.

"We expected you back for your mating."

I frowned, taking a long stretch of time to rifle through my memories of the fae realm, searching for the masculine voice.

"Alexi Oaksworn? Goodness, I haven't heard from you since the start of the industrial revolution. They have you on population?" I asked, trying to keep my voice easy and light.

There was a stiff pause, where only the sound of distant revelry echoed down the line.

"It's a promotion," Alexi said.

"So they say," I answered, staring at the ardent, tormented expressions now fixed on the lovers' faces on my television screen.

Alexi cleared his throat and I smiled as the flavor of his irritation reached me, bitter herbs and honey. "We requested your return for your mating season. We had several women of distinguished moth fae lineage waiting to meet you."

I swiped my tongue over my sharp teeth, recalling the ornately scripted "invitation" I'd received shortly before my mating season had started, the night I'd asked Victoria to spend it with me.

"I had no way of sending you my refusal, of course," I said. Not without coming in person, where I would be all but held captive until the breeding was complete.

"I see," Alexi answered, and the music was interrupted by the sound of leaves rustling in an oncoming storm.

"Am I the only male moth fae remaining?" I asked, slightly nervous to hear the answer. Would it make a difference in my decision? Probably not. But it might make the fae court desperate enough to be more aggressive in their demands.

There was a pause and then a slow, "No. You are not. There were two successful births in recent years."

Recent years could've been anywhere from the past three to the past hundred.

"Wonderful news!" I said, a little too cheerful.

"You are the last of your line," Alexi said, stern and just a hint hopeful.

I hummed, and my gaze trailed out the window. "I don't mind that. I've no…sentimentality in that regard."

Alexi sighed. "You've spent too long in the fast world, Elias. Why should sentiment be a factor?"

"What else should be?" I asked.

"Nobility, legacy, community, history—" Alexi listed off.

"I'm sorry, Alexi. I am unmoved," I said, cutting him off. I wasn't. Not *entirely*. But I didn't want to go back to the fae realm, where no one told a lie but no one told a truth either. Where progress moved at a glacial pace under the watchful eye of an ancient committee.

"You are so strange, Elias Goldwing."

Where I was *so strange* to those who were meant to understand me.

"Yes, I'm afraid so. Good day, Alexi."

The call ended without another word. I returned to my research, my hand clenched tight the remote as I hit *play*.

CHAPTER 22
Victoria

"E-ELIAS," I gasped, arching and swallowing a whimper as I ground down and then remembered myself and tried to rise up once more.

He snarled, tightening his grip on my hips and pulling me down to sit fully on his face once more.

Holy shit.

My brow furrowed and I whined, rocking, nudging my clit to his nose as his insanely long tongue stroked inside of me. This past week had been…insane. It was almost like Elias was taking out some kind of *revenge* on me, a punishment of pleasure for all the times we'd hooked up and I hadn't gotten off.

"I c-can't," I stammered out, trying to pull away again, head shaking, my sweaty hands slipping on his headboard.

Except I could. He'd proved that plenty of times.

I'd spent as much time at Elias's apartment—I was calling it that now, even if it was attached to a mansion—as I had at my own this week, squeezing every minute out of every day to juggle my work and the cats and…and whatever this was.

I moaned at the sound of a soft buzzing, and then Elias groaned inside of me as he shoved the little air pulse vibrator against my clit.

He *loved* using toys on me.

And really, I couldn't be mad about it.

His other hand reached up, alternating soft pinches on my nipples.

And still I resisted, my head filling with a dozen irritating thoughts that pecked and demanded my attention. Stanton had been a prick in emails and at our meeting this week, interrogating my study and acting almost *suspicious* of every answer I gave. Emma had reached out and asked me to come with her and Mom and Kathy to look at bridal gowns, and I was both delighted at our reconciliation and dreading the actual experience.

Elias had sent me flowers on Monday. My apartment super had left them at my door. A huge bouquet of greenery and late season blooms, like a wildflower meadow had been growing on my doormat. Thank god it hadn't been something cliché, like roses, but the gesture had thrown me for a loop. Maybe it was traditional for the fae to offer some kind of gesture after a mating season fling? I was too afraid to ask.

Suddenly, Elias growled and rose up, grabbing me around the hips and throwing me to my back on his bed.

"I swear I have to fill at least two of your holes to get you out of your head."

I gaped, thrilled by the words and shocked back into the moment, then cried out as he dove back down to feast on my core. His claim wasn't *entirely* true, although it was an extremely effective method. Mostly, I liked the way he talked, the slightly demeaning teasing he used. He was so…*sweet* after sex, and the contrast of this version of him short-circuited my brain.

Which, yes, helped me get out of my head enough to—

"*Victoria.*"

"I'm sorry!" I cried, my fists striking the mattress.

He purred and kissed around my pubic hair and then up to my belly button, licking in the divot. "Shh, no, darling, it's all right. I'm being selfish, aren't I? You don't need your pussy licked."

I mean, I didn't, but it had felt nice.

He rose up, bracing one hand by my ear. He passed the still throbbing vibrator into one of my hands and pecked my lips gently. "You need it pounded."

I sighed, relaxing, as he fit himself to my entrance and slid smoothly inside.

Elias laughed and grinned down at me. "One of these days, you'll cream all over my face." He kissed my heating cheek. "Tonight, I'll settle for you soaking my cock."

"Elias," I said, nose wrinkling, and then quickly my expression smoothed as he surged slowly out and back in again.

"Am I teasing you too much, darling?" He purred, nuzzling against my ear as I arched beneath him. "I do love to push your buttons," he said, pinching and tugging softly at one of my nipples as he drew out again.

"You-you know what I want," I gasped, one leg hooking over his hips, my knee brushing to the underside of his heavy wing.

"Mmm, I do," he murmured. "Really, of the two of us, you're the selfish one." He reared up, kneeling between my thighs, plunging in and out with far too much patience.

"Elias," I pleaded, my eyes squeezing shut. Was this what I was afraid of? A lover trying to prove that they could get me off? I didn't feel afraid now. I was hot and trembling and trying to throw my body into his, to grind my clit against his fur.

"I'll take my pleasure how I like it, Victoria," Elias growled, punctuating his words with rough thrusts. "With you wet. Gasping. Squeezing on my cock. Just. Like. That."

I clamped my hand over my mouth as I screamed, annoyed and delighted at his mastery over my body, still as shocked by the orgasm as I had been the first time but too busy swirling and drowning in sensation to care. Elias threw himself down onto me, his hands pulling on my hair, body weighing me to the mattress, pinning me for his thrusts as he groaned in relief.

The warm, dark pleasure I took when he came blended with my own heady satisfaction, my body still quaking around his, his jerks and shudders slowing until he lay unapologetically on top of me, my breath tight with his weight, but my body so sweetly relaxed.

"Your dirty talk is so…psychological," I mused, stroking his back, loving the feel of the feather soft velvet of his wings on the backs of my hands.

"Victoria," Elias sighed, and then he hushed me with a licking kiss. I recalled our conversation about aftercare and decided he probably preferred a quiet cuddle to my sexual analysis. I wrapped him tighter in my arms. He pulled from the kiss with a final brush of his lips and then rolled us to the side.

"The more I talk, the tighter you get," Elias said simply. He was quiet for a few moments, and then he gathered my hair in his hand, twisting it and lifting it from my sweaty neck, letting the cooler air of the room soothe my bare back. When did he learn how much I liked that?

"Was *Brett* really so bad in bed?" Elias asked, and there was something about the words that came out grudgingly.

I shrugged. "I don't know. It was a relationship that should've ended in high school. Except I didn't know how to…even communicate with myself, let alone with him. And he and my parents and his parents all seemed to think we belonged together, so that was what I thought too."

"You speak your mind to me easily enough," Elias said and then stiffened. "Don't you?"

I nodded and kissed the center of his chest. "And you listen." I smiled as he relaxed once more. "He's marrying my younger sister."

Elias almost sat up, but we were too tangled together, so he put me on my back once more and stared down at me. "I beg your pardon?"

I laughed. "I know how it sounds, but I think they make sense." He arched an eyebrow and I flushed. "For real this time. I've talked it out with Emma. They really are happier."

"And you don't mind?"

"No," I said, and then considered his question more carefully. "I don't mind. I don't look forward to what other people in our family circle will think or act or how they'll look at me. But Emma and Brett being happy together makes it feel like I made less of a mistake."

"You didn't make a mistake," Elias said roughly.

"I mean by staying so long." He humphed and I smiled, greedily combing my fingers through his hair and mane. He was so wonderfully soft to the touch. "The fallout was bad at the time. No one thought I'd made the right choice when I broke up with Brett. And even though I knew I had, I couldn't help but feel like it was because there was something wrong with me." I covered his lips before he could object on my behalf. "I've unraveled that in therapy. So we're all better off now. I'm going with Emma to look at wedding dresses next weekend."

Elias relaxed and slid down the bed slightly so that he could leave damp kisses on my throat and shoulders.

"I knew from the start I could make you come," he said, and I snorted at his easy arrogance. "You either need your mind silenced or it needs to be engaged, that's all. Left to wander, and it will distract you from your own pleasure."

"A very logical conclusion. What is your prescription?" I asked, smiling.

Elias lifted up, black eyes possessing my gaze, holding me trapped beneath him. "Why, myself, of course," he said, voice low and dark. He shifted, and my legs parted for him automatically. "I know your body, Victoria, and I am learning your mind. I am your lover now, and I mean to excel at the job."

I shivered, a wary note whistling at the back of my mind, but my body was already yearning in his direction, arching for his touch, trembling as his fur grazed against my breasts and belly. His mouth covered mine and swallowed my moan.

———

THE WARNING BELL grew louder by little increments.

I miss you. Any chance you'll come for a drink tonight?

I stared at the first three words of the text, trying to shake off the unsettled mix of excitement and confusion. I'd just left Elias's this morning. It hadn't even been a full day.

At the library till close and I've got an early morning. Tomorrow night?

I watched the text bubble float for a few moments.

I'll be patient if I must.

I rolled my eyes and fought my smile.

Brave of you.

Rafe's first supper club is coming up next month. 11.15. Make sure to schedule yourself off.

I stiffened. Next month. Two weeks ago, we'd been planning hookups on a sparse schedule, and now Elias wanted me in his bed every night and at his friend's debut supper club event in a *month*.

At least he hadn't asked a question. I could safely tuck my phone away and leave his demand on read. Just make it through my quiet work hours in the library.

A dinner was harmless. I liked Hannah and Rafe. And perhaps Elias meant this to be an opportunity to network with more people for the study?

He meant it to be a date. Don't be obtuse.

I shuffled my papers in front of me—a collection of studies on different species' biochemistry that Elias had found me—and gave myself a moment to imagine what it would be like to date Elias.

We already knew the sex was great. So there was that. Elias was smart, inquisitive, observant. Our conversations never stalled awkwardly into mutual ambivalence. But our interactions had been limited to a fairly specific area thus far. A spectacularly satisfying area, one that I was pursuing academically and personally, but still. A limited field.

It wouldn't stay that way, though. We'd discussed our backgrounds, and he'd shared his home with me, which was arguably some kind of secret artistic passion project, or an obsession.

Dating Elias would be—

My brain refused to paint in the rest of the picture, although there was a kind of cool glow in my chest at the thought, comfortable and a little bittersweet.

I'm your lover now.

I smiled and ducked my head, forcing my eyes to focus on the page in front of me, brushing away the whispers of memories from the past few nights every time they rose up.

The findings in the studies were wonderful. For the most part, various monster species had similar markers, although there were a number of species that didn't have prolactin at all, or significantly smaller quantities, like orcs. Species that mated had serotonin overwhelming the dopamine when copulating with their mate. I wondered about fae, but Elias said that it would be pulling teeth to get fae to submit to a study. He offered himself—with a wicked grin—for study, so long as I was his partner in the effort.

If I'd had the resources, I would've taken him up on the offer.

Purely for science, of course.

I made my way through the papers, taking as many notes as I could, not sure whether it added relevance yet but liking to order and organize the clutter of my thoughts.

Every so often, I'd be interrupted to track down a book or check a student out of the library, and my mind would wander back to Elias.

The flowers. The push for more time together. The possessive language in bed. Scheduling dates a month out.

Elias was a fantastic assistant to my study, mainly because he kept himself out of the work itself. It wouldn't *really* be a conflict to date him, aside from potential ramifications if we broke up. But that was a weak excuse to avoid something that would be…nice.

A throat cleared, and I looked up from my notes, freezing at the sight of Lyle's sly smile and a mass of glorious golden fur turned brassy under the fluorescent lights.

"Look who I found," Lyle said.

"E-Elias. What are you doing here?" I was stiff in the tall chair behind the desk, staring over the moth fae's shoulder into the room as if—

What? Who would care that he was here?

And Elias certainly seemed unbothered, wandering easily over to the gap that opened to my side of the desk, sliding behind it. I jumped off the chair and held my hands up in front of me to ward him off, but he just stopped against me, his warmth bleeding through the shirt he wore into my palms.

"I said I missed you," he murmured, not so quietly that Lyle couldn't hear.

My face was hot as Elias ducked to kiss the corner of my mouth. "I'm working," I said, my heart beating too fast in my chest.

"I know, I'll go. I just brought you some food and a mocktail," he said, smiling down at me, although his eyes narrowed as he searched my face. His head tipped. "I didn't know you were friends with an incubus."

"Lyle, this is—"

"We introduced ourselves," Lyle said, smiling, although now he was watching me too closely as well, aware of my spiking nerves.

"I've overstepped," Elias said, so lightly this time, I was sure I was the only one who could hear.

"You surprised me," I said, and my brow tightened. He *had* overstepped. Why couldn't I say so? I opened my mouth to admit as much, but he cut me off with another quick kiss.

"Just food and a drink. See? I'm on my way out now."

And sure enough, he was backing up once more, rounding the desk, nodding to Lyle and heading for the door. He paused at the far corner of the desk and looked back at me.

"Tomorrow?" he asked, and it was hard to tell with Elias sometimes, but I had the feeling he was nervous now too.

I softened, glancing down at the bag. I'd packed a granola bar and some grapes. Whatever he'd brought was bound to be delicious.

"Tomorrow," I said, forcing myself to add, "Thank you."

I just wasn't sure if I was thanking him for coming or leaving.

CHAPTER 23
Victoria

CHICAGO HAD CAUGHT on to the fact that it was fall, and the sudden snap of cold arrived, bitter and spiteful, turning the leaves an array of rust and orange and brown, ripping them off branches to swirl over sidewalks.

I lifted my chin out of the nest of my scarf and let the cold air bite at my face. Soon the lake would have its revenge on the city, bringing sleet and hail and rain, but today the sun was out and it was chilly and perfectly autumnal. I'd finally been able to comfortably switch from iced to hot coffee this morning, and I was happy.

"There's a rumor going around," Lyle said, walking through campus at my side.

My steps stuttered, and I resisted the impulse to blurt out, *About me?*

Lyle's steps slowed, and he glanced at me out of the corner of his eyes, burrowing deeper into his coat and scarf. "Stanton."

This time I couldn't resist, and I stopped. "About me?" Most students had their heads down, hurrying to class, and it was easy to catch a moment of privacy.

Lyle shook his head, frowning. "A few grad students have gone to the dean. Sexual harassment."

"*What?*"

Lyle stared back at me for a moment and then gutted me with three words. "Are you surprised?"

The blood rushed from my face, leaving me properly frozen all at once. I *was* surprised. Was that wrong of me?

"You're not the only student he's had an affair with," Lyle said gently, stepping closer. "It stands to reason that if he's had a pattern of successes, he's had a pattern of failures too."

I shut my mouth, shrinking into my shoulders. If I hadn't been pleased by Stanton's interest in me, would I have been able to find a moment he'd crossed a line?

Yes.

"Holy shit," I breathed out. "What…what are they doing?"

"It's fairly new. But there's talk of an investigation."

For a sick, guilty moment, I wondered what it would mean for my study. And then I blinked and shook myself. *A pattern.*

"God," I whispered, one hand lifting to cover my eyes.

Lyle caught me as I staggered and drew me into his chest, arms wrapping around me. And it was so easy to relax for once, a relief of white noise buzzing in my brain as I accepted the sanctuary of a hug.

"We'll hear more about it, but I wanted you to have an early warning."

I nodded. "Thank you."

———

I WAS STILL THINKING about the bomb Lyle had dropped the next day with my mom and Emma.

Stanton had been an escape from my facade of a relationship with Brett, and I'd been grateful for him at the time. And later, when the shine had worn off and the uneasy reality had settled in, I'd settled for accepting.

Now, I didn't know what I felt.

So I sat, holding a glass of champagne that was growing flat and warm, because the thought of drinking it made me queasy, and wearing a smile my mother had taught me as my sister tried on wedding dresses for her marriage to my former fiancé.

I was happy for Emma. I had no regrets about leaving Brett.

But I should've done it without an affair.

What had happened with Stanton? Had he seduced me, or was it the other way around? It'd seemed natural at the time, but could I pick out the overtures now and look at them differently? Did I even want to?

"Ben mentioned that you haven't called."

There was a soft giggle from the dressing room where Emma was being fussed over, and the sound helped me relax back against the overstuffed white couch.

"Who?" I asked, blinking at my mother.

Kathy rose up from my mother's side and wandered from the back room into the storefront. She and Mom had already had a handful of spats over the dresses they'd sent back to Emma, but I could tell Emma was too excited to really care about their bickering.

"Ben Stone," my mother said, and when I remained staring blankly back at her, she huffed and rolled her eyes. "*Ben*, Vicky. Your father and I introduced the—"

I jerked back, nearly splashing the champagne in my hand. "Oh! God, I completely forgot about him," I said, a laugh escaping me as I leaned forward, giving up the glass. I didn't want to drink anyway.

"Evidently. I imagine you don't like the idea of being set up by your father and me," my mother started.

"I don't," I agreed blithely.

"But he's a charming man, and he has a sister in academia—"

"Mom, I'm not—"

"Okay, first one is almost ready," a woman called to us from the dressing room.

"Vicky," Kathy said, reappearing with flushed cheeks and a strange and previously unheard of giggle. "Your friend is here."

He had asked where Emma's appointment was when I'd turned down lunch at the bar, but I'd never imagined…

"Ta-da!" Emma cried, bursting from the dressing room in a great heave of sighing satin.

"Hello, darling," Elias purred, following Kathy into the room.

"What do you—Oh!" Emma paused, one foot poised to step onto the platform at the center of the room, her mouth open and her eyes wide as she stared at the doorway.

Kathy stepped back, making room for Elias, or at least giving herself room to admire him.

My heart gave an awkward pang just at the sight of him. The lighting of the boutique's dressing room was designed to flatter nervous brides to be, but it made Elias's golden wings and fur absolutely radiant.

"Oh, dear," Elias said, shoulders hunching in a perfect imitation of sheepishness. "I didn't mean to interrupt a reveal."

He was holding a cup tray with four lidded drinks, and he was dressed in that devastatingly casual but meticulous way of his. And he was brilliant, and it was so obvious by the delighted fascination on Kathy's, Emma's, and my mother's faces that they'd never seen anyone like him before.

Moth fae were rare, as Elias liked to point out.

And even if they weren't, I knew few of them could possibly be as beautiful as Elias.

I was standing, although I couldn't remember rising, and Elias's eyes found mine, that gentle smile faltering for a moment before stretching wider.

"I shouldn't be here, I know," he said. "I just wanted to bring you all a treat, since I was passing by."

Liar.

"Vicky," my mother murmured, so sweet, all her carefully portioned sugar in two words. "Introduce us."

It was the perfect time to put Elias in his place, to draw the boundary wall back up between us, but I was too shocked to get the words out. And Elias was quick.

"You must be Victoria's mother." Elias's smooth, cultured tone was a perfect match for my mother's as he reached out a hand for hers.

"Grace," my mother cooed back.

"Grace. I'm Elias, Victoria's boyfriend."

The dense cushion of the couch rose up to meet me, my breath rushing out at once. Elias's eyes made a barely perceptible wince. What was he *doing*?

"Emma, I'm so sorry. You look *lovely*," Elias said with a sincere duck of his head. And it struck me suddenly that it was his *first* moment of sincerity since swanning into the bridal boutique. Everything else had been him playing yet another role.

But roles were for when he and I were alone. *Not* for him to come barreling into my life, around my fucking *family*.

"The beading is exquisite," he continued, delivering my sister a dazzling smile.

Emma blinked, her own smile shy and perfect in return. "Thank you. You just surprised us. Vic didn't mention you. That you'd be coming by, that is!"

"I shouldn't have," Elias said, teasing.

I rose up from the couch, and even though I wanted to shout at him, or snarl, or baldly correct the statement he'd just made, or ask him what the fuck he was thinking, I lifted the mask I'd been raised in, the one my mother would've demanded for such an occasion.

I smiled and said not quite sweetly, "You really shouldn't have."

"Well, I'm *delighted* to meet you," my mother chimed in, and she reached out and squeezed Elias's arm, and even *he* looked startled by that. No, grand Elias, rare moth fae, would not have expected an uninvited squeeze of the arm. It served him right. "Vicky is so private—who knows when we would've gotten the chance."

Elias straightened and looked at me, and it didn't matter if he was playing the role of charming, smitten, helpless boyfriend and I was playing the role of unflappable daughter of Grace Dempsey. We knew each other too well now not to see through the lie.

He had made a mistake.

I was angry.

"I should go," Elias said softly, offering Emma another quick smile.

"No, no," my mother, sister, and Kathy rushed to say.

"This is a special moment for you, and I'm a stranger," Elias laughed up to Emma.

Emma smiled back and shrugged. "Don't worry, this one isn't the dress anyway," she said easily.

"Before you go, we should arrange a dinner," my mother said, trying to catch Elias by the arm again. He was prepared this time, stepping out of the way, toward me.

"I'll walk you out," I said.

"Vicky," my mother huffed, laughing, beaming at Elias. Because he was beautiful and gleaming and my mother had a nose for good money and good reputations.

"Later," I said to her, not quite snapping, but enough for Kathy to hide a smirk behind her champagne glass.

"The coffees," Elias said to me, and I wondered if I imagined the slightly indignant stiffness to his posture, like I had *offended* him with my anger.

"No outside drinks allowed," said one of the staff, who'd

been watching us with smiles that were almost grimaces. "All the white."

Elias's laugh was slightly fragile. "Of course."

I walked ahead of him, steps silent on the thick carpet, out onto the sales floor where three young women were sighing at the dresses on display.

"Well, I mucked that up," Elias said under his breath, a wishfully friendly murmur. "I meant the timing to be more… or at least less…"

I threw my body into the heavy, tall handles of the door, and downtown Chicago arrived at top volume, a siren in the distance, tourists rushing out of the subway toward Magnificent Mile.

"Victoria," Elias said as I debated whether to hold the door open or turn my back on him without a word.

No. No, he deserved a few words.

He didn't flinch when I grabbed his arm but let me drag him down the sidewalk and into a too fragrant alley a few doors down.

"I just wanted to see you," Elias said, eyes wide and innocent, still holding that tray of coffees.

For a little flicker of a moment, I wondered what he'd ordered me.

"I wasn't thinking," he continued, voice too gentle for my temper.

"Yes, you were," I said.

He blinked at me. "I—"

"Elias. You were thinking. You are *always* thinking, planning, writing a script in your head for the rest of us to follow."

He straightened and frowned, glancing down the alleyway and out to the sidewalk in confusion. "I understand that that was the wrong time to introduce myself to your family. It interrupted Emma's time. I'm genuinely sorry."

He was. And he should be. And it was a solid chunk of why I was angry, but not all of it.

"Elias, look at me," I snapped. His brow furrowed—insulted, no doubt—but he did so. "You are not my boyfriend."

"Victoria—"

"You are not my boyfriend. You are trying to play a role, but this one requires a fucking invitation!"

He stepped back, eyes wide.

"Showing up at my work, insinuating yourself into a significant moment for my family? What the fuck, Elias?"

His mouth hung open for a moment, gaze vacant.

"Sending the flowers, trying to see me every day," I continued to list off.

"You object to seeing me?" he asked, his own tone sharpening.

"I object to you trying to force a romance between us!" I cried out. "Out of, what, thin air? You are assisting my research, and we are *fucking*. That is *all*."

I'd never really been that interested in theater, but I knew what I was seeing as Elias's expression smoothed and softened, then a perfect, gentle smile rounded his lips. He reached his free hand up to my cheek, and a sliver of a shiver traced through me, proving that the lines I'd drawn around us weren't *quite* right.

"I love you, Victoria," he said, husky and heavy and yearning.

Oh. It *hurt* to hear those words, so sweet, so carefully injected with all the meaning of the words. My cheek leaned into his palm, and I refused the sting in my eyes.

I sighed and Elias smiled, thinking he'd won.

"Elias, do you even know when you're lying?"

He stiffened, and his hand drew back. I lifted my head and waited a moment. Was I giving him room to object, or to let it sink in?

"This is not a game. You can't just decide to love, and have it be true," I said.

His hand dropped to his side, and his chin hiked up higher, staring over my head.

"I will do the interview with Otis alone. If you feel unable to continue working with me, I understand. Just please don't—"

"I would never risk your study," Elias rasped, staring out at the sidewalk.

I nodded. "We can discuss this more later, but I need to get back to my sister."

"Of course," he said, studying the alley, stepping toward a dumpster and tossing in the coffees.

Irrationally, that gesture made my heart ache.

"I apologize for my presumption," Elias said, studying me for a moment, then he turned and left the alley.

The dark eyes of his wings stared accusingly at me as he walked away, and I fought back the urge to call out to him, words tangling in my throat, a hot warning rising in my eyes, threatening to spill over. I covered my face with my hands for a moment, but my mother's eager voice in my head quelled any regrets. I just needed a moment to put the mask back on.

———

"THERE'S a lot of talk about you, you know," Otis, a shaggy yeti with a gruesome smile, said as he stood from the chair, his head nearly brushing the ceiling of the little campus study room.

"Oh?" I asked, gathering my papers.

"First it was because you were working with the moth," Otis said, shrugging. "But now it's just because everyone you interview is getting curious."

"Curious?" I repeated, steeling my expression as I looked up.

He nodded. "About your study. And about you. You're interested in us, but not in the usual way. You want to know what makes us the same and what makes us different. Generally, it's just the latter."

I was too aware of Stanton in the room, waiting in the corner. Too aware of Elias's absence. I couldn't think of an answer. I was having a hard time thinking at all this week.

"It's not one or the other. I think I just want to know *everything*," I said.

Otis grinned, carnivorous smile on full display.

"Academic minds," Stanton said. He'd been quiet today. I wondered if it was Elias that had made him interject so much last time, or if the rumors Lyle had told me about were now weighing on him.

Otis flapped his arms in a shrug, dangling hands slapping at his knees. "Whatever it is, I'm glad Elias called. It was nice to meet you at last."

My smile was easier to fake this time. Otis was terrifying but sweet. "It was nice to meet you too."

"See you at Nightlight sometime," Otis said as he lumbered toward the door.

I resisted the urge to crumple as if I'd been punched in the chest.

Stanton remained quiet as Otis all but crouched his way out of the doorframe and made his way off campus. I remained with my back to the room. I needed a moment by myself.

The door clicked shut and I sighed. I turned and then stiffened.

Stanton was still here, his hand on the door he'd just closed.

I swallowed hard and straightened, lifting my bag over my shoulder. "I know you probably want to discuss the interview, but I've got to get to my shift—"

"Vic, I need a minute," Phillip said, his voice rough.

Actually, all of him was a bit rough. He had dark circles

under his eyes, and his clothes didn't look so precisely casual and welcoming, more just wrinkled.

I crossed my arms in front of me, holding my bag to my waist like a shield, and waited for him to speak.

"I know you've heard the rumors," he said, staring at me out of those bloodshot eyes.

He looked older, like it had come over him all in the past two weeks. He waited for my answer, but I didn't want to have this conversation. I hadn't even begun to reconcile my thoughts since Lyle had spoken to me. Elias had bulldozed through that issue with an entirely new one to haunt me.

Phillip laughed, but it wasn't a happy sound. "Of course you have. Everyone has. Vic, I—" He stepped forward, and I stepped back without thinking. His eyes grew a little wild and then he recovered, taking a deep breath. "I want to remind you, Victoria, that anything that occurred between us in the past was consensual."

I frowned. "I *know* that."

He nodded. "Good. It just wouldn't be wise for you to be…contributing to this *witch hunt*. Not with the reputation of your study in the department."

I stiffened. Ah, yes, my scandalous study about sex. Supposedly scandalous, at least.

"A risk to me is a risk to your progress," he said, firmly. "That's all."

I clenched my fists into leather. "Understood, Professor."

He let out an uneven breath and sagged, eyes falling shut. "Vic—"

"No." I swallowed on the rock in my throat and tried not to tremble as he shoved a hand through his hair.

"Jesus, Victoria, it's my fucking career!" he cried out.

I haven't done anything, I wanted to say. And also, *Then you should've avoided flirting with your students.*

He shook and groaned, waving a hand. "I'm sorry. I'm going. I'm going."

I remained still, at the far end of the small room, until the door finally shut behind him. My legs folded, and a rush of relief and anger swept through me, a distant gratitude that there was a chair to fall into, a pang of *missing*—

I cut the emotions off, leaning down to rest my head against cool wood, breathing slowly. I was allowed three minutes, and then I would put this feeling away too.

CHAPTER 24
Elias

"I'M sure you're all wondering why I called you here," I said, my hands braced to the bar.

"Not really," Khell said, shrugging.

Rafe raised a hand, like a student waiting to be called on. "I've got a guess."

"Is this not...boys' night?" Theo asked, frowning and glancing at us.

I scowled at Rafe. "What do you mean, a guess?"

"You've got that edgy vibe that Khell had after his appointment with Sunny, when he just wanted to go hunt her down through the city," Rafe said.

"And that hopeless look Rafe had when he thought Hannah didn't want to see him anymore," Khell added, nodding.

"Is this a thing you guys do together?" Theo asked, reaching for his beer.

Rafe and Khell were still waiting for their drinks, waiting for me to deliver them something I'd chosen. I wasn't in the mood. They'd have to order like everyone else.

"You never fucked it up with Natalie and had to regroup?" Rafe asked him.

Theo stared at us. "No?"

"Strictly speaking, I didn't fuck anything up with Sunny," Khell muttered.

I crossed my arms over my chest, irritated and impatient. It had been like pulling teeth to get Rafe to talk about what went wrong with Hannah. I wouldn't dance around the topic. "I told Victoria I loved her. She called me a liar."

My three friends went silent and stared at me until my wings and antennae were twitching with nerves.

"Should I have called the girls?" I snapped.

"Probably," Theo said, taking another sip of his beer.

"*Were* you lying?" Khell asked.

They all stared at me once more. This wasn't helpful *at all*.

"Rafe, what did you say to Hannah when you flew out of here to go make up with her?"

Rafe shook his head at me, refusing my bait. "Elias. Were you lying?"

I snarled and threw my hands out. "I don't know! I don't— I don't *think* so, but I don't *know*!"

The bar was closed. It was a Sunday. I could shout if I wanted to. They didn't need to look so scandalized.

"Then why did you say it?" Khell asked, rising off the stool he barely fit on.

"What are you doing?" I asked as he rounded the bar.

"Coming to look for a drink," Khell said. "Why did you tell Victoria you loved her?"

I gaped at him.

"Get me one too," Rafe said to him.

"Did she need reassurance?" Theo asked me. At least one of them was paying attention.

"I don't…think so," I admitted, squeezing past Khell. "You might as well play bartender. I want a drink too."

Khell grinned at the invitation.

"She was angry with me," I said, taking Khell's seat.

"Why?" Rafe asked.

"I don't remember asking so many questions when it was you with the problem," I muttered.

"Well, you all knew a lot more about that situation," Rafe said. "Hannah and I guessed you *might* be involved with Victoria. And I knew you were looking to fall in love, but... you don't give a lot away."

"Victoria is very private," I said, thinking of that tricky little moment when her mother had said the same and I realized that I'd played my hand all wrong.

Playing a role.

Was she right?

"I thought it was time," I said. "You all fell in love quickly. And then from there it was wrapped up fairly neatly."

"You know that was partly to do with mating bonds, though," Khell said, and I scowled at the atrociously green concoction he placed before me, complete with a garish umbrella. Where on earth had he found that?

I frowned and passed the drink to Rafe. "There was a hurdle in our relationship. We overcame it. That's how it goes, isn't it? In the movies, there's arguing, then a confession of love, and then the couple is happy together!"

"Hurdles are a fairly regular relationship occurrence," Theo said.

"Have you been watching rom-coms?" Khell asked, brow furrowing. "Sunny loves to pick apart all the reasons why those couples would never last long-term."

"Then why are they so popular?!" I snarled. No one answered, and I sagged against the bar. "Victoria doesn't think we were in a relationship at all."

"Does she know you were trying to fall in love?" Rafe asked.

The bar was startlingly quiet. Maybe this whole process would've been easier if we were surrounded by crowds.

"It didn't seem prudent to say," I said slowly.

They were quiet.

"She said I was playing a role," I admitted, slumping further into the bar. That was what it was for, after all.

"Do you like her?" Rafe asked.

"*Yes*," I said, the word rising up without a thought, tearing out of me. "She's fascinating and brilliant, and the more I know about her, the more I feel I know about myself, like a mirror I'd never bothered to look into before, except the reflection isn't really a reflection at all, somehow. It's an entirely new person who I understand and yet don't know at all."

Khell hummed and set a second drink in front of me. This one was entirely clear, an absolute mystery that I would only solve by tasting. I drew it closer and studied the surface, my own face glaring back, a phantasmal version of me on the surface.

"I don't know how she feels about me," I said slowly.

They all sighed heavily.

"That's the worst part," Theo said, nodding.

"There's only one way to find out," Rafe said. "And trust me, it isn't by assuming you know. And it's not going to be by trying to replicate *my* relationship, or Khell's, or anybody else's. Do you think you and I are the same person?"

"Absolutely not," I snapped.

Rafe grinned, not taking it hard. Which was part of why I liked Rafe, and Khell and Theo, for that matter. I wasn't the… easiest person to get along with, prickly and proud. I'd heard the phrase "too smart for your own good" plenty from my mother. I'd always been too interested in the rest of the realms and this world for other fae to understand me. But these men dealt with me, not with a begrudging acceptance but a kind of fond amusement. I wouldn't *tell* them outright what that meant, to be not merely tolerated but enjoyed.

"Victoria doesn't sound like Sunny," Khell said.

I snorted, not dignifying the statement with an answer but

letting their point sink in. Except it sank in with uncomfortable pressure, directly at my chest.

"I like her a great deal," I said, my voice quiet. "I wanted to settle us. To be official." I winced at the juvenile term, but it was true. After my mating season had passed, after I'd had Victoria soft and satisfied and happy in my arms, I wanted to keep her that way. I wanted it to be *known* that I had done so.

"I tried to force that," I admitted.

"You all need to try having *conversations*," Theo said.

"You do like to be in control," Rafe said slowly.

I glared at him. "No, I don't."

"Yes, you do," they chorused.

"You choose our drinks for us," Khell pointed out.

"You booked Hannah's band because you wanted to make me face my feelings for her outside of MSA's environment," Rafe said.

I scoffed. "No, I didn't. I was just curious about her."

"Oh. Well."

"Their point is that you can't control another person or their feelings," Theo said. "If you want to fall in love, you just have to hope for the best, be honest, and wait for the other person to be on the same page with you. There's no orchestrating that sort of thing."

I'd designed the roles she and I would play for sex. I'd arranged the rooms, demanded the times, planned what I would do to her.

I like when you choose.

I'd let those words extend too far. My friends weren't telling me anything Victoria hadn't, in violently clear and brutally direct words.

"I'm not sure she wants me at all," I said. I'd been fairly sure before I'd gone bumbling my way into her life last week, but after witnessing her anger, her *honest* feelings, I had serious doubts.

"Do you want to give up?" Rafe asked. He'd sucked down the drink Khell had made.

I glanced down at my own, untouched, unknown. It could've been water, for all I'd been paying attention.

I raised it to my lips slowly. "I'm not...I'm not sure."

But I knew the real answer. I wasn't ready to lose Victoria. Except now I had absolutely no idea of how to go about keeping her. She was the only one who could answer that for me.

CHAPTER 25
Victoria

WHAT AM I DOING HERE? I stood at the end of the block, but Nightlight's glow was visible from here, warming the sidewalk, shadows of figures shifting and fading into one another.

What is the goal? What will I say?

Because I missed Elias.

I missed him, and I wanted to drag him in front of me to yell at him all over again, because my mom had been dropping little hints and questions about Elias ever since he'd appeared at the bridal shop.

Because I hadn't told her anything. Not that he was a fling. Not that he was helping me with my study. Not that he was no one.

Elias wasn't *no one* to me.

Which I supposed was my answer to why I was standing just out of sight of Nightlight, arguing with myself about whether or not to walk in. To demand an explanation…and maybe also to apologize.

Just a few steps… All I had to do was take a few more steps, peek through the window.

And then…

What? *Date* Elias? Why was that such a terrifying thought?

I swallowed as the door opened, light and sound spilling out, and turned my back on the bar, shrinking a little closer to the corner of the alley to let the flow of Wicker Park traffic sweep past me.

Sex with Elias was simple. Well, no, it was fucking spectacular. It was everything I'd ever wanted, been too afraid of or discouraged from asking for. But *Elias* was even more than that. He was smart and curious and intuitive. He was as interested in me as I was in him, not in the usual way of attraction, but at a deep "how does this person tick and what drives their choices?" level. I knew that hadn't been an act. That was who Elias was.

"Victoria?"

I startled, looking up and finding an unexpected face in front of me. "Hannah!"

The shadow behind her grew in size and then burst into a smile, dark wings spreading to shield us from the street. "Hey, Victoria! Looking for Elias?" Rafe greeted, one arm slung over his mate's shoulder.

I froze and the pair stared back at me, a subtle twitch of Hannah's elbow into Rafe's side, his face going slack with surprise and then recovering with a sheepish grin.

"I was trying to find him, 'cause the venue for my dinner club just dropped out on me, but he's not at the bar," Rafe hastened to add.

I blinked, glancing down the sidewalk, my shoulders dropping. "Oh. Umm… Yeah, I came to see if he was around."

"I told Rafe we should text him first, but—" Hannah started.

"I like the urgency of bursting into the bar without warning. Keeps the old man on his wings," Rafe said.

I smiled at that. "You could always surprise him at home," I suggested.

Rafe snorted, but Hannah tipped her head in curiosity, a

sharp light arriving in her eyes. "Have you been to Elias's house?"

"Of cour—" I paused as Rafe and Hannah both leaned in, the same intense focus in their gazes, and then recalled what he'd told me during his mating season. None of his friends had ever been to the house. "That's unusual, I take it," I said, pretending not to already know the answer.

Hannah relaxed and shrugged. "I've never been, but I'm still new to the crew."

Rafe shook his head. "I know it's nearby. And to be fair, he'd never been to my old place. I just assumed it was too tight for us all to have dinner there. Moth cozy, you know?"

Normally, I had a lock on my expression. But it had been a month made for fraying me at the edges, and I knew I was failing to hide my reaction from them.

"Told you," Hannah said to Rafe, nudging him lightly in the side. "He's ostentatious."

"It's not… He's more—" I swallowed hard and shook my head, pausing at the corner, staring blankly into the cars that turned around us.

"He's not at home, anyway," Rafe said, and it took me a moment to process the words, the gentle tone. I turned to stare back at him and found his smile uncomfortably kind. "We texted him at the bar. He's out looking for you."

I stiffened, my shoulders drawing in, and then caught myself, drawing in a breath. Why was irritation and defensive anger my first reaction? *I* was out looking for *Elias*, after all.

"He has good hunting instincts," Hannah said to me. "He'll find you…if you let him."

I chewed on my lip for a moment before a slow, tentative smile twitched at the corners of my mouth. "He's not just a hunter. He's Elias. He already knows where to look."

———

THE LIGHT WAS on over my back porch, striking soft golden wings and the pattern of huge amber eyes. The stairs creaked beneath me as I climbed, but Elias didn't lift his head, his smooth voice crooning softly to the alley cats who swarmed around him, yowling and croaking and mewling for pets.

"How long have you known where I lived?" I asked, halfway up the last flight.

"Since you agreed to let me work with you," Elias murmured, lifting his head. The light reflected off his and the cats' irises eerily—a reminder to myself that for as beautifully as Elias spoke, as handsomely as he dressed, as familiar as he sometimes seemed to me, he was not human.

"Have you come here before?" I asked, stopping at the top of the stairs and leaning against the railing post.

He nodded. "A few times. After you stayed with me."

The regulars came to rub against my legs, but some of the wilder strays remained near Elias, their crackling purrs and ragged fur a stark contrast to his brilliant elegance.

"Do you know that there's an opossum living in that cat tree?" Elias asked, pointing to the sprawling structure in the shadows of my porch.

"That's Fred. They have a peace treaty with the cats." Elias smiled at that, and my heart panged. "I went to the bar."

He froze for a moment, then sat from his crouch, the cats skittering away from his wings as he leaned against the wall. "I owe you an explanation."

I had meant to say the same, but it was easier to wait, to let him do the hard part of speaking first. Still, I needed one thing…

Elias's eyes tracked me as I crossed the porch, his hand flexing against his thigh as I sat down next to him. My thigh touched his and we both sighed, the cats sniffing at the soles of our shoes, one old clipped ear tomcat settling on Elias's lap for scritches, his purr thunderous in our silence.

"I've never been in love," Elias said after a long stretch of mutual quiet.

The sudden ache in my chest was revealing, but I lifted my chin and studied Elias in profile.

"Which is notable, given my life span thus far," he added with a skittish glance in my direction. "Some time ago, after Rafe and Hannah mated, I decided that I would…like to try the experience."

I inhaled deeply and held it there, letting the breath push against the crushing sensation in my chest.

"Rafe and Khell both fell in love with their clients, so I…"

"Looked for a similar opportunity," I supplied as he hesitated.

"It wasn't fruitful," he said. "They were just clients. The cases didn't even really interest me. Not much has, recently. Not until you."

I leaned my head back against the brick wall behind us, but found the gentle cushion of Elias's thick wing instead.

"Did you ask to assist me because you wanted to fall in love with me, or because it interested you?"

"Both," he said, so easily. He shrugged, and our shoulders brushed. "I don't think I could develop feelings for someone without that intensity of curiosity as well."

I stared at the brick of the building opposite us, the pattern of color, the veins where the wall had been repaired and patched, and considered Elias's confession. The more thought I gave it, the more the tightness eased.

"Are you in love with me, Elias?" I asked.

It had been a painfully obvious lie that day we'd argued outside of the bridal shop, but he'd looked so shocked when I'd pointed it out that I wondered if he really did *believe* himself in love.

He didn't answer quickly now, but shifted, twisting slightly to better search my face, take in my features. I remained still, allowing him to look his fill. Somewhere along the line, I'd learned to enjoy Elias's stare, when so many others made me uncomfortable. Aside from those awkward weeks leading up to our argument, Elias never looked to find what he already thought he knew was there. He *observed*, accepting what he found. He did so now.

And finally, he answered.

"Not yet," he said softly.

My breath caught, and a warm well of tears rose in my eyes, an unfamiliar, wide smile stretching over my face. Elias's own features eased, and our hands found one another as our knees nuzzled closer, fingers tangling.

"Are you in love with me, Victoria?" he asked, velvety and knowing.

I grinned and blinked back the tears. "Not yet," I said.

Not yet…but maybe I *could* be. Not *yet*.

He leaned in, and I closed my eyes in readiness for the kiss, a watery laugh escaping as it landed on my forehead first, then a sigh as it grazed down the bridge of my nose, and a sharp inhale as it nipped at the tip of my upper lip. And then we were quiet, breathing against one another, not hungry but curious, always curious for one another, learning what it meant to be *not yet* in love as we kissed.

How exactly did we fit together? It wasn't a perfect fold. Elias's mouth was wider, enveloping my small smile one nibble and caress at a time. I nudged my nose against his cheek, trying to press closer, and his arm wrapped around my shoulders, but it was a gentle, tempering embrace, our hands still clasped between us.

And I wasn't the only one owed an explanation.

It was easy to draw apart. I rested my head against Elias's arm, and his own forehead lowered to rest against my hair.

"I spent so long being my mother's daughter and Brett's girlfriend, the version of myself that *they* expected, that I…I'm still learning *who* I am," I whispered. Elias didn't so much as twitch, just listened. "My independence is precious to me."

"I overstepped," he said.

"A little. A *lot* when you introduced yourself to my family," I said, straightening. We leaned back enough for me to stare up at him, but our hands still held fast around one another. "But I shouldn't have said that you were nothing but a fuck. That wasn't true, and I knew it."

Elias relaxed slightly, just enough for me to know those words *had* injured him.

"I don't know what to call us, but I know it isn't just sex. But the more you forced me to acknowledge that, the more I tried to shut you out. And I know it isn't exactly fair, but—"

"Victoria," Elias sighed.

I shook my head. "I'm not trying to shut you out now. It's just that I'm not sure what I *do* want from you. It's more than what I thought I wanted, but I'm worried it might be less than what you expect."

"Victoria, I *was* forcing things."

"Yes, but, I mean, only what was already there."

Elias winced, and the ramble I'd been working up to died away. He met my gaze and offered me a crooked smile.

"It was very inconvenient to be constantly trying to appear with baked goods and coffees. I don't bake. I have a business to run, investments to manage. I was trying to be the kind of lover that my friends are to their partners. But it was annoying…even to me."

I blinked at that.

"I'm finding emotions very time consuming," Elias admitted with a heavy sigh, sagging back against the wall. "I would be glad to come to the university if you needed me to, or to any event with your family, when you're ready. But to be honest, keeping up with your schedule on top of mine was not ideal."

I tried to hide my laughter, but it rose up out of me in fits and starts, a snort through the nose and then a sudden bubble from my throat.

"I like your independence," Elias said, watching me, his own smile warming. "I appreciate knowing that you let me in when you trusted me, and not before. I shouldn't have jeopardized that."

Our hands squeezed at the same moment, and then he added with a little quirk to the corner of his mouth, "I also occasionally enjoy scheduling sex in advance."

I gasped and then laughed more in earnest. "So do I, actually. The anticipation is like its own foreplay."

"I was an idiot to try and model our connection based on one where the parties mate. It's a wholly irrational phenomenon," Elias muttered.

I wasn't so sure that love was always that rational on its own, but I was also glad Elias *didn't* mate. It would've sent me running to the hills if he'd told me that he and I were destined for each other in some permanent fashion. It would've felt too much like my mother and Brett, pushing me into that boxed up version of Victoria I'd lived in for so long.

"I don't want this to end, Elias."

Elias hummed and leaned into my side. "Neither do I."

"Can we just keep going, without following anyone else's pattern or model or whatever you want to call it?"

I looked up into his impenetrable gaze, a cool stroke of study caressing over my face and down my neck.

He nodded slowly. "Of course."

A sudden gust of wind set the cats who'd watched us into sheltered corners. I sat up, squeezing my fingers around Elias's.

"Would you like to come in?" I asked, and watched him think, and then overthink the offer. "I've missed you," I said, and his eyes widened.

"Yes," he said, very quickly, and then added, "I've missed you too."

————

ELIAS WAS SO SOFT. So warm. With the air cleared between us, I found it dangerously easy to wrap myself around his body, a touch I'd always been so greedy for and so cautious in accepting. He was freer with his touches too, hands stroking thoroughly up and down my side, over the leg I'd thrown across him, up my back, into the hair he'd tangled with his tireless fucking, and then back down again.

"I ran into Hannah and Rafe," I said, my eyes opening briefly as Hubert jumped up onto the bed and curled up against my bare back after a few moments of biscuit making.

"Ah. Rafe had something he wanted to discuss. Serves him right for showing up without warning," Elias murmured.

"The supper club venue dropped out," I said, recalling what Rafe had told me.

Elias stiffened, then relaxed once more. "I'll call in the morning." And he would take care of the problem for his friend was the unspoken message.

"How come you've never invited your friends to your house?" I asked, rubbing my cheek over his furred shoulder again. He wasn't as comfortable as a pillow, but I wasn't ready to quit the effort of cuddling him yet.

He liked cuddles.

"No need," Elias said, shrugging.

"Mmm, and you *need* dozens of unoccupied rooms?"

Elias was silent for a moment, perhaps too tired for the conversation, and then he roused. "You think it would be an appropriate offering of friendship?"

It was my turn to shrug. "I think your house is sort of like a work of art. Or many works of art, each of the rooms its own moment. I'm surprised you don't share it more often, is all."

Another long stretch of quiet, and this time, I was the one dozing when Elias spoke.

"You think I should host the supper club," he said.

It hadn't at all been what I was thinking. That had been

more along the lines of inviting his friends over for dinner, like he'd said before, or to…watch some kind of movie or sport? But the latter suggestion didn't really seem like an Elias kind of activity.

So I just hummed in answer and fell asleep, surrounded by velvety limbs and wings.

CHAPTER 26
Victoria

"YOU'VE BEEN FOCUSING on woodsy, earthy flavors and their contrasts. I was thinking perhaps a sort of art deco interpretation of Titania's bower. That would of course be where you, Khell, came in to assist."

I checked the time on my phone as the sound of several voices, rather than simply Elias's, floated through the halls of his house. I'd arrived a *little* early for our date, but I wasn't expecting him to have company. I paused on the threshold of the dining room, stripped bare of the stage Elias had arranged for my work, curtains thrown back and the soft glow of a cloudy day creeping in toward the small party gathered together at the center of the parquet floor.

Hannah was the first to notice me, and she drifted away as Elias picked up speed again.

"A modest nest erected there in the corner, perhaps a quartet of—"

Rafe made a small choking noise, and Elias turned to glance at him, finding me hovering at the door instead.

"Victoria!" He pulled his phone from his pocket and glanced down at the screen, blinking. "Forgive me, I lost track of time."

"I'm not in any rush," I said, smiling at the twin baffled expressions Rafe and Khell'ar were wearing.

Elias's head tipped, and his eyelids sank suggestively. "No, you usually aren't."

"This place is…unimaginable," Hannah whispered to me, distracting me from Elias's innuendo.

"He gave you the full tour?" I asked her as Elias turned back to his friends.

She nodded. "He started leading us here, but then Khell was asking about original finials and we had to start over from the front door."

"Believe it or not, I think he's a little shy of showing it off," I answered in a low tone. Elias flashed me a glare.

"He does seem…giddy," Hannah noted.

"Okay, no, I'm drawing the line at a string quartet," Rafe called. "I don't have the budget for that, anyway."

Elias crossed his arms. "One cello. *I'll* pay."

"We only have a month. I don't think I can really do your vision justice in that amount of time. I do have other ongoing commissions," Khell said, but I caught the way he started eyeing the space.

"I have some pieces in my storage unit we could look at repurposing," Elias said.

"Storage unit?" I echoed.

Rafe held up his hands, stopping Elias before he could continue. There was a tense moment of quiet, where both their wings spread slightly open, their stares challenging one another. Hannah's head tilted where she stood at my side, eyes narrowing speculatively, like she was gauging the threat Elias posed to Rafe.

"I need to see the kitchen," Rafe said, surprisingly imperious. "I won't know if this will work until I've seen what you have to support my culinary skills."

Hannah's lips twitched and she relaxed, twisting back to me. "Did we interrupt your work plans? Elias told us to come by for a quick meeting about the dinner club, but Rafe will keep him in the kitchen for another hour at least," Hannah said.

"Not today," I said, and she didn't press me further.

In fact, I was here because Elias had sent me a cryptic email reminding me it was time for my "annual check-up." I had a sneaking suspicion that somewhere in the house was a staged doctor's office. Which would hopefully be left *off* any tour he might be offering his friends.

———

INVESTIGATING the kitchen became marveling at the unstocked pantry, which led to an interrogation about Elias's eating habits that resulted in the whole group of us going up to Elias's personal apartment. Elias remained more or less silent as his friends peeked around the comfortable space, but his hand slid into mine behind our backs.

"I made that bench," Khell said, pointing to the beautiful hardwood bench inside the door, where Elias's shoes were lined up below.

"Yes."

"These are some of Sunny's pieces," Rafe mentioned. He pointed up at the wall, and Khell spun and marched over to examine the artwork.

"I ordered some," Elias said, with carefully simple answers.

"I like your style," Hannah said, and Elias straightened with a hint of a smile.

"I can't know if the kitchen downstairs will work unless I try cooking in it," Rafe said at last.

Elias shrugged. "So cook in it."

And so the evening became an impromptu dinner party. Khell called his human mate, Sunny, while Hannah and Rafe pressed Elias to include three others in the invitation—

another werewolf named Theo, his human wife, Natalie, and their son, Emmett. My head spun with new names and a web of acquaintanceship. Elias introduced me in relation to my study but was freely touching me when we passed near.

In spite of my previous claim to Elias that our connection wasn't solely about sex, it became clear to me that we'd never spent so long in each other's company before without sex as the topic or activity. He was surprisingly stiff with his friends, like he'd held himself apart from them for so long that he wasn't sure how to invite them closer.

They had no such concerns.

"I could do some amazing portrait work here," Sunny declared as Elias focused on mixing us drinks. He glanced up, nodding for her to continue. "You have great natural light, and all the different styles of rooms…just saying."

"Any time you like," Elias said easily. "I could get you a key made so you can come and go."

"This *would* be a great event space. Weddings or parties. Even a more upscale vacation rental," Natalie continued. Elias had unearthed a massive set of vintage blocks from a "toy room" that her son was determinedly building a cityscape out of on the checkerboard kitchen floor.

"I've considered it," Elias admitted.

"That's a lot of people coming and going in your space. A lot of insurance. Probably a liquor license somewhere along the line," Hannah mused, perched on a barstool as she watched Rafe cook, accepting small spoonfuls of flavors to test.

Elias only hummed in acknowledgement, then began to shake our drinks. I stepped closer, sliding my hand beneath his wings to rest against his back, noting the tense and then ease of muscle beneath my palm. His gaze was lowered to the ingredients and bottles he'd spread before him.

He's overwhelmed, I realized, although I couldn't guess the exact cause. So many people in his house all at once? The pressure of their suggestions? Or something simpler and sweeter?

He set the cocktail shaker down and leaned against me briefly.

"Ice?" Theo offered.

"Please," Elias answered.

"How many rooms could you use for the supper club?" I asked, catching Elias and Rafe's attention.

"More than just the dining room?" Rafe asked, surprised.

Elias straightened, shoulders lightening as he thought. "The entrance, obviously. Maybe the apéritif and hors d'oeuvres in the library. Time for introductions?"

Rafe brightened and nodded in answer.

"The dining room," Elias continued. "And what would you think of coffee and dessert in the solarium?"

"Can we scale back some of the interior design at dinner?" Rafe asked, arching a brow.

Elias tipped his head in consideration. "Would you be willing to make a spectacle of the kitchen between courses?"

Rafe hesitated, and Hannah nudged his thigh with the tip of her foot. "You love talking flavor. And a quarter of the club will be all of us here, so you can just talk to us."

"Chefs usually go to the table at some point," Rafe allowed. "And I keep a tidy kitchen. All right, but I get final say on anything you do in here. It can't interfere with the cooking."

"Fair enough," Elias said. "Do you have photos of the plating yet? I want to think about lighting."

———

ELIAS LOOKED ALMOST sluggish as we entered his room at the end of the night. I watched him stretch, rolling his shoulders, and hovered by the door.

"Do you want me to leave you for the night?" I asked. I

knew the signs of an overloaded introvert. To be honest, I was one at the moment too.

"Do you want to leave?" Elias asked, spinning to face me, words a little sharp.

I started to shake my head and then paused, thinking it over properly. "No," I said, more certain of my answer this time. "I want to stay, but I don't think I want to play patient, if that's all right."

Elias blinked and then sagged even further. "Oh, good. I agree. Do you know what I *do* want?"

"Hmm?"

"I want to lay in bed next to you, reading."

I smiled at that. "Can I borrow a book?"

And so we stripped in silence, Elias down to nothing and me to a camisole and my underwear. I found a battered thriller tucked between autobiographies and poetry collections and travel guides, and Elias held back the covers for me to slide in next to him.

We both sighed. Elias's arm reached to wrap around my shoulders and I settled closer, savoring the tickle of his fur and heat of his body.

"Your friends are fun," I said, opening the book.

"Mmm. I am lucky," he said, so quietly it was almost a private statement. "I don't usually enjoy thrillers, but that one is special. See if you can find my favorite character."

I nodded and parted the cover.

"I'm glad you were here tonight," he whispered.

"Me too."

———

I ROLLED the tension out of my shoulders for what felt like the hundredth time this afternoon, then snapped them tight at the first gust of bitter air rushing in from the lake. I paused at the top step of the campus building, my curls getting the best of me as they were tossed and tangled in front of my eyes.

"Here, let me help."

My breath caught at Elias's voice, and a moment later the wind softened, gliding around the shield of Elias's wings. Soft claws rearranged my hair into a knot at the nape of my neck, and I blinked up at the fae.

"Thank you," I murmured.

His brow was furrowed as he stared down at me, no doubt searching my expression for clues to my mood. I wasn't sure what he found. I didn't have the energy to hide anything, but I was feeling especially blank at the moment. Drained.

"How did it go?" Lyle asked, appearing at our sides.

I shrugged, and they exchanged a look over my head. "It was okay, really," I said, before they could start assuming the worst. "Awkward. And I'm not sure what I offered was of any use—"

Lyle cut in. "It's another example of his pattern."

Elias just found my hand with his, squeezing gently. I sighed, fighting the urge to lean into his chest. A month ago, I would've been utterly spooked to have Elias on campus for my sake, and I'd spent plenty of days leading up to my meeting with the team of HR representatives and investigators waffling on whether or not to ask Elias to come. He couldn't attend the meeting, and the only reason to have him here afterwards was because...I wanted him here. For support.

So why am I resisting? I wondered, the thought striking me suddenly. Tentatively, I gave in. Elias shuffled closer, bracing me as I propped myself up against his chest. There wasn't a logical explanation for it, but some tension bled away. *Pheromones*, I reasoned, knowing full well that wasn't the real answer.

Lyle glanced between us, his speech on Stanton's predator

patterns fading away. "It's done now," he said to me, and I nodded. "Have they assigned your thesis to a new advisor?"

I nodded. "Dr. Weathers. I had her for a class last year."

"Not an obvious choice, but she's open minded," Lyle said, nodding. "I asked them for a transfer, and they gave mine to Professor Jenkins."

Stanton was on probation with the university—barely a slap on the wrist considering—and if he could keep his hands off his students for a few years, it would no doubt pass. But it was on his record now, and an unavoidable reputation was attached to his name. After reporting our past relationship, I was mandatorily reassigned the advisor to my thesis, but the option was quietly available to all of us. Professor Jenkins made perfect sense for the biochemistry angle of Lyle's fear to arousal theory. Dr. Weathers was a less clear choice for me, but I'd already spoken to the woman and she was enthusiastic about stepping in for me, if not entirely sold on the methods of my study.

"Come on, let's go get lunch and we can do crisis planning," Lyle said.

"Are you worried about the study?" Elias asked me in a low tone as we walked down the steps together.

Lyle was ahead of us, leading the way, and Elias kept his wing around my side, his arm slung over my shoulder.

"A little," I admitted. "A new advisor might try to push an angle they're more familiar with, or this far into the work, they might not offer the same level of support," I said.

Elias hummed, and I could see his little inner gears working to solve the situation. He would probably pull an expert out of his rolodex of vague acquaintances with fascinating backgrounds. If things went sideways with Dr. Weathers, I might let him. For now, though…

I turned in step, placing myself in front of Elias, forcing him to stop at once, his eyebrows bouncing higher.

"May I ask a favor?" I asked, dropping my voice lower.

"Of course," he said, straightening expectantly, too familiar with requests.

"Tonight, will you fuck me until I'm so tired I can't even move?" I asked.

Elias froze for a moment and then his head dropped, wings folding closer to envelop us. "Can I use toys?"

I nodded quickly. "I want you to call me a good girl."

"So overused. I can do better," Elias said with a smug tilt to his head that made me fight my laughter. "I'll make you come."

"Until I'm dehydrated," I agreed. Aside from those first couple of times, Elias seemed to like asking permission for this now.

He rumbled, his hands cupping my hips, and I leaned back before he got the idea to spirit us away. I wasn't sure if he could fly while holding me, but now wasn't the time to find out.

"Gladly, my lovely little cock toy," Elias murmured in my ear.

My body throbbed eagerly, but I took one of his hands in mine and turned back to follow Lyle. My incubus friend glanced over his shoulder at us with a knowing curve to his lips but said nothing.

CHAPTER 27
Elias

THE BAR WAS MORE crowded than ever, and it was only ten. By midnight we might actually have to either create a line outside, or simply refuse anyone else entry for the night. The noise was almost unbearable to me, but we were too busy to retreat and leave Lulu and Nora on their own.

It was Halloween, and there was an uncommon number of humans in attendance. For the most part, they were fairly easy to spot at a glance—sexy little angels and men in cowboy hats—but a few had creative enough costumes to give me pause, wondering for a moment what unfamiliar species I was staring at until the light hit a smear in their face paint.

I noted, with a little bit of triumph, the way the humans mingled and flirted with monsters and vice versa. I was maintaining my theory that there was a genuine interspecies sexual lure, some evolutionary call to mix genes for best results, perhaps. The fae would be appalled by the notion.

I glanced to the corner of the bar where Victoria sat with her laptop, seemingly impervious to the roar of sound, the jostle of bodies at her back, the way strangers craned around her to try and catch the attention of my bartenders. She had a half finished drink and a basket of fries at hand, and she was chewing on her lip as she worked. She was dressed in a loose blouse, belted trousers, and a tweed jacket thrown over the back of her barstool, and she claimed her costume was Katharine Hepburn. I suspected this was a convenient, no effort costume, but considering I had told a young woman that my costume was an imperial moth, I had no room to judge.

Perhaps next year I would wear a vintage suit and hat and be her Spencer Tracy.

A sudden collection of cheers and groans rose up from one of the pool tables, and I stretched, staring over the crowd to where Rafe pumped his arms in the air, his slutty Little Red Riding Hood costume coming dangerously close to exposing him, if not for the tiny white bloomers. His Big Bad Wolf, Hannah, laughed from the side. Jessica Rabbit, or Natalie, struck a pouting pose that caught the attention of a few strangers nearby, and Theo's good humor grew far too narrow-eyed and predatory to be a convincing Roger Rabbit. Sunny and Khell, one pair of several Barbie and Kens in the bar, hurried out of the bathroom hallway, adjusting their clothes.

I mixed a few more of our specialty menu drinks, silently sympathizing with myself that I wasn't getting frisky in a supply closet as well for the evening. I had a significant consolation waiting for myself later tonight though, one I'd been keeping a secret from Victoria for a few days now.

I pulled my phone from my pocket and opened my string of texts with her. It was an amusing mix of filthy demands and everyday messages.

You're still leaking out of me.

How is Rafe's menu changing?

I can barely sit with how sore I am.

I typed out a new message.

> We have the opportunity for another
> demonstration tonight.

Out of the corner of my eye, Victoria straightened, picking up her phone. I spared myself the time for a glance, just long enough to catch her smile.

> Tonight? You won't be too tired?

I met her gaze and shook my head, then typed once more.

> However, they do need a volunteer. Or two.

I held my breath. Her eyes widened, met mine, and then flashed down to her phone once more, her thumbs moving quickly.

> You can't just say that and not give me any
> clues.

I grinned and searched for an appropriately illustrative gif. It was more than a hint, really.

Victoria's jaw dropped, then snapped shut. She went pale, and then flushed. A moment later, her tongue flicked out to wet her lips.

Lulu nudged me in the side, shooting me a glare and rattling off a list of drinks for me to prepare. I worked as quickly as I could, my phone buzzing once in my pocket, almost burning there with my anticipation.

Finally, a good ten minutes later, I could spare a moment. I looked at Victoria first, but she was focused on her laptop once more, hurriedly working, her expression placid except for a slight furrow of attention between her brows. My phone held the answer I sought.

I'm in if you are.

I grinned. It was precisely the answer I was hoping for.

———

GARDEN APARTMENTS WERE COVETED real estate for the Chicago monster species. Vampires appreciated the secure rooms without windows or ones that were easily shrouded. Orcs liked a deeply grounded space for their den. But a garden apartment with a saltwater pool? That was reserved especially for those aquatic beings who needed such a luxury for their survival.

I paused on the threshold of the stairs as Victoria's hand slipped into my coat pocket, her fingers fitting smoothly between mine.

"You're sure about this?" she asked, eyes tired behind thick framed glasses, searching my face.

I stared back at her for a moment, trying to anticipate the correct response, to guess at what answer she was searching for. And then I realized it would be better just to ask.

"You have concerns?" I asked.

She smiled and I had a strange, warm reaction to getting this particular puzzle right for once. "Usually there would be a little more discussion about the idea of a threesome than just a cheeky text."

"Mmm, I suppose I understand where you're coming from," I said, nodding. "I planned this, so I am sure, but my reasons are that I think you'll enjoy yourself. I know *I'll* enjoy myself. And I like the idea of watching you, and you watching me, and both of us having this experience together."

Victoria's eyes lit up and her smile grew as she stretched

to her toes, grazing a kiss against my jaw. "Well, I like those reasons. Thank you. Let's go and enjoy ourselves."

I wondered if I should say more. That I didn't think a pleasurable threesome would have any bearing on our budding, possible, hopefully, maybe relationship. That I wanted her to know she could share this with me, or enjoy something like it privately, and I would still be secure with how I felt for her.

Those words could wait.

"If at any point you aren't enjoying yourself, let me know and we'll stop," I said, pulling our hands free from my pocket, guiding her gently down the stairs. "That's all that matters."

Victoria nodded, but she was already studying our surroundings, cataloguing every detail, and I knew she was too excited now to continue to dwell.

After a brief tour of the apartment, I guided us to where Nico lounged, half submerged in their pool, and greeted us both with a languid wave. "I'm glad you could make it."

"Apologies for the absurd hour, Nico," I offered, slipping my shoes off and rocking on the balls of my feet, the tile cool and smooth beneath my toes.

Victoria's hand clung tightly to mine, her expression holding a rare shyness as she smiled back at the kraken.

They shrugged in answer, one webbed hand reaching up to slick back sage green hair. They bobbed down into the water, the gills on their ribs expanding for a breath. "I keep strange hours in my season. And I just had some time to rest from my last visitor."

That caught Victoria's attention. "You have a mating season too?" she asked, glancing back at me.

Nico nodded, smiling, revealing sharp teeth. "Not so often as Elias's. And I'm near the end of the egg drop now."

I nodded. They didn't look as bloated as I would've expected.

"Must've been a very accommodating guest," I teased.

Nico blushed, their pale blue skin warming to a deep

purple. "Astraeya. I had to tell her to leave you something to work with."

My eyebrows rose at that news. Curious. Technically, Nico worked for the agency, although mostly as a driver rather than a partner. But Astraeya had to feed, I supposed, and she and Nico were friends. Hopefully, she wouldn't mind the kraken having shared that tidbit with me.

"She has been stressed," I reasoned.

"Mmm. There's been another mating," Nico said, bobbing up once more and floating in our direction.

Victoria sat on a cushioned bench near the pool, unlacing her boots, her jacket draped to the side. She watched us gossip with a neutral expression, mostly studying Nico in the water. I tried to picture them from her perspective as well.

Nico was broader than a human, muscular chest built for long swims, trapezius extending farther down their back and spreading wider, similar to those of us whose bodies needed the structure and strength for flight. Instead of wings, there was a stretch of dense skin that expanded at their underarms for easy gliding along the floor of the sea. They had high, sharp cheekbones and features more flat against their face, eyes set wide beneath a long brow. There were the gills too, of course, along their ribs and behind their jaw.

Was Victoria able to find the kraken attractive, or did their features fall too far outside of human familiarity? Then again, did mine? She had never called me handsome, not that I could recall, although she seemed to enjoy tracing her fingertips around my face in the aftermath of lovemaking.

Below the water, Nico's body flared like a gown, nearly amorphous at some moments, and then extended into long, flexible limb-like tentacles.

By the time Nico was done filling me in on the latest scandal at the Agency, Victoria was standing, her blouse discarded and her trousers falling loose down her bare legs. It suddenly struck me how small she was, how *human*. Nico might be too much for her body to handle.

You just don't entirely like the idea of how much she might enjoy them, a voice hinted in my head. I smiled at the taunt and hurried to shuck off my own clothes. I enjoyed the spark of jealousy, a rare emotion in my life. My suspicions about how *well* Nico's physiology would suit Victoria's needs were more than half the reason I'd arranged this liaison. The rest was due to how much *I* enjoyed a romp with Nico.

Victoria paused at the ledge of the pool, still wearing her bra and underwear, and glanced over her shoulder at me with a reserve in her expression that chilled some of my eagerness.

"We can't really use this in the study," she said softly, glancing back at Nico. "I don't think it would be appropriate."

Nico laughed, and I finished stripping, stepping to her side and finding the warm spot at the base of her spine that fit the curve of my palm perfectly.

"That's what the interview is for," Nico said brightly.

Victoria looked to me for confirmation, and I nodded, shrugging. "I assumed there might be a conflict of interest with this part, but Nico had already promised an interview. When their laying came up at the same time, it just seemed… too exciting a temptation to resist."

Victoria leaned into my touch, a new phenomenon I was relishing in since our reunion, and rose up on her toes to graze her mouth over mine.

"Don't stop, please," Nico called gently, the sound of water lapping at tile heralding their approach. "I like to watch."

Victoria's breath caught against my mouth, but she didn't pull away as I cupped her face, drawing her in for another, deeper kiss. My arm circled her waist, holding her against my chest, and I slid my hand down from her cheek to trace a long muscle from her neck to shoulder, then moved to her breast, cupping it through the gauzy cotton. She sighed into my mouth, tasting of the spiced liquor I'd crafted with cardamom, ginger, vanilla, and green tea.

I found the front latch of her bra and paused to lean back and enjoy the picture of her, arched back over my arm at her waist, the thin bra parting to reveal small breasts with perfect dark peach areolas that tightened and pebbled in the cool, humid air.

Nico was watching too, and I smirked, holding Victoria's slightly nervous gaze as I drew the cups of the bra away from her body, showing her off to the kraken's worshipful stare. Her pupils widened, and her breath hitched as I circled a soft claw around the tip of her breast. I repeated the motion, back and forth, one nipple and then the other, until she was swallowing the start of a whimper and her eyelids had drooped shut. Her head hung back, hair loose, throat flexing with a swallow. Perfect surrender.

My chest burned, and my cock ached where it was starting to thicken, coremata flirting against the waistband of her underwear.

"Are you getting wet?" I whispered into her ear.

She nodded, eyes fluttering open, a glance skirting over Nico and then fixing to me, her cheeks coloring with a blush. She liked exhibitionism as much as she liked voyeurism, apparently.

She really is perfect for me, I mused.

I'd been determined to believe as much that very first moment I'd found her name on a sticky note. It was preposterous to realize that now—now that I did know her and had discovered all the ways we matched together.

"Show us," I said, stroking my hand over her cheek, keeping her face lifted to hold her gaze. I wasn't sure if I did that for her comfort, or for my own selfish need to remain the one connected to her.

The whine escaped, and I swallowed it with a kiss, my

tongue laving over her bottom lip as she shifted against me. In the water, Nico groaned softly.

"So lovely," they murmured, and Victoria shivered.

"Spread your legs," I said, nipping at her lip. Her foot nudged against mine. "Very good. Now hold yourself open so Nico can have a good look at you."

Victoria's stare was blazing, her breaths short and quick, and her arm moved to cross in front of her. A darker flush spread over her cheeks as we held each other's stare, and I wondered for a moment what in particular had her so embarrassed.

And then Nico answered the question without prompting. "Ohh, she's just started to drip."

Victoria's eyes slid shut, and I let out a long, slightly pained sound of approval. I scattered kisses over her cheeks, an apology for the ruthless teasing and in gratitude for her perfect response.

"May I?" Nico asked.

Finally, we gave our attention to the kraken waiting in the water for us. One long tentacle mottled with emerald and indigo was swaying up out of the water, its tip curled back to reveal the pale underbelly, where little rounds of flesh were pursing and relaxing like lips begging for a kiss.

Victoria gaped for a moment and then roused from the haze of desire, the hand not holding the lips of her sex reaching out to the extended tentacle. Nico met her partway, sucker clasping around the tip of her middle finger. Victoria's eyes widened as Nico's lids hooded.

"They're exceptionally sensitive right now," I explained. "The more suckers that have somewhere to touch, to exert pressure and receive feedback, the more pleasure Nico experiences."

This caught Victoria's attention too thoroughly to be distracted by the promise of what those little suckers might offer *her*.

"Do you masturbate with them?" she asked, abrupt and direct, her study jumping to the front of her mind.

Nico laughed, and the sound was deeper than I expected, bouncing off the walls of the bare room. "Oh, yes. Sometimes even accidentally," they admitted, drawing their tentacle away from Victoria's hand, folding it in on itself, rubbing the rounds together. They shuddered in the water in response, and Victoria brightened with interest. Nico preened under her attention. "I could manage on my own, really, but I'm a social creature. I like new textures. New tastes."

Victoria had forgotten about my orders to her, straightening at the edge of the pool, her toes curled over the ledge, panties around her ankles. When Nico's tentacle snapped out and wrapped around one leg, tugging her closer, she flew forward with a yelp. I growled and reached for her, but Nico was faster, another tentacle whipping out with a splash of water, coiling around her waist and lowering her more gently into the pool. The two long ropes of muscle stroked between her legs as she sank, and Victoria's moan was surprised and ragged.

For a moment, I remained standing, unsure of what to do with myself. But she twisted in Nico's hold, searching for me, and I found myself jumping down into the water, my wings growing heavy as the delicate fibers grew saturated.

"May I kiss you?" Nico asked her, floating in place so it was easy for me to catch up with them.

Victoria hesitated and Nico glanced at me, as if they were both waiting for permission. Her hands were braced against Nico's broad, flat chest, but it wasn't a caress. It wasn't a push to back away, either. Her head turned, and I inched closer, almost brushing against her back. She wanted instruction.

Slowly, to give her time to declare her own wishes, to watch every little shift of her face to know if I was guessing correctly, I reached up to cup the back of her head, my fingers tangling in the now damp strands. Victoria softened between us, her nape relaxing into my grip, head tipping back at my instruction, offering her mouth to the kraken.

This was a privilege I'd never experienced before. Victoria might claim she had reservations, but she'd gifted me with a trust so thorough, I found it somewhat daunting at the moment.

Daunting, and thrilling.

"Open your mouth, darling," I coaxed.

She did so, back arching as Nico played between her legs, moaning as they dove down and thrust a long, thick tongue into the welcome of her cry.

CHAPTER 28
Victoria

THE TUGGING, suckling sensation on my clit was almost oppressive, and I squirmed and whimpered against the kraken as their tongue—nearly a tentacle on its own—fucked into my mouth. My hands squeezed strangely dense flesh, and my eyes clamped shut at the sudden and forceful claim on my body. Something burrowed at the opening of my sex, and I shuddered and almost choked against Nico's kiss. If that was what you could call it.

And then a soft scratch combed at the back of my head, fur brushing closer to my shoulder blades. I softened at Elias's touch, then moaned and sucked on Nico's tongue, my body relaxing and finding harmony after the brief struggle. Nico liked that, groaning loudly, more twining touches surrounding me, surrounding Elias too, pulling us closer together, his cock nestling against my ass.

I rocked my hips back to greet him, rubbing myself over Nico's tentacles, and they both wrapped their arms around me. Nico drew away from the kiss, their head falling back, and I glanced down to find Elias's hands wrapped around a tentacle on either side of me, stroking and rubbing and squeezing.

"I forgot how much I like fur," Nico mused in a rasp, sagging into the pool, dragging us both down to our chins.

Elias nuzzled against my ear, his breath raising goose bumps where the warm water droplets cooled in the air. I joined him in playing with Nico's tentacles, finding a large, swollen sucker near the base that almost joined to Nico's muscular hips and massaging it in my hand, circling my fingertips around the edge. Nico shouted and Elias huffed out a laugh.

"Finger it," Elias urged.

I hummed, curious, and dipped my index finger into the pinching ring. Nico thrashed once and then grew even more limp in the water, upper body falling backwards as I added a second finger. I was grinning, fascinated, when a tentacle rose up from the water and wrapped around my own chest, suckers hunting until they found my breasts. The pull was immediate, stronger than even Elias's most urgent kisses.

"Two can play at that game," Nico said, but their smile was wide and toothy and sharp.

The tentacle that had been teasing my entrance now thrusted in earnest, making my jaw drop and a small, tight sound of surprise escape. It pulsed inside of me, growing thicker rather than pushing deeper, and I tried to see the mechanics but the view was too tangled and distorted.

"It has a flexible mass," Nico explained, head tilted. "It can be long and thin, or shorter and thicker. You really don't distract easily, do you?"

"She's simply too good at thinking. It's the opposite of single-mindedness—she too easily shares her focus away from pleasure and toward her academic curiosity," Elias answered them. "You could come from me playing with one little sucker at a time. She needs every part of her body occupied before her brain stops coming up with questions."

I nudged my elbow into his side.

"Is that not true?" he asked me, surprised by my offense.

"It's true, just rude at the moment," I murmured.

"Apologies," he said, kissing me softly on the cheek, before adding in a darker tone, "Spread your cheeks. I want your ass."

I huffed and ducked my head but did as he asked.

"Don't be embarrassed," Nico said, rising up from the water and coiling closer. "I'm going to have his."

Elias hummed in agreement as he probed gently at my ass, patiently waiting for me to relax in the water.

If I was honest with myself, I wouldn't have been able to see this through without Elias. His presence was a reminder, not just of safety and familiarity, but that there was someone here who knew what I needed, whether that was over-whelming stimulation to reach release or simply allowing me the freedom to enjoy sensation without expectation.

I smiled, arching back to rub my head against Elias's shoulder. I knew why he'd done this, why he'd arranged for this night, this experience between us. If there was ever a way to prove he was willing to enjoy an unconventional relation-ship, arranging us a date with a many-limbed, breeding kraken was a good start.

"Oh *fuck*," the three of us said in unison.

Elias started to wedge and then nudge and slide inside of me, the incredible pressure sending me out of my head and back into the pool with Nico and Elias. Nico's tentacles held us up as they explored our bodies, mine floating between the tender twining holds, pinned between the intrusions in my cunt and ass. The sound of lapping water and small splashes grew loud in my ears, along with the sound of my own whines.

Nico was floating close now, and their body gave me some-thing to anchor onto, my arms wrapping around those silky, broad shoulders, keeping my head above the water literally and figuratively as a tentacle thickened and pulsed in my core. Elias's fur brushed up and down my back, feathery under the water, his breath ragged in my ear, one of his hands stroking my hip. He didn't move or try to thrust, but he groaned as Nico's tentacle reshaped itself, as if it were able to toy with both of us.

More tentacles tangled around my legs, pulling one up high, suckers toying over my toes and the tender flesh of my instep, surprising me with the erotic throb that raced up my leg to my cunt.

"M-may I?"

I blinked, realizing I'd been staring blankly in the churning and sloshing water over Nico's shoulder, my mouth wide on a leashed cry. One of Nico's tentacles was stroking up my shoulder, sliding around my throat, and I tensed, shaking my head roughly, knocking it against Elias's temple.

"No," I said, my voice a little rough. I liked it sometimes when Elias cupped his hand around my throat, but the thought of the tentacle coiling around my throat and squeezing the way it was around my legs and waist and breasts shocked me in a way that dragged me out of the moment.

"Please," Elias rasped, catching the tentacle and pulling it from my shoulder to his. My eyes widened and I twisted, watching him bare his throat and groan as Nico accepted the offering. "Do you mind?" Elias asked me.

I chewed on my lip for a moment, watching Nico's tentacle flex around Elias's neck, the tip curling up to poke and prod at Elias's mouth, seeking entry. "I only mind having too many places I want to look at once."

"Then look up," Nico said, their smile warm and sweet. They punctuated the offer with a thrust and swelling inside of me that made me shout and arch, turning my stare up as they'd instructed. I moaned at the sight of the mirrored roof over our heads that reflected the pool, the closeness of us, Elias's wings draped in the water, Nico's searching limbs, my own face warped with pleasure.

Elias whimpered as I pulled one hand from Nico's shoulder, finding Elias's hip in the water, nestled against my own, bracing against them both as I started to rock. My mothman and the kraken both groaned, closing in as if to stop me from moving. But I wanted friction. I wanted pressure. I wanted Elias to lose his restraint, and I wanted to watch Nico come undone. I wanted to join them.

"Fuck me," I gasped, ordering them both.

Elias bucked, and I wasn't sure if it was because he was aroused by my command or because Nico had followed it first, every tentacle inside and out of me seeming to swell and respond to my words. A kind of tightness rolled down the length of one long, thin extension, rubbing over my chest until it reached a nipple, the sucker pinching roughly around the tip, tugging a sharp cry from my lips.

Elias sagged against my back, his moans tight from the tentacle around his throat, his hips urgent but thrusting gently and shallowly into my ass, driven by Nico's own motions inside of him. He whined, and I wasn't sure I'd ever heard that exact note from him before. I tried to twist to look back, but Nico caught my face with a hand, drawing me in and nipping at my lips.

"I'm sucking on his prostate," the kraken said, and then we shared a grin as Elias moaned loudly. "He's going to come soon, but I won't stop. He'll stay hard for you."

Elias was right about me. It took a lot of stimulation to keep me from thinking, and I still had the two brain cells necessary to find interesting potential in that claim.

"Can you do the same to my—"

Nico didn't wait for me to finish the sentence, the tentacle in my cunt twisting, a sucker finding a tender, spongy spot inside of me. I started to shout, solely from that first touch, and then I screamed as it pulled roughly, my body tensing so tightly it had to shatter, to break apart into a million pieces, all rattling and quivering and lighting up with warm electricity at the same time.

———

I SIGHED as Elias hauled me out of the bath, bundling me into a massive, thick towel. My body was strangely sensitive and yet numb at the same time, but his touches were gentle, clearly aware of how I would be feeling after Nico's onslaught in the pool.

After my reality was rearranged when my G-spot was suckled for the first time, Nico had settled for good old-fashioned fucking, one tentacle after another massaging inside of Elias and me, apparently working the eggs out of their engorged lengths. I'd had a brief concern for where those eggs might be going, but in a moment of my lucidity, Nico had assured me they were settling to the pool floor and would be cleared away. They had no intention of becoming a parent anytime soon either.

"Where are we sleeping?" I whispered, using a corner of the towel wrapped around me to rub the fur on his chest, my tiny attempt to help dry him off.

"In a guest room," Elias answered, and when I leaned against him, not caring whether he was damp or not, he hummed. "That pleases you. Was I...wrong to suggest tonight?"

I shook my head quickly, leaning back to catch his eye. "Not at all. Tonight was..." I trailed off and laughed, wrapping the towel more securely and holding it shut with my fists under my chin. "Amazing, fun, overwhelming, incredibly hot—all of that, of course. I just want to be alone with you now."

Elias's smile was soft, dark eyes glittering. The dense hair on his body puffed up suddenly, trembling all over and scattering little droplets of water. His wings thrummed behind him, casting off a sudden cloud of mist.

Well. I'd wondered how he would ever manage to get dry, but I supposed that answered that.

"Come," he said, wrapping an arm around my shoulder and tugging me toward the door.

I'd been a little delirious when we'd finally gotten out of the pool with Nico—it hadn't even occurred to me that the kraken could leave the water, but they'd walked away on their tentacles with a surprising grace—but as Elias shepherded me, the layout of the apartment came back to me. We stepped out of the bathroom and into a cozy bedroom with a large bed, one corner of the blankets and sheets already pulled aside to welcome us. There was a small LED spherical lamp on a dresser in the corner in a shade of peachy pink, just enough to give the room a dim, cozy glow.

"Will you braid my hair for me?" I asked as Elias tenderly buffed the towel over my skin once more.

"Of course. Lie down on your stomach, darling."

Elias shoved the blankets to the foot of the bed as I lay down on the mattress, but the room was warm and I was tired enough not to question the choice. He accepted a damp hair tie from my wrist, straddling my back and gathering and untangling my hair with his claws.

"Did it bother you, to see Nico and I kiss? To know they were fucking me?" Elias asked me, barely tugging on my hair as he braided it down my back.

I chewed on my lip, debating my answer, wondering why he was asking this *now* and what he wanted to hear. I decided on honesty.

"No. I liked it. I would've liked watching the pair of you together, even from the side, like I usually do," I said, folding my arms beneath my head and turning it just enough to see the looming shadow of him out of the corner of my eye. "Did it bother you?"

Elias snapped the tie around the end of my hair, draped the braid over my shoulder, and then leaned down to kiss my cheek, bracing his hands on my lower back.

"I did experience some jealousy, especially as they watched you in the height of your orgasm," Elias said. His voice was light, considering, approaching his own discomfort with curiosity. Then he laughed. "I enjoyed it, actually. I expected to enjoy watching you with Nico, but I was surprised that even the tinge of possessiveness I felt added to my arousal and urgency."

I lay still beneath him, eyes wide at his answer, processing in slow motion. He'd been jealous. He'd enjoyed it. He'd *organized* this for me, a night together, with another person. And now we were alone, and he was as affectionate and thoughtful as ever. His fingers dug into my tired muscles, and I gave up my weak attempt at analysis in favor of relaxing into the bed with a low moan.

"You tensed a great deal tonight," Elias murmured. "You brace against your orgasm, did you know that?"

I grunted, not really caring at the moment, as his thumbs smoothed a line up either side of my spine.

"The first time I made you come you were sleeping, utterly relaxed. It was quite easy compared to when you're awake and thinking and fighting against the process."

"Elias," I said, wrinkling my nose. As much as I liked studying others' sexual responses, I wasn't in the mood to have my own picked apart. Maybe in the morning.

"I want a relationship with you," he said.

I stiffened, but only for a moment. Elias's hands were spreading and kneading, and I was so *tired*, and it was impossible to resist the effect his touch had on me now.

"I didn't plan tonight as a last hurrah to your independence, if that's what you're worried about," he said, and he bent once more, placing a wet kiss on the nape of my neck, adding a teasing circle of his tongue. I tried not to squirm, and tried not to tense either, now that he'd pointed *that* out.

"I want a relationship with you, but it doesn't have to follow any set of rules except the ones we make for it. We don't even have to make rules," Elias said lightly. I tried to lift myself to roll over, but Elias was heavy and he didn't give me a chance, just started working on my shoulders.

"I think a solid relationship does need to be mindful of *some* boundaries," I said.

"You're right. But *our* boundaries, not anyone else's," Elias said. "I don't want a perfect cardboard woman who…who… Honestly, Victoria, I wouldn't even know what to expect."

"Fits in with your friends, charms your coworkers, dresses to attract you but not to provoke others, agrees with—"

"My friends don't fit in with each other, and none of us care a whit. I don't *have* coworkers, I have employees and acquaintances, but even if I did, why you should charm them, I have no idea. You are attractive to me at every moment, and I don't particularly care who else thinks so. And if you *ever* agree with me for the sake of peace, I will hear the lie in your voice and I will pester and press and irritate you until you *spit out the truth*."

The speech was, from Elias at least, a veritable *tirade*. It was snappish and sharp, sarcastic and dismissive. The ensuing silence between us was brittle and expectant, as if Elias had said more than he might've intended to, or at least in not so pleasing a tone as he would've wished.

"Let me up," I said.

Elias sighed, murmuring my name in a plea, but he slid to the side, flopping back onto the bed at my side, looking remarkably defeated, more than I'd ever seen him.

He wanted me. *Me.* Head to toe and every cold, analytical, reserved nook and cranny in my mind.

I leaned over him and his eyes met mine, his features rearranging to hide the blatant droop of disappointment that had stolen over him.

"Do you know what I don't want?" I asked.

There was a flash of hurt in the wince around his eyes, but he blinked and lifted his chin up, waiting. Still, that hint of his thoughts bruised my heart, and I knew what he expected to hear. *I don't want you*, or at least *I don't want a relationship*.

"I don't want the mysterious, aloof, prestigious fae who can't be more to me than an attractive unknown," I said.

Elias's brow furrowed and he blinked at me.

"That man is *lonely*, Elias," I said, and the connection of his gaze flickered as he tried to shut his eyes. I grabbed his face, catching his attention once more. "I don't want you to get along with my family. I don't want you to use your influence —that you only have because you're the only one of your kind locally, which has got to be *isolating*—to help me with my study. You *deserve* to be known, Elias. You deserve to be thought highly of because you're an interesting, creative person, and you deserve to be thought poorly of because you're kind of a snob."

His eyes were crinkling at the corners, lips twitching. "So are you," he said softly.

I nodded. "I want you to be jealous," I whispered, bending my head down to graze my lips over his. "And I want you to enjoy it."

"Victoria," he started, and I covered his mouth with my hand.

"You're fantastic in bed, and I'm so grateful that you've learned what pleases me. But I *like* when you're selfish and you use me to get yourself off. I know that for you, half of the pleasure of sex is knowing that you've satisfied your partner, because *I'm the same way*. So we're going to have to compromise sometimes."

Elias lunged up to kiss me, but he was smiling, teeth scraping my bottom lip as he caught it, sucking and scratching and laving with his tongue, his arms and wings gathering me closer and rolling us onto our sides.

He buried his face in my throat, nipping and nuzzling there as he growled out happily, "Say the word and I'll use your sweet pussy like the good little cock toy that it is. I'll use you so thoroughly you'll be leaking my cum for days. There won't be a creature with a decent sense of smell in all of Illinois that won't be able to tell how hard I fucked you."

The massage had warmed my body up to his touch, but there was nothing like Elias's particular brand of filth purred into my ear to make me consider just *one* more round of sex.

"Not tonight, though," Elias said, and I shook off the impulse to pout as he tugged the blankets out from under him and then tossed them over us both. "You took *two* tentacles at once from Nico, *and* me in your ass. Your body needs rest."

It was proof of how true that statement was that the arousal Elias had stirred up in a moment now cheerfully simmered down and melted away.

We cuddled closer. We'd roll away for cool sheets and our own pillows as we fell asleep, but I had grown so attached to these moments when he was warm and soft and holding me tight that I sometimes found it difficult to fall asleep without him.

"How did you know I was lonely?" Elias whispered.

I smiled, fumbling in the dark until I found his soft, fluffy mane of hair, smoothing it gently, antennae tickling the back of my hand. It had been fairly obvious the first time he'd shown me his house, all those empty rooms, all the time he'd spent arranging them perfectly, for no one.

"Because I was too," I said instead, since it was also true. "And I knew that…when you feel like you don't fit the shape of what you're expected to be, or you can't find a reflection of yourself in those around you, it can seem easier to isolate yourself intentionally, rather than just *feel* that way. You can't fail to be what someone else wants you to be if you don't let anyone near enough. And you can't stand out in a crowd if there's no one else in the room."

Elias's arms around me squeezed briefly.

"It took me quite a while to realize Khell and Rafe liked me, even when I was intentionally proving to them that I was an irritable ass," Elias said, laughing softly.

"I couldn't hide much from Lyle. And he didn't need me to. It was such a relief," I said, nodding against his chest.

One of his hands remained on my back, warm and broad, holding me to his chest, and the other lifted, stroking through my hair, lulling me to sleep. I was nearly there when Elias whispered my name once more.

"Hmm?"

"Be mine."

Perhaps it was like the first time Elias had made me come, easier when I was all but asleep, or perhaps we'd simply reached the understanding we'd been strolling toward for months.

"I am," I said, sighing and sinking into the dark with the brush of lips on my forehead and his soothing fingers in my hair.

CHAPTER 29
Victoria

IN ALL MY worries about my family's reaction to Elias and vice versa—that they would make it uncomfortably obvious that they'd never spent time around any other species, that Elias would find them banal and petty, that if they found out about his oh so prestigious fae pedigree, they'd relish it like he was some kind of European royalty—I'd never considered the reality.

That they would fawn over him, and Elias would *love* it.

I lifted Emma's mocktail into her reaching hand as she crossed to me from the dance floor, panting and smiling brilliantly. She and Brett had made a deal to curb their own alcohol consumption for the night, and Elias and I were in charge of keeping glasses in their hands before any of Brett's finance bro friends could start a chant for shots.

"Mom and Aunt Jen are monopolizing your boyfriend," Emma said, nodding her head to where my mother was indeed holding court with family and friends, her arm linked through Elias's.

"He's thriving under the attention," I said, waving a hand.

Emma raised her eyebrows at me as she sipped her drink.

I laughed, reading her too easily. Which was wonderful. We'd spent a lot more time together in the past few months, and even had a double date with Brett and Elias which, while slightly forced in its amicability, hadn't been as awkward as I'd feared. I had my sister back, and she was incandescently happy.

"I don't mind, actually," I said, surprised to find it was the truth. I shrugged, glancing back across the room to find Elias watching me. "It suits him, and it keeps Mom's spotlight off me. It's better they all get along than not, anyway."

Emma nodded, smug married smirk curving up. "That's very long-term thinking of you."

I blushed but didn't argue.

As much as Elias enjoyed the preening praise from my mother, he did tend to grow bored with her quickly, and he turned a cold shoulder on her if she picked at me in front of him. My father, however, had entirely won Elias over. Their mutually quiet habits, love of antiques, and business acumen made them easy companions, and the three of us had recently gained the upper hand against my mother, spending New Year's with just immediate family and partners rather than hosting another one of my mother's socialite parties.

I'd been open to the idea of a relationship with Elias, then I'd accepted that I was in one, and yes, lately I was thinking of it in more of a potential future sense than just a pleasantly present situation. We made each other happy, and not by squashing ourselves into perfect *traditional* romantic boxes.

"Do you think Mom knows?" Emma whispered in my ear.

It took me a moment to realize what she meant and then I laughed, shaking my head. "She'd never even consider it. Don't worry. I see Dad heading her way now. Your escape is nearly here."

"She'll never forgive me," Emma breathed.

I snorted. "Don't fall for that. She'll be fine. Elias already has a half dozen speeches ready to fool her into thinking it's charmingly romantic."

Speaking of Elias he'd made his escape and was walking

toward us, Brett at his side. It was strange to see them together. The high school football quarterback turned investment firm partner, something like my first love and first heartbreak, although they were faded versions in my memory now. And at his side, casting his all-American good guy looks into washed out shadows, was Elias. My enigmatic mothman who owned a slightly less abandoned mansion—now that it was serving as the venue for Rafe's bi-monthly dinner club and an *occasional* event space—and a wildly popular cocktail lounge, and who consulted with a sex work agency for *fun*.

I might've spared Brett a glance, a smile. Emma loved him after all, in a way I never could, and he loved her in return, every bit as much as I would've demanded for her sake. But Elias's gaze had me in its grip, the depth and darkness as potent now as it had been that disgustingly hot day we'd met.

"Our cue," Elias said as the obnoxiously loud and thumping dance music shifted abruptly into a tender classic, an old Ella Fitzgerald number my parents sometimes danced to in the kitchen—the sweetest memory I had of them from growing up.

"Don't forget to turn your phone off," I said to Emma.

Dad was leading Mom out to the floor, her giggle and smile only for him for once.

"Ready?" I heard Brett murmur to Emma.

"I've been waiting all day," she answered.

And then Elias and I took each other's hand and hurried to the dance floor, his arm hooking around my back, spinning us as his wings spread open, catching a few gasps from nearby guests. My skirt flared around my legs as we turned, and I caught the flash of my mother's smile, her laugh, and then a quick peek at Emma and Brett, easing around the edge of the room toward the exit.

They had a plane to catch, a flight to the Maldives to start a honeymoon a day earlier than my mother would've preferred. It was the most selfish choice Emma had made for the entirety of the wedding planning, and I was outrageously proud of her.

"We don't have to linger in their place, do we?" Elias asked, murmuring the words in my ear.

I shook my head, leaning back in the frame of his arms, his wings blocking the view of the door my sister was fleeing through.

"It would be entirely unwise of us to linger," I said, smiling.

Without Emma on hand, my mother's focus would turn to me, and that was bad enough without the added temptation of wedding talk.

"Then let's make our own escape as soon as the song finishes," Elias suggested.

"Not now? I think Emma and Brett are safely away."

"Not yet," Elias said, holding me tighter. "I want this dance with you."

———

ELIAS'S GROAN licked into my mouth, vibrating in my throat, the ragged edge matching his uneven pace inside me. I tried to match his thrusts, whining, rubbing myself against him. I was tensing, clawing my fingers along his back like it might drag me further to the edge, even as the edge kept inching away.

Elias said I fought my orgasm, but I swear I was only fighting for one.

"Oh, Victoria," he moaned, head thrown back. His hand braced against the headboard, hips shifting against mine, deeper and harder, snapping. "Look at me."

My eyes flew open, and I hadn't even realized I'd been squeezing them shut. I opened my mouth to say that I couldn't get there, I *wanted* to, but it had been a long day with the wedding, and some of my mother's comments were stuck on a loop in my head, and it was late and he should just—

Elias's gaze swallowed mine, his brow tightening. "God, you're so beautiful," he gasped. "Oh fuck, Victoria, I'm going to— You feel so good—"

He just wanted to see me. That was all he needed.

Suddenly, my heart burst, cascading warmth and an unbearable shattering sensation that made me want to weep. I wrapped my arms around his back as Elias's mouth fell open, a deep shout of elation exploding out of him as he stiffened, burying himself deep inside of me.

"I love you," I said, the words bursting out of me as I knot my legs around his hips.

Elias bellowed, shock and then sudden overwhelming ecstasy of his own relief stealing over his features, tearing away his strength, sending him collapsing down against me, pinning me clumsily to the mattress.

He groaned again, bucking, and managed to lift himself just enough to nuzzle his jaw against my temple. "Say it again."

"I love you," I said. It was just a whisper, but repeating the words made some of the fragile, sharp bits in my chest seam back together. I pressed my face into his throat, and there were tears after all, pooling in the hollows above my cheeks. "I love you."

Elias shuddered and let out a small laugh, a light, relieved sound. He hadn't said the words yet, not since our argument months ago, but I didn't have a moment of doubt. He loved me too. Our vow of "not yet" was old now, every day having chipped away at my defenses, his habitual solitude erased with every conversation and touch. Dinner parties and books read side by side and the slow, urgent hours of learning each other's and our own bodies all over again.

Elias's hands stroked my sides, and he eased back until his

face could hover over mine, eyes lined at the corners with his smile.

"You love me," he said.

I laughed and nodded. "I do."

"Because I'll finish without you?" he teased.

I grinned and arched for a kiss, humming against his lips, prompting him for a little more *attention* with a circling of my hips, still holding the tip of him inside of me.

"I love you too, Victoria," he rasped, brushing my hair back from my face, greedily studying me once more. His smile brightened, and he mouthed the words, "I love you."

Maybe he'd just realized too. He'd been hunting for love when we'd met. Perhaps it had surprised him once it arrived.

"What do you think?" I asked.

He blinked, and I knew he understood my question. "Mmm. I see the appeal. It's…wonderful, actually."

"It is nice, isn't it?" I asked, closing my eyes for a moment just to enjoy the heat and softness and ache of the emotion. I loved Elias in all his unraveling mystery, his curiosity, his ageless superiority that he was still learning was actually fallible after all.

"Victoria, darling," Elias called, the hands on my sides moving to my breast, one wandering down my middle to tease at where we were still joined, then up to my clit. I tensed and then reminded myself not to brace, opening my eyes to his once more. "Are you tired, my love?"

I was exhausted, actually. Exhausted and elated and giddy and sated and *needy* and relaxed.

"Why do you ask?" I asked, even though I could guess.

He wet his lips, sitting up slightly and staring down at me, drinking me in one inch at a time.

"Well, you're still quite wet," Elias said slowly.

I nodded. "Some of that is you, but yes, I am," I said, and I rocked into his fingers, my eyes hooding as the warmth of affection became something a little more potent and pressing.

"And I'm rather parched," he continued, grinning. "Would you mind terribly if I helped myself?"

I sighed, desire tingling down my spine, and spread my legs so wide I could almost hook my heels over either edge of the bed. Elias's cock slipped out of me, followed quickly by his release and my glossy arousal.

"Take your time," I offered with a inviting wiggle of my hips.

Elias chuckled, the sound dark and delicious. "You may regret saying that," he muttered.

I doubted it.

EPILOGUE

ELIAS - ALMOST ONE YEAR LATER

PAPER CRINKLED AS I SHIFTED, hefting my languid girlfriend more comfortably onto my lap as my coremata curled back around my slick and sated shaft. A soft giggle ghosted into the fur, around my throat and I reached up between us, tugging the toy stethoscope from her neck and dropping it to the floor somewhere behind me.

"My, my, Dr. Dempsey, that was a *very* thorough appointment," I murmured, nuzzling Victoria's flushed cheek and pressing a kiss at the rosiest spot.

She leaned back, grinning at me, curls a riot from where I'd clutched and tugged on them as she'd licked me and played with my ass. "Fine, you were right. It *was* more fun to play physician than psychologist."

I nodded, trying to restrain some of my smug satisfaction. "Much more hands on."

Victoria rolled her eyes, but her sigh was sweet, ruffling my mane as she curled against me once more.

"Congratulations," I whispered, squeezing my arms around her waist. I would lift us off this examination table in a moment or so, carry Victoria up to our personal suite and start her a bath, but my favorite moment of sex with my partner was directly afterward, when she was entirely at ease with herself and me.

Victoria was like all the city's stray cats she loved to care for—her trust was slow earned and the sweeter for it, but my patience had been well worth the wait, and every month I discovered a new facet to her affection. She'd recently discovered she liked having painted toenails in strange colors—vivid blues and acid yellows and a truly atrocious mouldering purple—and after a long soak in the bath, she would offer me her delicate feet for whatever new shade she'd found discounted at the nearby pharmacy.

"It doesn't feel real yet," Victoria said, sighing and then barely breathing the words, "Doctor Dempsey."

She'd defended her dissertation on monster sexuality and the role societal taboos and shame play, both for and against sexual satisfaction, to resounding success. I'd known she'd pass, rare as that was on the first try, but she'd planned our little session tonight as a balm to potential revisions. The triumph had made her especially sexually aggressive, and I was already considering how I might achieve similar results for her in the future. It was fun to be *her* toy for once.

"MSA will have to give you a raise for your consulting work," I said, and Victoria snorted.

"We both know *that* won't happen," she said.

She was starting to float back into her head. I shifted and sat up. "You could come work with me for Astraeya."

It wasn't really an offer I could make, except that Astraeya had dropped some hints about being interested in Victoria's new studies in human and monster relationships.

Victoria's arms looped around my neck as I stood from the

table and headed towards the door. I would clean up the mess we'd made of our torn and tossed clothing in the morning.

"I'm always happy to help Astraeya, you know that. She's the reason I have you, not to mention my doctorate now," Victoria said with a kiss on my cheek.

"*I'm* the reason you have me. I found that sticky note!"

"Mmm, but aren't we lucky she wrote it?"

I huffed, hiding my smile. "I suppose so. I take it you still prefer the idea of your own sex therapy practice?"

Surprisingly, Victoria was quiet. I waited until we reached the attic suite, setting her down on the bed and searching her eyes.

"I do," she said slowly, chewing on her lip. "But I think I want to focus on the new study more first. Less lucrative—"

"Not a concern," I reminded her, and she glared at me.

"—but I can look into publishing my dissertation now, which will bring in income—"

"We have plenty of that," I continued, and she pressed her lips flat in stubborn irritation. I sank to my knees in front of the bed, and Victoria blinked. "Darling…"

"Elias," she said, her tone warning me against pushing the topic of my finances as a means of supporting her work.

"What are we?" I asked her, and she sat up straighter, her blouse askew and her lips swollen from my kisses.

But she knew the answer. "Partners," she said softly.

"In what way?" I prompted.

Her shoulders lowered and her lips curved, then her hands covered mine at her sides. "All the ways we can be," she answered, leaning forward.

I grazed my mouth over hers but didn't give into her pleading kisses for more, sitting back on my heels. "You got me through a summer of social events planned by Sunny and Natalie, strangers tromping through my house and ruining my beautiful lawn with kitten heels and wedding archways. I fed and clothed and fucked you to sleep through the past few months of prep for today." Victoria laughed and her cheeks blushed, but she didn't deny the claim. "Besides, you know how I feel about this new study."

Victoria arched a brow. "You think it's your idea."

"It *is* my idea. But I'm not as brilliant as you, and so I fully plan on playing my role as your assistant to the fullest once more. Agreed?" I rubbed her hips, tugging her closer to the edge of the bed, her already rumpled skirt rucking up to reveal where I'd torn her hose in my eagerness to get inside of her.

"Agreed," Victoria said, leaning in for a nibbling kiss on my lower lip. Her voice lowered. "If you promise to still let me play your role as your good little toy."

I growled, rising up, leaning in so she had to brace against the bed to keep from falling backwards. My claws found the edge of her skirt and slipped beneath the fabric, stroking up her bare hips. We were lucky she'd passed on her first defense, because my mating season was just around the corner.

"Oh, my darling love," I hissed, bucking between her legs, drawing out a husky, pleased laugh. "*Always*."

THE END

Afterword

Welcome to the Monster Smash Agency!

This series is a fun model for me where I post in progress chapters on my Patreon and then later rewrite, edit, polish and publish the series wide!

I bounce between various series in progress including this series and the Dragonkin books! While the next Dragonkin book is my upcoming project, later this year I'll be working on Astraeya's book, tentatively titled Sweet on the Swamp Beast (or Succubus, undecided.)

If serial chapter reading isn't for you, there's also lots of spicy art, some bonus content, and some options for physical reward tiers.

Also by Kathryn Moon

<u>COMPLETE READS</u>

The Librarian's Coven Series
Written
Warriors
Scrivens
Ancients

Standalones
Good Deeds
Command The Moon
Say Your Prayers - co-write with Crystal Ash
Secrets of Summerland

The Sweetverse
Baby + the Late Night Howlers
Lola & the Millionaires - Part One
Lola & the Millionaires - Part Two
Bad Alpha
Faith and the Dead End Devils

Sol & Lune
Book 1
Book 2

Inheritance of Hunger Trilogy
The Queen's Line
The Princess's Chosen

The Kingdom's Crown

Tempting Monsters
A Lady of Rooksgrave Manor
The Basilisk of Star Manor (novella)
The Company of Fiends
Sanctuary with Kings

<u>SERIES IN PROGRESS</u>

Sweet Pea Mysteries
The Baker's Guide To Risky Rituals
The Knitter's Guide to Banishing Boyfriends
The Florist's Guide to Summoning Saints (coming fall 2025, I hope.)

Monster Smash Agency
Games with the Orc
Howl for the Gargoyle
Lessons with the Mothman
Book Four (coming late 2025)

Dragonkin Series
The Alpha of Bleake Isle
The Alpha of Grave Hills (coming summer 2025)

Acknowledgments

Elias and Victoria's book felt risky and new somehow. I wasn't even sure if it *ought* to be properly a romance where they said I love you's at the end. But I've always tried to give myself permission to follow even the most unlikely story and now at the finish line of their story, I'm glad I did. I'm especially grateful to everyone who's joined me on this journey, guided me, propped me up when I wanted to wobble, and read my work! Authors are incredible people, and they make amazing friends!

Special thanks in the Lessons with the Mothman crew includes my babe Whoop for being my brain and for take a little shadow version of her own Elias and run with him. My beta babes, Ash, Jami, and Gia! Jess and Meghan, for editing and tidying my words. Sophie for my beautiful cover, with extra lamps. All of the astonishingly talented artists who provided art (shared on Patreon) and most especially my patrons who were willing to take a chance on a weekly chapter update model.

As always, thank you to my family and friends, my readers, and my little furry supervisor, Coraline.

Kathryn Moon is a country mouse who started dictating stories to her mother at an early age. The fascination with building new worlds and discovering the lives of the characters who grew in her head never faltered, and she graduated college with a fiction writing degree. She loves writing women who are strong in their vulnerability, romances that are as affectionate as they are challenging, and worlds that a reader sinks into and never wants to leave. When her hands aren't busy typing they're probably knitting sweaters or crimping pie crust in Ohio. She definitely believes in magic.

You can reach her on Facebook and at ohkathrynmoon@gmail.com or you can sign up for her newsletter!